Pamela Taylor

A Feeling in the Bones

Second Son Chronicles - Volume 8

Black Rose Writing | Texas

ISBN: 978-1-68513-087-9
PUBLISHED BY BLACK ROSE WRITING
www.blackrosewriting.com

Printed in the United States of America
Suggested Retail Price (SRP) $21.95

A Feeling in the Bones is printed in Book Antiqua

*As a planet-friendly publisher, Black Rose Writing does its best to eliminate unnecessary waste to reduce paper usage and energy costs, while never compromising the reading experience. As a result, the final word count vs. page count may not meet common expectations.

This series is dedicated to the hope that thoughtfulness, compassion, respect, and rational dialogue can triumph over bigotry, greed, mistrust, and self-righteousness to create a world that is truly a better place for all of humankind.

I'm particularly grateful to Linda Kirwin for her help and guidance. Though her project started as a beta read with critique, she quickly grasped what I was trying to do in this series and became a valued editorial consultant. Thanks also to the members of the DFW Writers Workshop who listened to readings and offered their food for thought. And a very special thank you to Jeffrey – himself a second son – who was my first reader and who encouraged me in the early days, when I was unsure if my vision was worth pursuing.

Praise for
The Second Son Chronicles

**2021 Next Generation Indie Book Awards Finalist
–Fiction Series**

**2021 American Fiction Awards Finalist
–Historical Fiction**

**2021 PenCraft Awards
Historical Fiction Runner-up**

2019 PenCraft Awards 2nd Place

**2020 Eric Hoffer Awards Finalist
–Historical Fiction**

"A healthy blend of drama, politics, history and action make the story engaging on every level, and the protagonist's journey makes for brilliant storytelling and character progression."
–*Pacific Book Review*

"A fine-grained and emotionally satisfying medieval adventure."
–*Kirkus Reviews*

"In the genre of historically inspired fiction, Taylor has done a marvelous job of combining fact, history, and fun."
–*IndieReader* "Highest Rated" list

"Historical fiction lovers will enjoy this tale of knightly adventure."
–*Sublime Book Review*

"Reading Taylor is like slowing down to absorb history through entangled plots, culture of the period, and significant protagonists rather than dry textbooks."
–*Authors Reading*

The Royal Family

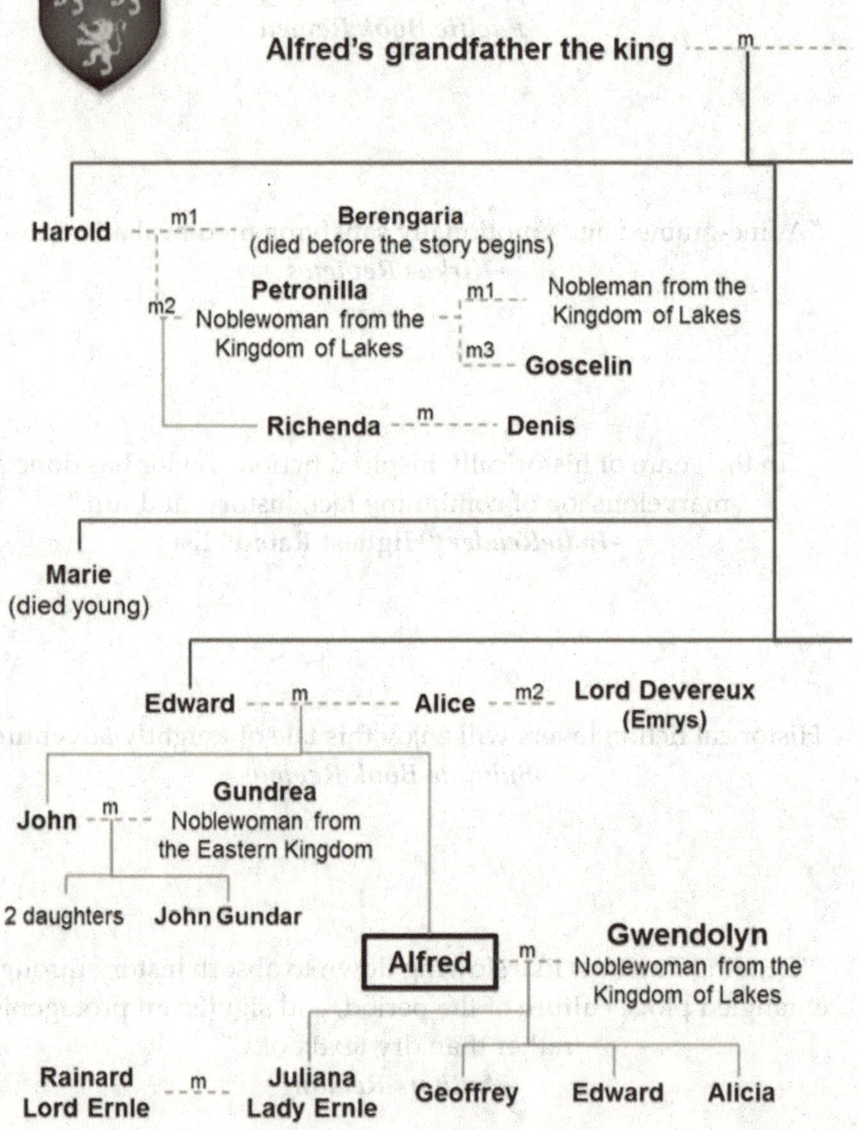

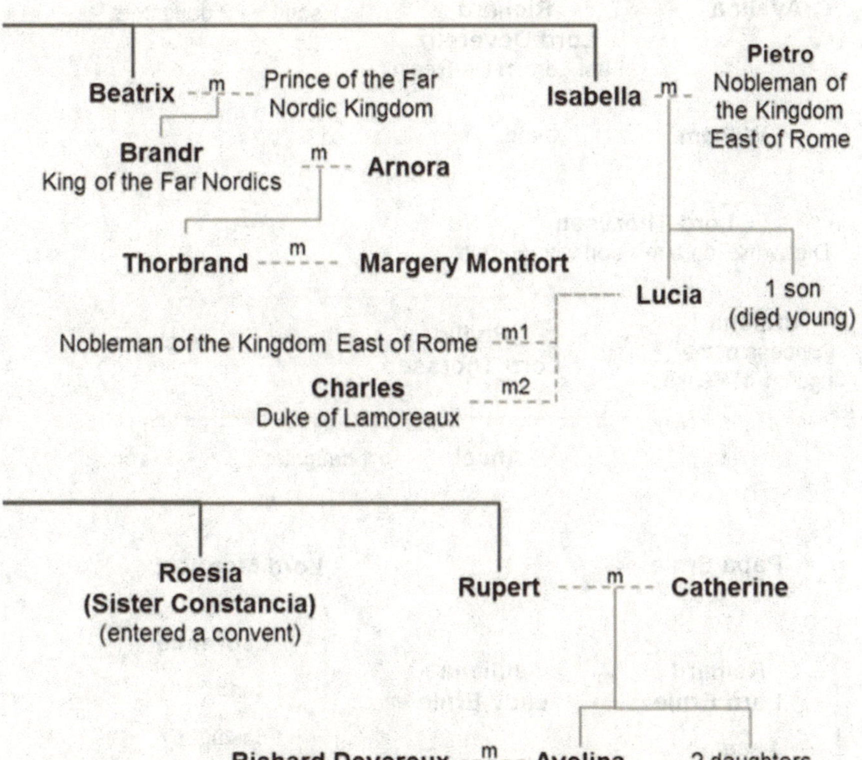

Juliana
Princess of the Kingdom Across the Southern Sea
(died before the story begins)

Beatrix —m— Prince of the Far Nordic Kingdom

Isabella —m— Pietro Nobleman of the Kingdom East of Rome

Brandr —m— Arnora
King of the Far Nordics

Thorbrand —m— Margery Montfort

Lucia

1 son (died young)

Nobleman of the Kingdom East of Rome —m1—

Charles —m2—
Duke of Lamoreaux

Roesia
(Sister Constancia)
(entered a convent)

Rupert —m— Catherine

Richard Devereux —m— Avelina

2 daughters

The Nobility

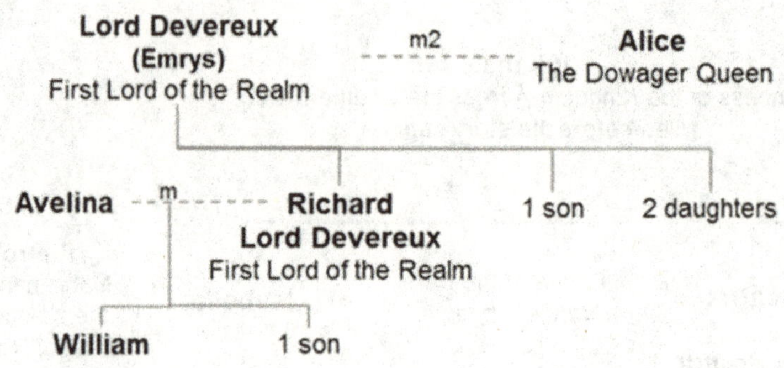

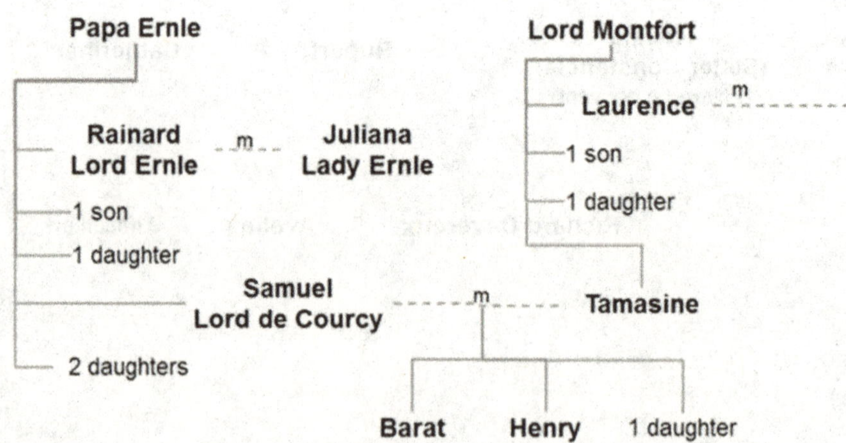

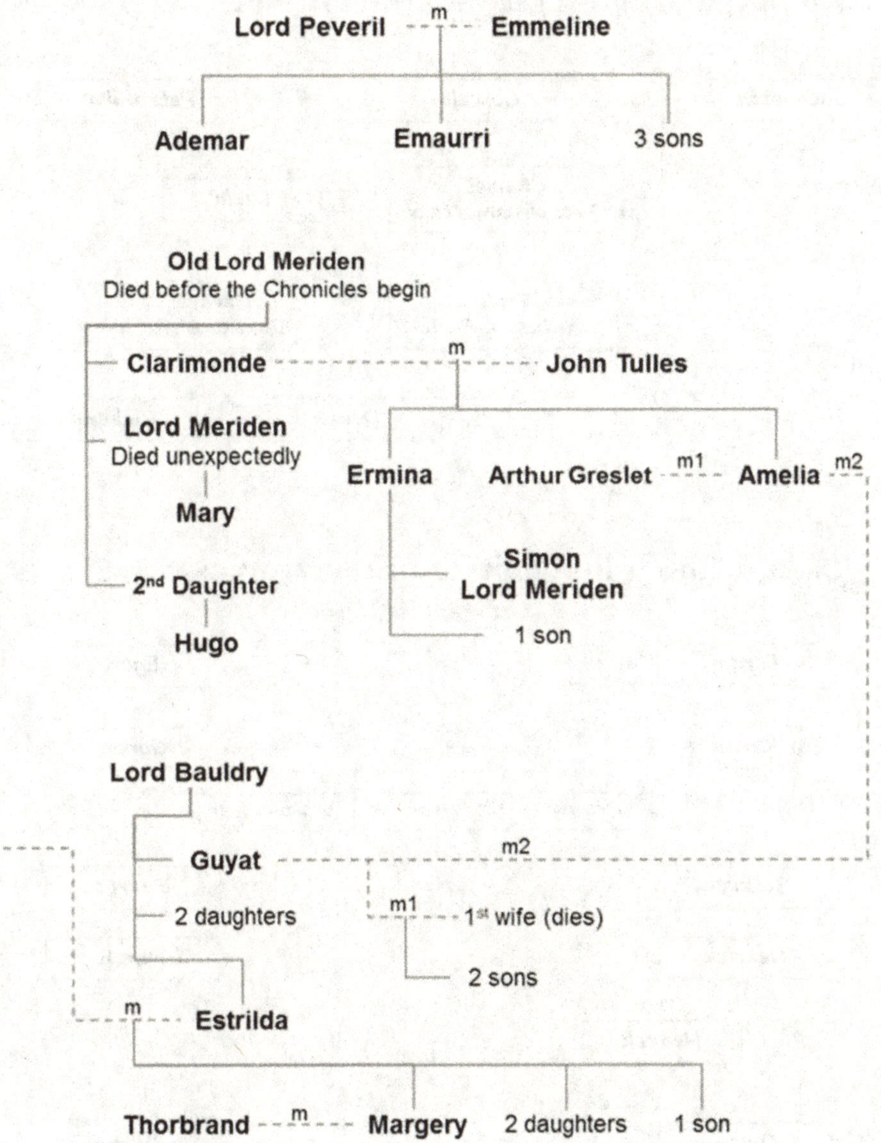

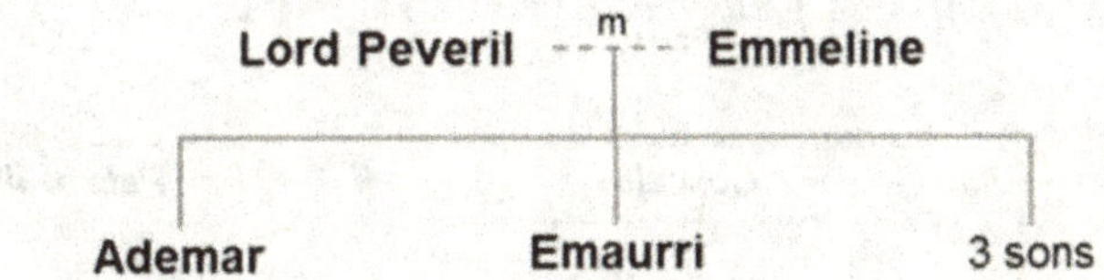

Lord Peveril
m
Emmeline
Ademar
Emaurri
3 sons
Old Lord Meriden
Died before the Chronicles begin
Clarimonde
m
John Tulles
Lord Meriden
Died unexpectedly
Mary
2nd Daughter
Hugo
Ermina
Arthur Greslet
m1
Amelia
m2
Simon
Lord Meriden
1 son
Lord Bauldry
Guyat
m2
2 daughters
m1
1st wife (dies)
2 sons
m
Estrilda
Thorbrand
m
Margery
2 daughters
1 son

Royal House of the Kingdom Across the Southern Sea

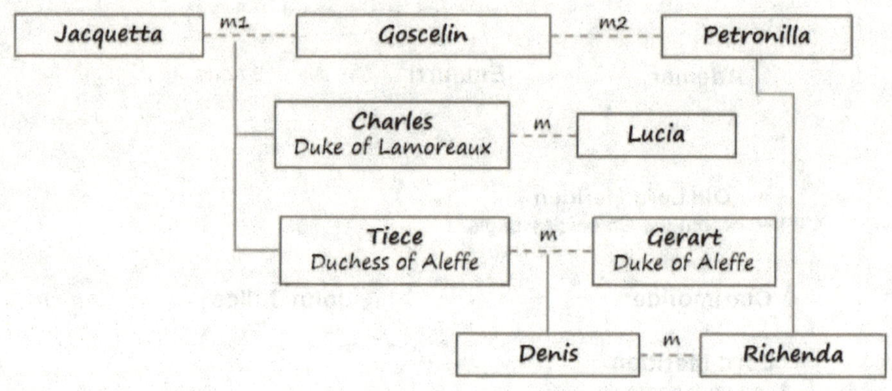

Lords of the Unorganized Territories

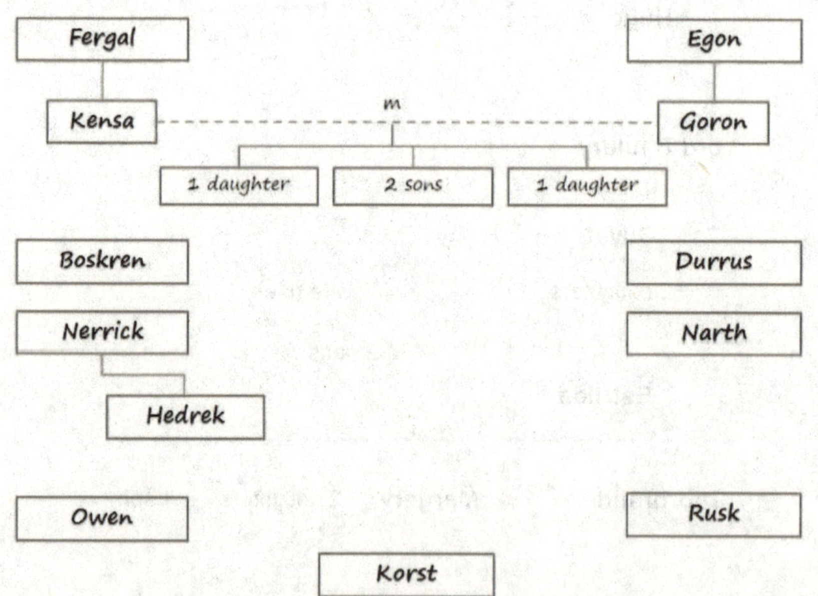

KINGDOM OF PEAKS
KINGDOM OF LAKES
EASTERN KINGDOM
UNORGANIZED TERRITORIES
KING'S CASTLE
KING'S CASTLE
KING'S CASTLE
LAKE ST. JOHN
LAKE ANNE
JUNO LAKE
LAKE ST. ANNE
LAKE OF ROSES
GODWIN
GWENDOLYN'S COTTAGE
DEVEREUX
NEUKIRK MARKET
PEVERIL
BAULDRY
MONTFORT
OUR RIVER
GREAT NORTH ROAD
FOOTHILLS
ABBEVILLE MARKET
BRIDGE
MONASTERY
GREAT TRUNK ROAD
PORT ROAD
PORT FERRY
PORT
ERNLE
MERIDEN
GREAT WOOLSCOT
THORSSEN
FISHING PORT
SOUTHERN SEA

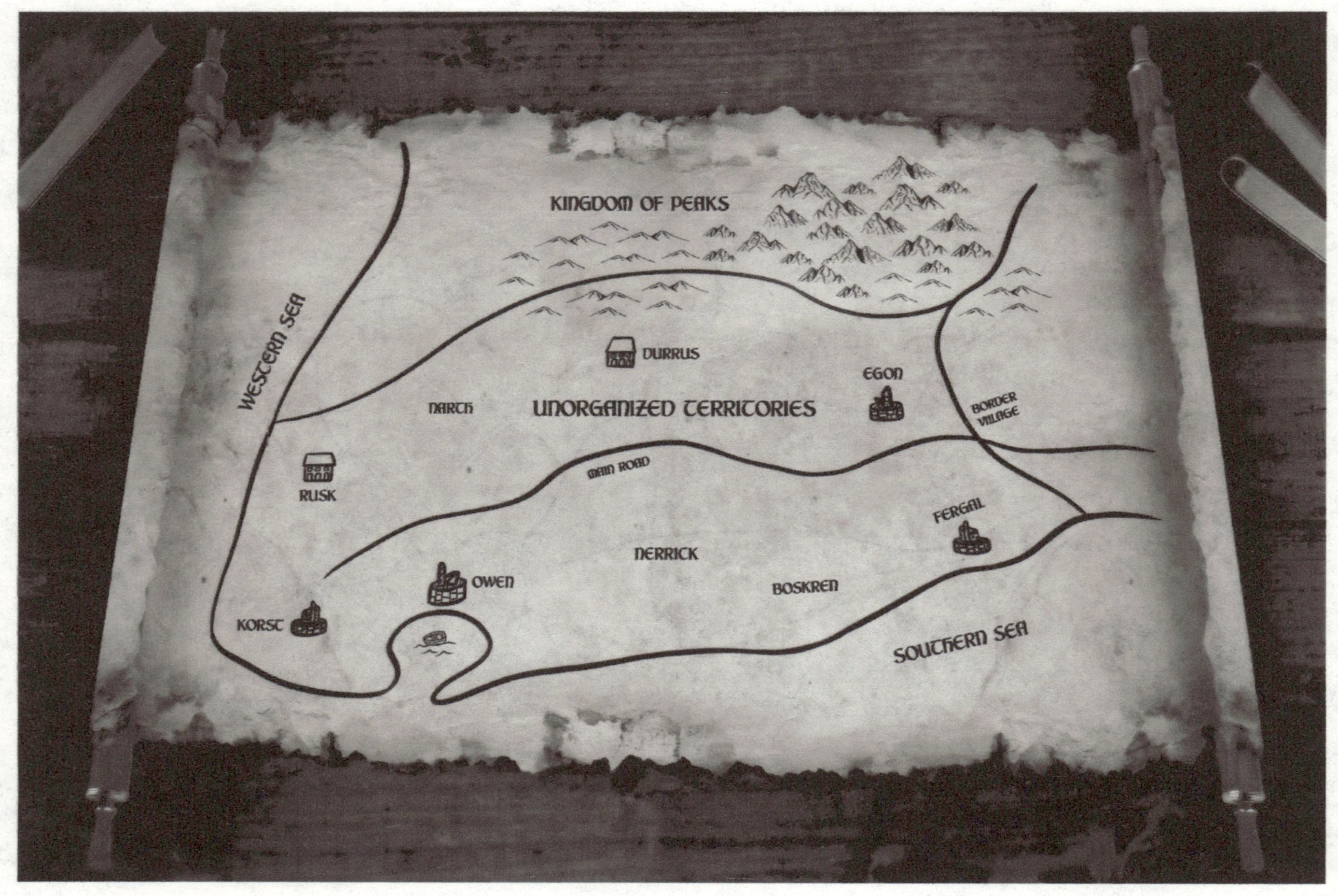

KINGDOM OF PEAKS
WESTERN SEA
DURRUS
EGON
BORDER VILLAGE
NARTH
UNORGANIZED TERRITORIES
MAIN ROAD
RUSK
FERGAL
NERRICK
BOSKREN
OWEN
KORST
SOUTHERN SEA

A Feeling
in the
Bones

When Peveril Castle first comes into view, Geoffrey gasps. "They must be able to see the whole valley from up there. They can probably see people approaching when they're still miles away."

"You're not wrong about that, Lord Geoffrey," says Sir Evrouin. "Makes it a strategically sound location. Take a good look as we get closer, though. Try to look at it through a commander's eyes – an enemy commander's eyes."

We're riding with a routine patrol – something I haven't done in far too long, given the campaign to suppress the Teuton threat and this past summer's papal inquisition. What a pleasure it is to be out with a troop once again – and especially to be doing it with my son. The early October air has the briskness of autumn, but there's plenty of time to complete this patrol before any risk of serious cold.

I'd allowed Geoffrey to make the arrangements for us to accompany this patrol, the only stipulation being that it had to be after all the excitement surrounding his sister Juliana's wedding. With his sixteenth birthday looming next year, it's time for more serious lessons in the art of kingship, so I've begun giving him responsibility for some things I'd ordinarily do myself. Small things, as yet, where his inexperience is no detriment, but sufficiently important for him to learn and to start developing some confidence.

An hour later, as the hill begins to loom above us, Evrouin turns in his saddle to address my son. "So what do you think now, Commander Geoffrey?"

"Well . . ." Geoffrey pauses, and I can almost see the calculations running through his mind. "An all-out assault from this side doesn't seem to make any sense at all. It must be more than a hundred feet up to the top."

"Closer to two hundred," says Evrouin.

"Even worse. And the hill is steep and mostly grassland, so there's nothing to impede the view of the defenders at the top. Cavalry's no help. By the time the horses struggled up that hill, they'd be too tired to be of any use in a fight. And most of them would get picked off anyway before they made it halfway up."

"So what would you do?"

"I think I'd send my scouts out to look for a better approach."

"Good thinking," says Evrouin. "So your scouts come back with the following reports. There's a village just ahead at the base of the hill, and the hill continues on around until you reach a river. The river flows beneath the castle on the back side. But it's a two-hundred-foot sheer cliff up to the castle from the river. On the side opposite the village, the hill is wooded and begins a slow descent toward the valley. That might be an easier way up for foot soldiers, but just before you reach the castle, there's a deep ravine at least as wide as a castle moat with sides almost as sheer as the cliff on the back and a stream flowing through the bottom toward the river."

Geoffrey furrows his brow. "And my orders are to take this castle?"

"That's right."

"Even if we had cannons, I don't know if we could aim them high enough to do any damage. And the higher we aim them, the shorter their range, if I understand what Sir Tobin's been teaching us. Most likely, the balls would fall short on the hill somewhere. So it seems my only option is a siege, sir."

"Well assessed, Commander Geoffrey," says Evrouin. "Which is why Peveril Castle has never been taken and only rarely come under assault. It only takes a couple dozen experienced longbowmen on the ramparts to make short shrift of anything trying to advance up that hill. Give some of them cross bows and the outcome is even deadlier. The attackers will turn tail in the blink of an eye."

As they've been talking, we've come to the edge of the village, but Geoffrey's obviously still thinking about military questions. "Sir Evrouin?" he asks as we make our way through the village toward the stable.

"Yes, Lord Geoffrey?"

"I wonder, sir . . . . Cannons might not be of much use to an attacking force, but what about for the defenders? Could they keep an army far enough away from the base of the hill that even a siege might be impractical?"

"You've hit on exactly what part of this mission is about. We don't know much yet about using cannons mounted so high above the intended targets. So the two engineers on this patrol are going to be working out the slope of the hill and the distances involved so we can try to figure things out. I'm still not convinced, though, that the cannons could entirely replace the bowmen."

"Why's that, sir?"

"Once the enemy works out the range, all they have to do is reposition themselves inside that range, potentially edging farther and farther up the hill. And there'll almost certainly be an ideal spot where the firing angle couldn't be adjusted enough to have any impact."

Geoffrey's thoughtful for another long moment. "That could be another tactic the attackers might use intentionally, right, sir?"

The smile on Evrouin's face is as big as the one I'm trying to suppress – it's important for my son to concentrate on learning from his military tutors and not rely on simple fatherly approval. "Sounds to me like you've been paying close attention to Tobin's lessons, lad. Keep it up. We're still figuring all this out and counting on your father to keep the peace long enough for us to know what we're doing before it really matters."

Time for me to release that smile. "Nothing I'd like better, Evrouin."

By now we've arrived at the stable. "Welcome, Your Grace," calls Peveril, striding toward us from the far end of the building as we dismount and turn the horses over to the grooms.

"Nice to be back when I can actually see the place," I reply. The last time I was here, I'd temporarily lost my sight after the cannon explosion in the war with King Charles.

"I came down with the pony carts. Emmeline's waiting at the top, fussing over having everything just so for your visit." He pauses to glance around. "Sir Evrouin – anything you and your troop need, just ask the stable master. And he'll have a pony cart ready when you want to come up in the morning."

"If it's all the same to you, my lord," Evrouin replies, "I'll ride up. Want to get a good feel again for what the slope of the hill is like. But the engineers will be doing their surveys tomorrow. I'm sure they'll be grateful for the cart for their equipment."

"Very well. So . . . Your Grace . . . Lord Geoffrey, come with me." We follow him back in the direction from which he'd come. Our gear has already been loaded onto the specialized baggage cart that's pulled by two ponies – they'll come up last. "Geoffrey, why don't you ride with me in the first cart, and I'll point out the sights," says Peveril. "It's only two people to a cart, so the ponies aren't over-taxed, and your father's done this before, so he has a pretty good idea of the place." Geoffrey doesn't hesitate. Thoughts of military strategy completely forgotten, he's an eager lad off on a new adventure, though he does manage to preserve just a bit of the decorum suitable to his position.

When we climb out of the carts at the top and he gets his first good look out over the valley and to the hills beyond, the only word to describe his expression is awestruck. "So what do you think of my home?" asks Peveril.

"I . . . I've never seen anything like it, sir. Is there really a cliff down to the river at the back?"

"Come . . . I'll show you." They make their way toward a spot on the back wall where there's a view over the parapet. "Two hundred feet straight down."

"So Sir Evrouin wasn't making it up."

Peveril chuckles. "Indeed he wasn't. It's our best protection."

"And the ravine on the opposite side?"

"Also there. But it's easier to see from inside the keep. I'll show you tomorrow."

Inside, Emmeline is eager to greet us – and just as her husband did, she takes my son under her wing. "Your rooms are all ready" – a quick glance to acknowledge my presence, before turning her attention back to Geoffrey – "and I've given you one of my favorites. It's just to the left at the top of the first staircase, and the view down to the river and out to the land beyond is breathtaking. I don't get up there very often anymore," she looks down at her walking sticks, "but I'll tell you a little secret if you promise not to tell Pev."

"I promise."

She leans her head close to Geoffrey's and whispers conspiratorially but loud enough for any of us to hear, "I made the steward carry me up there so I could be sure it was all just as I remembered it and everything was done perfectly for you."

Peveril's smile speaks volumes about how much he adores his wife, and she diverts a quick smile in his direction before returning her attention to Geoffrey. By now we've reached the base of the staircase, where the steward is waiting to show us to our rooms. "Freshen up from your travels and then join us in the sitting room," says Emmeline. "Emaurri and his wife will be with us for supper, if you've no objections, Sire."

"That would be delightful."

Conversation over the meal inevitably turns to who will be returning as our ambassador to the Kingdom Across the Southern Sea. Both Peveril and his son have held that post at various times, the father most recently. When he was taken hostage last summer in a plot to coerce me to withdraw my support for King Denis, it was the first time any of our ambassadors had ever faced danger. He was eventually released, unharmed, when the architect of the plot tried to enlist the support of the wrong person. But the fact that it happened at all – and the period of several weeks during which our spies could find no trace whatsoever of where he was being held – left Peveril and me both feeling just a bit shaken.

"For my mother's sake," says Emaurri, "to spare her the worry, I really think I should be the one to go this time, Sire."

Emmeline smiles and moves her head ever so slightly from side to side in that gesture mothers often adopt with children whose ideas are a bit naïve. "Tell me, Alfred, why is it that he thinks a mother would worry any less about her son than about her husband?" Emaurri manages to look a bit sheepish. Without waiting for a reply, she continues, "In truth, I think there's almost no likelihood of such a thing happening again. After all, we know who was behind it and why."

"And we know Denis has given Suidbert a role that will keep him out of any further mischief," I add.

"Mischief?" Peveril asks. "Is *that* what it was?"

"Alright, madness then."

"Foolishness, more like," Peveril chuckles.

"In any event, Alfred," Emmeline resumes, "Pev and I have talked about it, and neither of us has any concern about him returning, if that's what you should decide." She pauses for a sip of wine. "In fact, we've even talked about me going with him. It's been so long since I've done that, and I do miss it. Now that Gwendolyn's shown me I can still do things I once thought were lost to me forever, I think I'd like to try."

Emaurri's face is a portrait of astonishment. "Mother, I . . . I had no idea."

"She surprised me too, Son," says Peveril.

"Well, you may have surprised these two, my dear," I tell her, "but you've made *my* life ever so much easier."

"Oh?"

"I don't have to worry that what's best for the kingdom is at odds with what's best for people I truly care about. You see, I'd really like Emaurri to continue with the Territories. I'm convinced that nurturing the relationship he's started with Hedrek, in particular, and also with Goron is in everyone's best interests. So I was dreading the possibility of having to disrupt that. If you're agreeable, Emaurri?"

"As you wish, sir. And if I can make my mother happy at the same time, then it seems imprudent to say otherwise."

Emmeline giggles, but I can't help but laugh out loud. "Spoken like a true diplomat, Emaurri. Or maybe I should say 'a true Peveril.' Only you or your father would use the word 'imprudent' in that context."

Peveril and Emaurri both grin. Emmeline raises her glass. "To exciting times ahead for all of us!" And everyone joins her in the toast.

Geoffrey's naturally been quiet throughout this exchange, but now takes the opportunity to propose his own toast. "To Lady Peveril!" A sentiment we can all share.

As the evening comes to a close and we prepare to find our beds, I stop at the door to the corridor. "A word, Peveril?" He follows me out, closing the door behind him. "You didn't actually say anything when we were discussing postings. Do you have any hesitation about returning to Denis's court?"

"It's generous of you to ask, Alfred, but I've no qualms about the assignment. I'd go, even if for no other reason than to make her happy. She's right about the lack of danger though. Even if someone there still wishes you ill, they'd be foolhardy beyond all reason to risk a second encounter with the Teuton's dungeon master. And besides . . . having Emmeline there removes even the possibility that I'd consider walking home alone in the middle of the night." He pauses before adding,

"Between you and me, Alfred? I suspect eliminating that temptation might figure into her reasons for wanting to come along."

•   •   •   •   •

Evrouin arrives at the summit at midmorning. "If my horse could speak," he says as we meet him in the courtyard, "I think he'd be giving me a piece of his mind right now for refusing your offer of a pony cart, my lord."

Peveril chuckles. "The only cavalry advance I've ever thought might have the slightest chance of succeeding here would be Peaks highlanders, with their horses that are accustomed to the mountains."

"You'd be right about that, sir."

"So, Sir Evrouin, you've come to survey my little aerie for those new weapons."

"Sort of, sir. At the moment, we don't know if they even make any sense from these heights."

"Truth be told, I don't want the damn things. But I know Jasper would be remiss if he didn't at least consider it."

"The commander told me as much, sir. We'll try to stay out of your way while we do our work."

"I presume that involves some of your famous drawings?" I ask.

Sir Evrouin has a remarkable talent for rendering sketches that look identical to what a man's eye sees. His drawings – from both our vantage point and the enemy's – of the spot chosen to meet King Charles's invasion force helped our commanders plan their battlefield tactics. And his renderings of the proposed fortifications of our port made it easier for our allies to understand our intent.

"It does, Sire. From up here and from below. My engineers started their surveys at first light. We should finish by the end of the day."

"Then we'd best let you get on with it."

"Sir?" My son addresses Peveril.

"Yes, Geoffrey?"

"Why don't you want the cannons? I mean, why wouldn't you want to have the most modern weapons?"

"Well, for a start, I think they'd spoil the beauty of the place – the place that's my home. But beyond that, I'm concerned they'd just attract an opponent's attention – make them more determined to try to take the place for themselves in order to gain a tactical advantage. As it is, the landscape is so daunting that an enemy quickly comes to the conclusion it's not worth the cost in men and animals of even attempting an assault. But if they thought they could capture a prize where there were already cannons at the top and they didn't have to figure out how to haul their own up here, it might change their calculations dramatically. So to my way of thinking, installing cannons here would only make us more vulnerable – not safer."

"Have you discussed that with Jasper?" I ask.

"Briefly . . . while we were there for the wedding. Same time he let me know what this patrol would be up to here."

"And his reaction?"

"He's not convinced either way yet, but did acknowledge I was making a legitimate point. I think he wants to withhold judgment until they can assess the feasibility of even considering it. Can't fault him for that."

"Do us both a favor, if you will. Before you head back across the sea, talk it over with Samuel. He's spent a lot of time here and could have some insight that might sway Jasper's decision."

"Should have thought of that myself."

The pony carts are waiting in the courtyard when we emerge the next morning. So is Peveril. "No need to go down with us," I tell him. "Evrouin will have the troop mounted and ready to ride out when we get there. In fact, it's only my exalted rank that will save us from a tongue-lashing for being late."

Peveril chuckles. "Your visit has been delightful, as always, Alfred. Emmeline sends her best wishes to Gwendolyn."

Once down in the village, we join the troop and point our horses' heads east. The first half hour or so of the ride passes in quiet companionship. Geoffrey seems rather more subdued than usual, almost as if something is troubling him. Finally, he lets us in on his musings.

"Papa? Sir Evrouin?"

"Aye, lad?" Evrouin replies.

"I've been thinking about what Lord Peveril said about not wanting cannons. His argument makes some sense . . . at least when you think about things from a defensive perspective. But isn't any kind of weapon used for both offense and defense?"

"Aye, that it is."

"So wouldn't it be an advantage to have them for both? What I mean is . . . it seems like Peveril Castle could be strategically important if we were invaded from the east. If they could stop an advancing army before it got any deeper into the kingdom, wouldn't that be an enormous advantage for us?"

"Good thinking, lad," says Evrouin. "Now tell me, is that offense or defense?"

Geoffrey looks thoughtful for a few moments. "I'm not sure. Maybe a bit of both."

"Right again."

"So why isn't Lord Peveril thinking about that?"

"I'm not sure he isn't," Evrouin says, "but maybe he thinks his concerns outweigh everything else."

"Seems to me Geoffrey's hit on a very good question that he and his mates should discuss with Sir Tobin," I chime in. "What do you think, Evrouin?"

"That he has, Sire."

We ride on in silence for several minutes. "There's one other thing I want you lads to consider in coming to your recommendation."

"What's that, Papa?"

"Lord Peveril is right about something else. That castle is his home. It's been the Peveril family seat for over two centuries and will be for generations to come. So he has a right to have a say in how his home is used."

"But don't the lords Thorssen have a hereditary obligation to keep watch over the sea and the mouth of the river?" asks Geoffrey. "Doesn't that mean the lords Peveril have some sort of obligation to the kingdom as well?"

"Might there not be a difference between keeping watch and active engagement with an enemy?" I ask then quickly add, "Don't answer that now. Discuss it with your mates."

"Don't forget, lad," Evrouin says, "we don't know yet what's even feasible for that terrain, so take that into consideration too."

"And, Geoffrey, I want to hear what you come up with. So when you're ready, ask Coliar to schedule some time for you to report your conclusions and how you arrived at them."

"Yes, sir."

Now I just have to remember to see Tobin straightaway once we're back home to give him the details of the problem we've set for the lads so he's not caught off guard. There's no doubt in my mind Geoffrey will bring it up in their very first training session.

By late morning, we reach the site where the two armies faced each other when Charles invaded in his ill-conceived attempt to remove me from the throne. Nature has worked her magic, and the broad grassy meadow shows no sign that hundreds upon hundreds of men and horses once trampled this spot beneath their feet as men and arms clashed. Evrouin calls a halt in a spot that seems approximately where our command tents stood at the time, invites Geoffrey to join him at the front of the column, and begins describing how the armies were arrayed. "Once they got settled in opposite us, there was a parlay just there," he points, "halfway between the two camps. Nothing came of it, of course. King Charlie had no intention of backing down, and we had no intention of letting him advance any farther. But the formalities had to be observed. The fighting got underway the next morning."

As he goes on to describe how we surprised Charles's forces when they attempted a sunrise cavalry charge, my eye is drawn inexorably to the evergreen grove off to my right – on what was Charles's left flank. This is the first time I've been here since that fateful day, and the memories are rushing back. I turn Altair's head and begin a slow walk toward the grove. Behind me, I hear Geoffrey call, "Papa?" and Evrouin's gentle remonstrance, "Leave him be, lad. He needs to make his peace with what happened that day."

I urge Altair to a trot and we quickly arrive at the edge of the grove – not a stealthy approach through the woods this time. The events of the day play out in my mind. Samuel and his men sneaking up from behind the cannon position. One of our archers quietly felling the man tending the fire. Realization dawning among those manning the cannon that they weren't alone in the grove. The hurried loading for one last shot before turning to face the threat. The ear-shattering explosion. The heat. The wind. Sirius rearing up in fear. Sliding to the ground, unable to stay in the saddle as my horse pawed at the air. And something I've never remembered before – Sirius's scream as a huge chunk of hot iron penetrated his chest. Then utter silence. And impenetrable blackness, my sight a victim of my proximity to the explosion.

I dismount and stand beside Altair's neck. Sensing the depth of my emotion, the horse lays his big head over my shoulder and rests it on my chest. I stroke his muzzle as tears well in my eyes. It seems somehow fitting that Sirius's son is with me as I finally get to say a proper goodbye to the horse that almost certainly saved my life that day. That Samuel and I both survived when everyone else in the grove perished in the explosion was nothing short of miraculous.

I wipe the tears from my eyes and look around the grove as the memories recede into the background. Nature has worked her magic here as well. Here and there, a chunk of metal is just visible in the undergrowth. Ahead and to the left, a piece of iron is lodged in the trunk of a tree, but the tree itself seems no worse for its injury. I chuckle to myself, imagining the utter confusion of someone coming on this place for the first time and trying to puzzle out what might have happened. And with that little half laugh comes the realization that my soul has now healed as thoroughly as my eyesight – that in some peculiar way, actually seeing the place again rather than trying to recall what I couldn't see in the immediate aftermath of those events was the salve long-needed for the last of my wounds.

Mounting up, I urge Altair to a canter to return to where the troop is waiting. "Are you alright, Papa?" Geoffrey asks as I rein Altair in and resume my position in the column.

"Never better, Son. I trust Evrouin's told you all about the skirmishes here?"

"Yes, sir." The enthusiasm of youth resonates in his tone. "You never told me about those polished shields. That was brilliant."

"I thought so too at the time. Never hurts in a battle to have a little surprise to spring when your opponent least expects it. Now, Evrouin, something *I've* never seen is the route our army used to drive Charles out of the kingdom. Care to show it to us?"

"My pleasure, Sire. It's our route to the border. There's a stream not too far ahead – just beyond what would have been the back of Charles's encampment. We can water the horses there and have a bite to eat."

After a brief rest, we resume our trek eastward, Evrouin pointing out how our forces separated Charles from his supply wagons and captured the two cannons. When we break camp the following day, I return to my usual habit of taking a different position in the column each morning and following each midday break. Another habit learned from my grandfather. And I've long since learned he was right about the kind of loyalty that arises from ordinary conversations with ordinary men-at-arms.

As we approach the stone markers on either side of the road that mark the border with the Eastern Kingdom, Evrouin calls a halt. "We'll make camp here for the night," he says. "Standard practice, Lord Geoffrey, for a patrol that inspects the border."

"In case anyone's watching, lad," adds the knight riding beside my son. "Lets them know we're here and keeping an eye on things, but staying clearly within our own land."

Over a supper of dried meat and bread, Geoffrey asks Evrouin what inspecting the border entails. "Depends on where," Evrouin replies. "Most all of them have stone markers about an hour apart at a horse's walk where there isn't anything else to mark the border. Going north from here, that's what we should find, and part of our job is to make sure they're all in place and all in the right place – that nobody's moved one, trying to encroach into our territory."

"But how could you know if a marker's been moved?" Geoffrey asks.

"The markers that aren't along a main road like those two," he gestures toward the road, "are shorter. Well, the part that sticks up out of the ground is shorter. The rest of the stone block is buried deep in the earth. So if anyone wanted to move it or just do away with it, they'd have to dig it up. And that would leave signs that someone had been digging there – signs that would be obvious for months – maybe even a year – if you know to look for them.

"So going north from here, we'll be looking for a marker every hour – or every half hour at a trot – until we come to the spot where a stream makes a sharp bend to the east. From there, the stream is the border until you get to the northernmost point, at the Kingdom of Lakes. There's an ancient stone circle there that marks the point where the three kingdoms meet."

"What about to the south?" asks Geoffrey.

"The land in that direction is mostly wild woodlands. About half a day south of here, there's an ancient hill fort that spans the border. Everyone knows if you keep to your side of the hill fort, you're safely within your own lands. Then about an hour south of there, where the land has flattened out, the marker is a long stone wall. Some say it's the remains of a Roman fort, others think it's a garden wall that's the only thing left of a Roman villa."

"Have you seen it, sir?"

"I have, lad. And I'm more inclined toward it being a garden wall. Doesn't seem thick enough to have been part of a fortification."

"Another possibility," I interject, "is that it was once part of a fort, but much of it has been pillaged for building stones."

"Could be, Sire. Anyway, south of that, the land gets even wilder. Not even any forest folk living down there. And the closer you get to the sea, the marshier it gets."

"Will we be patrolling south, sir?" asks Geoffrey.

"Not every patrol in these parts goes that way," Evrouin replies. "Once a year at most – usually longer in between. Nobody down that way to help, really, and no way the border markings can be moved. The usual route here is through the valley, then north, then back through the hills and past the quarries before heading home." Evrouin doesn't miss the look of disappointment that Geoffrey can't mask. "But I don't think Sir Jasper would mind if we took a little side trip for the heir to the throne to see some of the history of the land he'll one day be in charge of."

Truth be told, I haven't seen those sites either and am just as intrigued as my son. And when we arrive at the hill fort the next day, it seems the other knights are equally fascinated. "Look at those defenses, lad," says the knight riding next to Geoffrey. "See how they made those dips in the land – like moats – all around so an attacker has to actually climb four hills to get to the top? And every hill gets steeper as you go up."

"The moats don't provide any shelter either," says the man behind. "If the defenders were lobbing spears or rocks at the men in the moats, they'd have to climb one way or the other to get out."

"And forget using rain as cover for an assault," says the man who spoke first. "Those moats would start filling up pretty quickly and the grass on the hills would be slick straightaway then turn to a muddy morass as it got trampled."

I wonder who the ancient people were who built this place – and how long ago they built it. No doubt it was before men in this part of the world began writing chronicles. But if the Romans came here, they might have encountered the descendants of those original builders and might have recorded their notions about the history of this place and others like it.

Everyone dismounts to climb the hills and have a look around. Much to my disappointment, we men forego the final climb to the top lest someone watching on the other side mistake our intentions, but Evrouin deems it safe enough for Geoffrey to give it a try provided he stays carefully on our side of the summit. He doesn't have to be asked twice, though it takes quite some scrambling to make it up the steep slope.

"You can really see a long way from up there," he reports when he rejoins us to return to our horses. "The land on the other side is much flatter toward the south, so the approach would be a lot easier. But attackers would still have to negotiate all these hills and moats. And the defenders would be able to see them coming from quite some distance away."

"What about the terrain to the north and due east, lad?" asks Evrouin.

"Hilly, but not so much as what we rode through to get here. The hills aren't as high and they drop off to a plain pretty fast."

Another mental note for myself – ask Samuel about our vulnerability here. Based on Evrouin's questions, I'm confident he expects to have the same conversation with Jasper. Is it only Fortuna's favor that's protected us so far?

We make the trip to the Roman wall and back at the trot. Evrouin wants to be sure we have time to return to last night's campsite. "Jasper would have my hide if anything happened to you, Sire, because I decided to camp in these wild hills." It's slower going through the hills as we give the horses their heads and let them pick their own path on the sometimes-rough woodland track. The full moon is rising as the hills give way to the valley, so there's plenty of light to return to the main road and set up camp. The dilemma of the Roman wall remains unsolved. There's no doubt it's been pillaged, but with only the single wall remaining, there's little to confirm if it's an outer wall of a villa compound or if it was once part of a fort. But there should definitely be something in either our library or the one at the monastery to shed some light on the Roman occupation of this area.

The next morning, we turn our horses' heads north, finding nothing amiss as we make our way toward the stream. "This is always an easy patrol," Evrouin tells Geoffrey, who's riding at the front, alongside our captain. "Rarely anything to do but observe and report back. Those border stones are always right where they're supposed to be. And I'm not sure there's a knight alive who can remember ever having to repair a deep rut or a small hole in a road in these parts."

"Why's that, sir?"

"On account of the Peverils keep everything to rights."

"But I thought the main roads were the king's responsibility."

"That they are, lad, but the Peverils have even more need for smooth roads than the rest of the kingdom. You'll see why when we come to the quarries."

About an hour north of the point where we picked up the stream, we arrive at a small village. Well, two villages, really – one on each side of the stream. A clapper bridge spans the water between them, a sure sign that the notion of a border is of no consequence to the people who live here as neighbors. Half a dozen men are standing at this end of the bridge, where the slab from the bank to the first pillar is missing. Evrouin calls a halt to see how we can help.

"Stone be washed away in the flood after that big storm back in the spring," says one of the village men. "Same as the four houses that be closest to the stream this side and yon." He points toward the village opposite. "All summer, we just be wading across. Bits of time we have after tending to flocks and fields and gardens, we needs be building back those houses. But now winter be on its way, needs be fixing the bridge. A man could catch his death of cold wading across in winter."

Evrouin beckons to the two engineers in the patrol. "Anything we can do?" he asks.

One of the men wades into the stream to examine the remainder of the bridge. The other asks the villagers, "Did the slab wash completely away?"

"We be finding it downstream a ways. But 'twere cracked. Like something heavy slam against it. 'Twere thinner than the other slabs, so mayhap dinna' take much to crack it. We bring it back in the wagon anyways and try to put it back in place, but first time a man walk on it, it break. That be the pieces just there." He points to two slabs of stone lying on the bank where the other engineer is just climbing out of the water.

The two engineers huddle in conversation for a bit, then one of them asks, "Do you have any spare planks of wood? Maybe something left over from rebuilding the houses?"

"Some. Not be much, but ye can have a look-see." One of the villagers leads the way toward a small barn. They return with a cart filled with scraps of wood and a bucket about half full of nails. Most of the men of the patrol get busy, supervised by the engineers, as the rest of us watch while they create a triangular-shaped wooden frame that they place in the water, abutting the stone pillar that supports the next slab. Two men hold the frame in place against the flow of the stream while the others place the two pieces of the old slab on top and pile some broken stones they'd found at the base of the pillar onto the end to anchor the frame to the bank.

"That should be good enough for people or a man with a small animal, like a sheep or a small pig, to cross – but no more than one animal at a time," one of the engineers tells the villagers. "I wouldn't try it with a horse or a cow or a loaded cart, though. We've made the frame as strong as we could with the short planks we had, but it can't really carry a lot of weight. The stones should hold it in place for a time, if there's not another flood, but this is really just temporary.

"That pillar," he points to the one nearest this bank, "was also damaged by the flood and needs some repair. We're headed to the quarries next, so I'll send someone from there with a new, stronger slab and everything they'll need to repair the pillar. If you're careful, this should hold until they get here."

We reach the first quarry almost simultaneously with Ademar, Lord Peveril's eldest son, who's in charge of the family businesses. "Your Grace . . . Lord Geoffrey . . . seems my arrival is timely." He offers a smart bow that we both acknowledge. "Father said you might be interested in seeing the workings of a quarry."

"That we would, Ademar," I reply, "but first, I think two of these men need your help with a bridge repair for some villagers near the border."

The engineers explain what's needed, and Ademar points to a nearby shed. "See Nick Ditton over there, and tell him I said to organize whatever's required. We'll take it from here." Then he turns his attention back to us. "What say we start at the beginning, Geoffrey, at the rock face?"

"I'd like that, sir."

We arrive just as a huge slab of rock breaks away from the face and lands on the ground below in a resounding crash, sending a cloud of dust into the air. Geoffrey's eyes are as big as saucers. "How do they get such a big chunk off all in one piece?"

"It's all a matter of knowing the rock, lad," Ademar replies. "You see, rock breaks along its natural seams – those grooves and lines you see in any exposed rock anywhere. An expert quarryman can look at those seams and visualize just exactly how the rock will break apart. So his job is to encourage it. If there's already a crack forming, they'll use wedges to widen the crack. They pound the wedges as far into the crack as they can and then soak them with water. The wood will expand and nudge the crack open. So they keep repeating that until the crack shows signs of being ready to give way. They might have to work on a couple of seams simultaneously to get the stone out. And if the seam goes really deep, they might have to drive in long picks to use for leverage to get it to finally break away from the face.

"In winter, they'll just let the water do all the work. Fill a crack with water, and when it freezes, the ice works just like the wet wedges, widening the crack. Keep repeating that, and you can sometimes get a nice slab to fall away completely on its own. Rather like that one just did, though it had quite a bit of help from wedges and picks. It's always nice to get a slab intact like that because then we can break it up into the right kinds of pieces for building stones. But it's not unusual to get much smaller pieces. We collect everything, though, even the little rocks you can hold in your hand, because the stone masons want those for filler when they're building walls."

"Looks like hard work," I remark.

"It is, Sire. Both at the rock face and afterward. Which is why a full day's work for a man here is shorter than for most jobs. And why we make sure our men are well fed."

"I'm glad to hear that, Ademar, though I'd have expected nothing less from your family."

"It serves two purposes, Sire. We work our quarries slowly. Our stone is the lifeblood of the estate, but when it's gone, it's gone, and then what do we have to create wealth for the family? Yes, we have the forests and could cut timber, but that has to be managed carefully as well. It's an asset that could be depleted quickly unless whoever is in charge exercises restraint.

"So taking good care of our workers goes hand in hand with not over-working the quarries. It also means we get the very best quarrymen anywhere to be found."

As he's been talking, we've been watching the preparations for the next step in the process. A man who must be the master stone-cutter walks along the top of the slab, studying the surface. The slab is thinner at one end than the other, and he decides that's where they'll start work. "Alright, you four," he calls to a group of men standing to one side. "Really nice seam here about a foot and a half back from the edge. Let's take the chase-masse to it and see if we can get it to break off cleanly."

"What's a . . . what did he call it?" Geoffrey asks.

"A chase-masse. Stone-cutting tool with a long wooden handle and a metal head, sort of like an axe. One end is sharpened and the other is flat. Watch how they use it."

The men work in pairs, starting from the center of the slab and working in opposite directions toward the side. One man places the sharp side of the tool on the seam and holds it there while the other strikes the flat end with a heavy iron hammer. When they reach the side of the slab, they return to the center and repeat the process. "Going slowly again," says Ademar. "They want the rock to split of its own accord."

"What happens if there aren't any seams?" asks Geoffrey. "How do you break it apart then?"

"They drill holes close together and then use a chisel to remove the rock between the holes. That makes a channel where they can use the technique with the wedges. It's harder going, but sometimes you just have to force the stone to break where you want it to. Come with me. I'll show you."

He leads us toward a covered area where men are working on three stones, each about two hands thick and about four times the size of a regular building stone. "This stone's pretty hard, so we use star drills."

Geoffrey inches toward the workmen for a closer look. "Ye be wanting to give it a try, lad?" one of the men asks as he stops working. "Here." He holds out a metal shaft that's sharpened on one end and flat on the other along with a small, heavy hammer. Geoffrey takes one tool in each hand. "So what ye do, see," continues the workman, "is ye put the sharp end of the drill in that hole I be starting and give it a right whack with the hammer."

Somewhat tentatively, my son does as instructed. "Ye best be pounding a lot harder than that, lad, else ye be here nigh on to next Whitsun afore ye make a decent hole. Here . . . give me the hammer and ye hold the drill." He gives the drill a resounding whack and Geoffrey's entire body shudders with the force. "Now," says the workman, handing the hammer back to Geoffrey, "ye turn the drill just a wee bit and give it a whack."

This time Geoffrey delivers a much more forceful blow to the drill. "That be better," says his tutor. "Now, ye be turning the drill and whack it again and do that over and over until ye be getting a hole."

Geoffrey repeats the process several times then hands the tools back to his tutor. "I think it might still be next Whitsun before I could make much of a hole," he says, "but thank you for letting me try."

"Do they do this all day?" I ask Ademar.

"At some quarries, yes, but not here. It's jarring work – hard on the bones and shoulders – and if they get too tired, it's too easy to get injured. So my foremen insist they take regular breaks. There are lots of other tasks that need doing around here, so they rotate who's working with the drills."

"What's that over there?" Geoffrey points to his left. "It looks like a smithy."

"That it is," Ademar replies. "That drill you were using, Geoffrey . . . it'll get dull quickly on this hard stone. A driller might go through a dozen or more in a day. So at the end of the day, he drops off the dull ones at the smithy and picks up freshly sharpened tools for the next day's work. The blacksmith keeps our horses shod too. And makes fittings for the wagons and for the wheelwright. That shed over by the barn is the wheelwright's workshop."

As he speaks, Ademar leads us past the smithy toward a large barn. "Shelter for the wagons and for the horses at night or when the weather's bad. Storage for hay and oats. Our big draft horses require a lot of food for the work they do. Have a look inside at one of the wagons, Geoffrey."

I follow my son inside the barn, just as curious as he is. The wagons are sturdier than any I've ever seen. "And look, Papa," says Geoffrey. "Two axles in the rear."

"A load of stone is unimaginably heavy," says Ademar, who's clearly enjoying how enthralled his guests are with an operation neither of us has ever observed firsthand. "We have to do everything possible to make sure a wagon doesn't break down when we're delivering a load."

"And is that why you maintain your own roads, sir?" Geoffrey asks.

"Precisely, lad. We can't risk a broken wheel or axle in transit. Maybe next time you're here, I can show you what it takes to load a wagon, and you'll understand why a breakdown on the road would be such a catastrophe. We've already made our last delivery for the year. The days are getting shorter and the weather will be closing in soon, so we won't have any more deliveries until after the spring thaw."

"Do you keep the quarry operating during the winter?" I ask as we leave the barn.

"We don't shut down completely. But we only do what the weather permits. If we have a really mild winter, we may be able to get a fair portion of the first load ready for the following year. Mostly, though, the men do what needs to be done indoors, out of the cold wind and snow. And if it's too bad, everything shuts down except taking care of the horses and the other necessities of life. It does me no good to have men getting frostbite working out in the cold."

By now we've made our way back to where Sir Evrouin waits with the rest of the patrol. "Is there anything you need here, my lord?" Evrouin directs his question to Ademar.

"Not at the moment. And don't give a second thought to those villagers, Sir Evrouin. We'll see they're taken care of."

"Thank you, sir. We'll check in at the other quarries, as they're on the way, but if my past experience is any guide, they'll have things well in hand."

Ademar smiles. "You let me know if they don't, Sir Evrouin. And you, Sire . . . Lord Geoffrey . . . visit us again sometime."

"We might just do that," I tell him, "if you promise not to put us to work."

Ademar laughs out loud. "That's a promise I can easily make. My father would have my hide if I did."

We turn our horses' heads west and resume the homeward journey.

We arrive home to find the castle deserted. That is, if a place crawling with guards and servants and stable boys and knights in barracks and horses in paddocks can be described as deserted. "They all be gone home or to the country manor for the harvest festivals," says Osbert as I shed my clothes and eye the steaming bath eagerly. What a treat after weeks on patrol! The sentries and kitchen boys have certainly not relaxed their vigilance.

I still marvel at the financial enterprise behind the king having a hot bath waiting when he returns from a journey. How long has it been since I increased the amount of money I give Osbert to take care of such things? I make a mental note to be sure his next purse is a bit fatter than the last one. And one thing I won't have to worry about – Osbert will make sure the kitchen boy at the head of this particular enterprise doesn't pocket the extra for himself and that everyone who plays a role benefits from the king's largesse.

"In that case, it'll be just you and me and Geoffrey for supper," I say.

"Aye, m'lord. I be telling Matthias 'tweren't any need to fuss, but he say ye be needing something nice after all those days of camp food." The steward has definite opinions about what's proper for a regal repast, even when it's just a simple supper.

"Much as I hate to admit it, Osbert, a tasty meal wouldn't go amiss this evening."

The following day, I forego my morning ride – Altair's had plenty of exercise these past weeks and deserves a bit of lazy grazing. Instead, I make straight for the barracks and manage to waylay Sir Tobin before he goes out to meet the lads. He listens thoughtfully as I describe the problem Evrouin and I set for the boys to grapple with. "It's as if you were reading my mind, sir," he says.

"Oh?"

"The boys' enthusiasm for all things modern seems to know no bounds. I've been scratching my head trying to devise an exercise for them that would force them to think about modern and traditional side by side, depending on who their opponent might be. But something real like this . . . I suspect it'll spark their imaginations far better than anything I could conjure up."

"Be sure they don't just rush through it, Tobin – that they actually look at things from every perspective, including Peveril's. Geoffrey knows that's the expectation. But at their age, it's far too easy to get caught up in whatever your mates are excited about."

"You needn't worry, sir. It's going to take some time for the engineers and armorers to work through the details your patrol brought back. The boys will have to assess things several times as they get new information." He pauses, clearly mulling something over.

"Something on your mind, Tobin?"

"I was just wondering, sir, if you might want progress reports as they go along?"

"Not this time, Tobin. Let's let them wrestle with this on their own."

Since I'm already nearby, I make my way to the knight commander's office where I find him with Evrouin, poring over the drawings and figures of the landscape around Peveril Castle. They both jump to their feet as I appear in the doorway. "As you were, gentlemen." Evrouin scrambles to pull another chair up to the table before they both resume their seats. This is the first time I've seen the drawings. "I'm still in awe of your skill, Evrouin. Looks like we're right back there riding through the valley looking up the hill."

"I just draw what I see, Sire."

"So what's the next step, Jasper?"

"Precisely what we were talking about, Sire. Quite a bit of work to do yet to even know what's possible. We may even have to make a model of the place to figure out the tactical position once the experts work out what the weaponry can and can't do."

"Well, I'm afraid you're going to have an eager bunch of trainees pressing for answers to all those questions."

"Evrouin told me about the problem you posed for the lads," says Jasper.

"I'm sure Tobin will keep them from making a complete nuisance of themselves, but I wanted you to have my personal gratitude for helping them out. They're probably a bit young yet to tackle something so complex, but it's not too soon for Geoffrey to begin learning to think deeply about such things."

Jasper nods his understanding. "Seems to me it was a successful patrol all around, then – both for my purposes and yours. Evrouin says you went all the way down to the Roman wall."

"Indeed it was and indeed we did. You know, one would think, at my age and in my position, that I'd have seen every inch of the kingdom by now. But I'd never actually been all the way to the eastern border and didn't even know those ancient sites were there. It was a good education for me as well."

Japer smiles broadly. "Our duty is to serve, Sire. Truth be told, not many people *do* know about them. And it's one reason we rarely take a patrol down that way. The rough wildness of the place is a natural barrier, and we don't want to send any signals that we think it requires defenses beyond what nature has already provided."

I leave them to their day's work and make my way back to the castle to my own. But Jasper's remarks linger with me. Is that traditional strategy still wise?

My secretary makes it a habit to present matters related to the king's justice only once a month, and today's the day. Signing the affirmations of sentences handed out by magistrates to assorted miscreants is usually just a formality – Rainard's already reviewed them before they appear on my desk. But as he and Juliana have been away on their wedding trip this month, I'm reading each one more carefully this morning. There's one that brings a smile to my face. A repeat offender and inveterate spinner of yarns, the man called Asa who appealed his case to me a year ago has once again been sentenced to spend some time in jail for theft and lying to the sheriff – with an extra week tacked on "to contemplate the merits of telling the truth." Apparently, the two days I added to his earlier sentence for the same purpose were insufficient to needs. For the magistrate's sake, I hope it works this time, but I've no intention of holding my breath to find out.

As I finish signing the last of these documents, Geoffrey wanders in from the outer room. Coliar knows to allow him free access if I'm working alone, but it's unusual for him to come in the morning unless Tobin has given the boys some time off from training. He waits patiently while I finish signing the last document, then holds out a folded message. "For you, Papa. It was inside my letter from Denis." Geoffrey and Denis began their correspondence right after Denis was crowned. They share many common interests, but both of them seemed to recognize instinctively that this was a method Denis could also use to seek my advice when it would be unwise to do so openly. Usually, that takes the form of Denis asking Geoffrey's opinion on the matter in question, knowing my son will discuss it with me. This is the first time the young king has included a completely separate missive, apparently for my eyes only. "I think he must want to tell you something really secret," says Geoffrey.

"Or maybe it's just too long and complicated to include in his letter to you – or something that didn't fit with your own correspondence. Does he have anything interesting to say?"

"He wants to buy some horses from us. He's discovered that their breeding program was badly neglected while his uncle was king, and he and his stable master both think some new stock is needed to revitalize it. They'll need more draught horses to transport the new weapons to a battlefield, and Denis liked the looks of the ones Master Elvin's been breeding. He'd also like a couple of mares so they have some new bloodlines. So I'm going to get Elvin's help to make some good choices for him."

"And have you thought about what price you might ask for these horses?"

"I thought maybe Elvin could help with that too."

"He could. But don't forget this will be a trade deal between two kingdoms – not just one man selling a horse to another. You need to be sure to put the right value on something we have that Denis wants."

"How do I do that, Papa?"

"Well, I'd suggest you talk to Lord Thorssen, who knows a bit about trade between kingdoms, and to Lord Guyat, since he's in charge of the Treasury."

"I can do that."

"But I have another suggestion. Is there anything Denis has that we might want?"

Geoffrey furrows his brow in thought. "How would I know that, Papa?"

"Asking questions seems like it might be a good start."

"Then I'll start with you. Is there something you think we want?"

"I seem to recall they once imported a few horses from across the Roman Sea. A different style of horse altogether – lighter of bone than ours and remarkably fast and agile. When we stopped at the battlefield on that last patrol, I remembered how we approached the cannon emplacement from the rear. The men firing the weapon were intently focused on their work and didn't even realize we were there until we'd killed one of their number and were about to kill more. We'd have succeeded, too, if the cannon hadn't exploded. What if we had some lightly armed men on fleet horses who could get in behind the cannon positions, quickly dispense with a few of the men managing the firing, and get out just as fast? Would that be a useful tactic? The idea's only just occurred to me, so I don't know if it's forethought or folly."

"But it sounds like another thing my mates and I could discuss with Sir Tobin."

"Indeed. Talk to Carew as well. He was there that day. And he was also in charge of creating the training plans for how to fight in the presence of the new weapons. He'll have some ideas." My son's excitement at being handed another big responsibility is written all over his face. "Then, once you've decided on your trade, bring me your proposal." Geoffrey suddenly turns thoughtful again. "Something else on your mind, Son?"

"I'm not sure. I . . . well . . . it's just that . . . you've always said I should also think about whether or not doing something is a good idea in the first place. Does that apply to this too?"

"Why don't you think about that as well and let me know what you decide."

"And talk it over with other people?"

"If you think that seems helpful. Just remember that when you bring people into your confidence, you need to be sure it's the right people – people you can trust to be discreet and respect that confidence." This is hardly a matter of great import to the world, but it's not too soon for him to start learning how to choose his conversations. In point of fact, I hope he *does* discuss this with his mates – and even with Edward – as an important exercise for them all in learning how to be reliable advisors.

"Alright, Papa. I think maybe I should go see Elvin now."

"Then off you go."

When the door closes behind him, I open Denis's letter.

My dear Alfred,

I hope you will forgive this ruse, but there are things I wanted to tell you without having my words scrutinized by all my advisors. I long for the day when I come into the crown in my own right so such subterfuge is no longer necessary. There is no doubt that my minders have my best interests at heart, though in this matter, I see no need for their interference.

But enough of moaning over the fact that I am straining at my bonds and eager to take the bit in my own teeth. All in good time.

There is actually some quite good news to report. We have just returned from a state visit to the Kingdom East of Rome, which exceeded everyone's expectations. We have only ever had a casual friendship with this kingdom, but everyone is of like mind that this visit laid the foundations of a much more substantial alliance. The Duchess of Lamoreaux accompanied us, and it is my opinion that her presence and her high rank within our nobility proved most advantageous to the conversations around strengthening our ties. I was unaware that her first husband had familial links to their royal house, though not so close that he was ever likely to figure in the succession. But that relationship had not been forgotten in the land of her birth.

This visit began as a test for Suidbert in his new role as ambassador at large, tasked with arranging state visits. Though my father and Lord Greville were both reticent to bring him back to court so soon, lest he disrupt the emerging congeniality, Petronilla and I eventually prevailed in our view that leaving him isolated presented more opportunities for mischief. It did not hurt, I think, that his role requires him to be away from court at least as often as he is here. And Petronilla took your suggestion to pander to his vanity a bit by casting this role as more important than it probably is in reality. This was all done in private, as you might imagine, to avoid ruffling other feathers, but it seems, at least so far, to have been sufficient to support his high opinion of himself.

We began with the Kingdom East of Rome because the nature of our past relationship there was such that little would be lost if Suidbert proved inept or if he chose to purposefully subvert his mission. Thankfully, his desire to be seen as important has guided his actions so far, and the whole business was perfectly planned and orchestrated. I made a point of thanking him in open court, though without too much fanfare, to give him the opportunity for some small amount of preening in the presence of his peers. With any luck, this will be sufficient oil for the mechanism to ensure he performs flawlessly in the next mission we have set for him – an invitation to the King of Peaks for a state visit here at my court.

Which brings me to the second point of this missive. To keep Suidbert occupied, we are sending him to the Peaks now to convey an invitation for a visit sometime in the spring. This means he will be passing through your kingdom in a week or a bit more from the time you receive this letter. I have given him instructions to present himself to you for the purpose of conveying my greetings and the reason for his presence in your lands.

Alfred, we have not told Suidbert that we know he was responsible for the abduction of Lord Peveril. The only way he would be aware we have that knowledge is if the Teuton king has told him, and I'm convinced that man would rather keep Suidbert dangling on the end of a string than to reveal he told us the truth of the matter. Petronilla agrees with me that leaving Suidbert to wonder what we may or may not know is likely the best approach to ensure his good behavior – and leaves us with a trump card to play should that behavior turn sour.

So the formal appearance at your court is yet another test for him. If the man has any sense, he will be exceedingly nervous that you may have somehow discovered what happened and rather apprehensive about how you might receive him. I look forward to hearing from you how he performs, perhaps in a private note from Geoffrey if you deem that appropriate.

I trust you will reassure Geoffrey that I have no intent to snub him by writing to you in this way and that you will feel free to share with him any part of my news that is appropriate or consistent with what you may have told him about the events of this past summer. I also look forward to learning what he is able to organize relative to my desire to revitalize our horse breeding program.

And now to prepare for the final autumn hunts and look forward to the Yuletide, which will be upon us in short order.

Denis

Over the past few days, people have been returning from the harvest festivals – or in the case of Lord and Lady Ernle, from their sojourn at Gwen's cottage on Lake St. Anne. "It's a beautiful place," Rainard remarks during our private family supper the first night they're back.

"So different from when we had to stay so secluded during Uncle John's reign," Juliana adds. "We crossed the lake to the village two or three times every week. Such friendly people there. And, of course, they all know Hamon and his family and remember you, Mama, from your summer holidays there as a girl."

"How are Hamon and Agnes?" asks Gwen. The caretaker/steward and his wife went to great lengths to protect us while we were in hiding there.

"Quite well," Juliana replies. "All their children are married now and living in the village. But they still help their parents with whatever needs to be done around the cottage. And Father Bartholomé's just the same as ever."

"I swear, that man never ages," says Gwen. "He must be around sixty by now."

"You'd never know it by how spry he is," Rainard chuckles.

"Anyway," says Juliana, "we're only stopping long enough to collect the dogs before heading for Ernle Manor. It's important for us to spend some time with the people there straightaway – even our first

Christmas there as lord and lady. We'll be back here for Twelfth Night, of course."

"That's assuming you can spare me, sir," says Rainard.

"I think we might just be able to muddle through."

"Oh, Papa, don't be silly." Juliana laughs. "Of course he can stay if you need him, but . . ."

"But, yes, you do need to take up the reins of the estate. I wish I could afford you the same luxury Grandfather gave Gwen and me of a year to solidify our marriage, but in the circumstances . . ."

"Don't think twice about it, sir," says Rainard.

Alicia has been looking up from her food after every bite, obviously hoping for a lull in the adult conversation, and now she has her chance. "Will you bring Primrose and Holly with you when you come back, Juliana?"

"We'll see when the time comes."

"You should bring them. And I'll take care of them again."

"Sela said you did a very good job while we were away." Juliana's lady's maid proved a godsend when my youngest daughter's dog had puppies and she insisted on keeping all of them in her room, much to Nurse's consternation.

"She told *me* I was *perfect*." Alicia's emphatic nod leaves no one in any doubt that this is the final opinion on the subject.

Over brandy after supper, Rainard returns to the topic of their continued absence from court. "I don't think it will hurt to postpone the discussion of the new trade routes until after the New Year," I tell him. "God knows, we've postponed it enough times already given that ridiculous papal inquisition and all the other events of the past summer. But I'm determined to get to a decision and start putting the wheels in motion on that matter as early as we can next year. And I want your voice heard in that conversation. You'll take your father's seat on the Council, of course."

"Sounds like I should spend some time with my father to get caught up on what's gone before."

"Can't hurt. But it won't take long. We hadn't gotten very far." I pause for a sip of brandy. "Which brings me to the question of what role you want on the Council."

"Is there any reason I need to take on something different, sir? Not that I'd mind, of course, but it will take some time to prepare someone else to take over supervision of the magistrates, and until young Meriden comes of age, you're actually short of people to assign things to in any event."

"True. So maybe your first job is to find your successor and begin preparing them." A small smile crosses his face. "Something amusing about that, Rainard?"

"I know who wants the job."

"Oh, dear."

"The irony is, she's completely prepared to do it right away, so it would solve one of your problems. But we both know . . ." He leaves the thought dangling in the air.

We both *do* know that the magistrates – not to mention everyone else in the kingdom – are far from ready to accept a woman in such a position of authority, even if she *is* the king's daughter. And yet most societies will readily accept a queen regent and some, even a queen regnant. Is that because there's an unspoken assumption that a queen is surrounded by male advisors whose function is to mold her will?

"She knows it too, sir," Rainard continues, drawing me back from my musings, "but that doesn't mean she doesn't relish the notion of doing something so important and so completely unexpected."

"Well, let's hope something else comes along soon to capture her imagination."

He chuckles. "I rather think she's going to take us both on this journey of the unpredictable for quite some time to come."

They stay here one more day before departing for their domain. As their carriage pulls out of the inner courtyard, Rainard's father falls in step with me to go back inside. "I constantly marvel at the change in my son," he says. "A person meeting him today would never know he was once so shy and uncomfortable at court and in society. Thank you, Alfred, for all you've done to draw him out."

"I'm pretty sure, sir, that I had very little to do with it."

•   •   •   •   •

The next day, just after the midday meal, Coliar finds me in the library perusing two new acquisitions that Abbot Warin has found for us. "Lord Suidbert has arrived, sir. Matthias has already arranged lodgings for him. Will you see him alone or do you want the court assembled?"

"Ask Matthias to get him settled in, then bring him to me in an hour. Let's give him the pleasure of hearing you announce him formally. But I'll see him in the private reception room. No need for the court this time."

For Emmeline's sake, I'm grateful that the Peverils are already on their way back across the sea. I suspect, though, that Peveril himself might have found it rather amusing to watch the weasel squirm when they came face to face. He'll get that pleasure soon enough at Denis's court. Today's the day for *my* amusement.

At the appointed time, the tableau is set, just waiting for the visitor to arrive. Wearing a small coronet to give Suidbert the added sense of his own importance at being received by a king, I sit at my writing table, quill in hand, in apparent concentration on what is actually a blank piece of paper. The formal knock. The opening of the door. Coliar appears in the doorway and announces, "Your Grace . . . Lord Amboise de la Fontaine Suidbert, Ambassador at Large for Your Friend and Ally, King Denis of the Kingdom Across the Southern Sea." Interesting. Not "His Most Excellent Grace" as he chose to style Charles but "Your Friend and Ally." Suidbert's invention to avoid reminding me of the past or Petronilla's instructions?

Coliar steps aside and Suidbert enters with his familiar air of importance, stopping four paces inside the door for a formal bow – also toned down from previous performances, with only a single flourish of his right hand and no elaborate footwork. Either he's been instructed or his previous displays were as much to ingratiate himself with Charles as they were for the recipient of his obeisances. My wager is on the latter. But his attire is as rich as ever, and the plume in his hat looks like more than one pheasant made a contribution.

I lay down my quill and push the paper aside then rise and gesture to acknowledge his bow. "Lord Suidbert . . . please . . . take a seat." He waits until I've chosen my own. "To what do we owe this visit?"

"I bring personal greetings from my king, Your Grace," he takes a chair facing me, "and from the regent, our dowager queen. They both hope I find you in good health and send their very best wishes to your lovely queen and the rest of your family."

"And for that we are exceedingly grateful." Though it might not be noticed by someone unfamiliar with last summer's events, it's obvious to me that the studied formality and careful deference are a shield for his inner anxiety. A slight hesitation in meeting my gaze. Shifting in his seat twice then a third time, trying to get comfortable. "But this seems rather a long journey just to convey those sentiments."

"You are quite correct, Sire. My visit here is but a courtesy call . . . a stopping-place, if you will, in the middle of a longer journey."

"And what, pray tell, is your mission?"

"I bear an invitation to the King of Peaks for a state visit to my master's court come the spring. My king is eager to discuss trade and other matters."

"May I take it this means the discord in your kingdom is now well and truly healed? Both the invitation you bear and the fact that you bear it on behalf of your new king."

He wiggles in his seat again, then looks me directly in the eye. "You are quite correct that I am pleased to now occupy an important position in the service of our kingdom. And though I have only recently decided to return to court, I find the mood there far less acrimonious than in recent years." Yes, Suidbert, it's all about you. I expected no less.

"The time of your arrival is actually quite fortuitous, Lord Suidbert. This being Thursday, it's the evening of our weekly court dinner, and I hope you'll accept my personal invitation to attend." Let's see how he fares surrounded by the entire court.

"That would be my honor, Sire."

"Excellent!" I rise, and he quickly gets to his feet. "Until this evening then. And perhaps you'll do me the favor of conveying my greetings to the King of Peaks and, when you return home, to King Denis, Queen Richenda, and the lady Petronilla."

"I shall indeed, Sire." He bows then walks backward to the door before turning to exit.

I remove my coronet then wait until Coliar returns. "That didn't take long," he says.

"He's gone?"

"Aye, Sire."

"I invited him to the court dinner this evening. If you will, please, make sure everyone knows he's unaware that we're privy to his role in Peveril's kidnapping – and we'd like to keep it that way. Oh, and tell Matthias to seat him at the far left end of my table, beside Lord Devereux." Honored guest, but not a particularly favored one. Then again, maybe after a bit of wine Devereux can get a sense of Suidbert's true feelings about being part of Denis's court.

"Of course, Sire. Anything else?"

"Not at the moment. I'll inform the family when we gather before coming to the dining hall."

Suidbert departs the following day, staying only long enough to bid me a proper farewell when I return from my morning ride. Geoffrey waylays me in the entrance hall. "Can we go talk?"

"Come on. I'm just headed up to see what Coliar has waiting for me this morning."

"Maybe in the garden, Papa? I think this should be private."

"Of course." Whatever's on his mind isn't so serious as to require a visit to the hut in the woods, but he's definitely troubled about something, though he says nothing more until we settle on a bench beside the garden wall.

"So it's about what I saw last night, Papa. Edward heard some noise in the corridor and wanted me to see what it was." My sons share the same room my brother and I occupied when we were boys, before John went into the knighthood and I came of age and got my own apartment. "I opened the door just a crack and looked out. Down the corridor to the right was that Lord Suidbert with his arm around one of the guards, and they were laughing together about something. And then they both went into Suidbert's room."

God's beard, Suidbert! Can't you keep it in your trousers for just one night?

"Did they see you?"

"No, they'd already passed our door – that must have been what Edward heard – and their backs were to me. Besides, I didn't step out into the corridor – just poked my head around the doorpost."

"So what did you tell Edward?"

"Just that it was guards passing and laughing – one of them must have said something funny. Papa, I remember from before that everyone said Suidbert was like King Charles – that he prefers men – but . . ."

"Men of that persuasion, Geoffrey . . . well, if they don't have a patron like Charles, then they have to find other opportunities to satisfy their urges. And I think you're old enough now to know how strong those urges can be."

"But with a complete stranger?"

"Is that really so different from when a man goes to a brothel?"

He looks thoughtful. "I suppose not. But one of your own personal guards?"

And then recognition dawns. This is absolutely personal. "You know, Son, it occurs to me that might actually have been the point." Geoffrey tilts his head, his expression one of complete puzzlement. "Suidbert was on his best behavior all day and all through the court dinner. Not a word or a step out of place – the perfect protocol for an ambassador. But he's still nursing a grudge left over from when Charles convinced him I was behind everything that went wrong in their world. I can't help but wonder if the noise they were making was intentional – if Suidbert wanted someone to pop out into the corridor to discover the source and then tell me what they'd seen. He'd have expected me to confront him before his departure this morning."

"So he left disappointed? Wouldn't that just add to his grudge?"

"It might. But regardless, he knows in his own mind that he's mocked me with his actions, and that might just be enough to satisfy him. Who knows? It might even give him more satisfaction to think he's pulled something over on me, and I'm totally in the dark about it."

"Does that bother you, Papa?"

"Not at all, Geoffrey. Thanks to you, I now know *two* things about Suidbert that he's completely oblivious to my knowledge of. I still have the upper hand."

The smile on Geoffrey's face tells me he's satisfied with his new understanding. Then he wrinkles his nose and asks, "Why are adults all so complicated? Why are they always playing some kind of elaborate games?"

I can't help but laugh. "Sometimes seems that way, doesn't it? In truth, though, most of the game-playing is part of statecraft. You just get to see a lot more of that because of who you are. The people who are most important to us, though . . . no game-playing there. Just honest, enduring friendships we can place our trust in." I pause to let him take that in. "And speaking of friendships, how are you coming along on working out what we might want from Denis in exchange for our horses?"

"Carew is taking me to talk with Sir Jasper and Sir Evrouin this afternoon. I think I'll be ready by the end of the week."

"Just let Coliar know."

• • • • •

Thus it is that I'm not surprised to find a meeting with Lord Geoffrey on Coliar's list of items requiring my attention on the following Friday. Nor that the first document on the stack for my review is a single page in my son's handwriting.

"I told him, Sire," says Coliar, "that it's customary for the lords to give you something to study before they present their proposals in person."

"Well done, Coliar. Is there anything urgent in this stack?"

"Not particularly. Nothing will suffer if you devote the rest of the morning to Lord Geoffrey's business."

"Then show him straight in when he arrives."

"As you wish, Sire." He takes his leave and I turn my attention to Geoffrey's document.

Proposal for Trade in Horses with the Kingdom Across the Southern Sea

King Denis has expressed an interest in acquiring some breeding stock from our stables.

I have discussed the request with Master Elvin, and we have chosen a stallion and two mares from among our draft horses and two mares of different bloodlines from among our other breeding stock.

Following your suggestion to determine what we might ask in return for these horses, I have gotten advice from many people about your notion of our possible future needs for faster, lighter horses. I have talked about this with my mates, with Sir Tobin, with Captain Carew, with Commander Jasper, and with Deputy Commander Evrouin. We have come to the conclusion that, since war will be different now that everyone has cannons, other things will be different too, even if we don't yet know quite how. So it would not be a bad idea to try out some possibilities and see if they are useful. I also discussed the price of horses with Lord Guyat.

So I am recommending that we offer to trade our draft horses to King Denis for an equal number and gender of their horses from across the Roman Sea and that we allow him to purchase the other two mares.

Simple and to the point. Not bad for a lad's first attempt at proposing a trade deal. There's really nothing here for me to object to, though I wonder what he has in mind as a price for the broodmares. When he arrives, I make him take me through his reasoning for coming to his conclusions and engage in a small negotiation about the proper price for the mares. I'm quite proud of him. And, try as he might, he can't hide his pride in himself.

"So what are you going to tell Denis?"

"I thought I'd tell him this is what I think you'd be likely to agree to so maybe it's what he should suggest."

"Excellent. And would you also tell him from me that Lord Suidbert seemed a little nervous when he first arrived but was on his best behavior throughout our meeting and the court dinner."

"Of course, Papa." He pauses, clearly thinking something through, then asks, "You don't want me to tell him about . . .?"

"I think not."

"But . . ." Then understanding dawns. "That's how you keep the upper hand, right?"

Denis was right – the Yuletide is upon us far more quickly than one expects. Perhaps it's the shorter days that make the time seem to pass faster. Brandr's trusted ship captain, Thorvald, is wintering over with us for the third year. After taking Beatrix, Thorbrand, and Margery Montfort back to the Far Nordic Kingdom – home for the first two and a new home for Margery – he returned with a letter from Brandr.

My dear Alfred,

What an absolute joy it was to welcome home my son and his betrothed! He has chosen well, and Mother assures me you're as pleased with the union as I am. Lady Margery is quite delightful and will make a wonderful queen someday. I'm even hopeful she'll eventually succeed in winning Arnora's acceptance, though I rather doubt Arnora will ever forgive me for allowing our son to make his own choice without her approval. But that's a cross I can easily bear so long as I know our alliance is secure and the young people are well suited for each other.

Mother also tells me you intend to resume your pursuit of a trade route through the Southern Nordics port. When you're ready to begin the negotiations, Thorvald and his ship are at your disposal. A ship arriving under my banner will not be challenged there, and Thorvald knows his way around the kingdom and its court. He has in his possession a letter from me to their king, by way of introduction for your emissary. The most important thing, I suspect, will be to assure him from the outset that you have no interest in fishing in the Northern Sea. He is fiercely protective of his fishing fleet and considers the entire sea to be their private domain. It's understandable, since their catches are not only an essential source of food for his people but also valuable for trade with his neighbors to the south and east. As you might imagine, a reliable supply of dried, salted, and pickled fish are part of his complex strategy to maintain his balance of power with the Teutons.

We look forward to welcoming you here for the wedding, Alfred. Summers in this land are lovely – our reward from the gods, I think, for enduring what winter sends our way. And you can rest easy that I don't expect a prompt reply. Winter, after all.

Brandr

At least once the Council agrees on an approach to opening a new trade route we can execute the plan straightaway. And yet, this latest gesture, freely offered, serves to remind me that Brandr has asked nothing in return for his generosity. The family connection is strong, of course, but I can't help but wonder if he might have deeper motives.

The Yule season passes in a flurry of celebrations, not least of which is Alicia's overt display of delight when Juliana and Rainard arrive the day before Twelfth Night with Primrose and Holly among the traveling party. "We'd have been here sooner," Juliana tells us over a quiet family supper, a brief respite in the festivities before the following night's banquet and entertainments, "but I had an idea that turned out to be a rather good one. I remembered from years ago, when you went to Goron and Kensa's wedding, Papa, that the New Year was a very auspicious day for them. So we decided to visit and find out how they celebrate."

"What an excellent idea!" says Gwen.

"Well, it's really much easier for us," says Juliana, "being so much closer to the border. Anyway, we took small gifts for the children and explained our gift-giving traditions. The children were overjoyed, of course." She laughs softly. "Kensa thought it was a lovely practice, but I couldn't quite work out Goron's reaction."

"I don't think he objected," says Rainard. "To me, he actually looked quietly pleased that his children were so happy."

I couldn't be prouder of my daughter's instincts. This is how sharing of cultures and ideas *should* be done. Not by challenging their core beliefs. Make a special point, Alfred, to let her know just how important what she's doing is.

"How did you get on with Goron?" I ask Rainard.

"Well enough, I think. We'd met briefly at the wedding, of course, but this was the first time we'd had lengthy conversations. He seems quite interested in learning more about our system of justice. I described it in broad terms, of course, but was uncertain how much detail to offer without talking it over with you, sir."

"If he's that keen," I reply, "then I've no objection to your letting him see how we do things. Invite him for a visit and show him around, if you'd like. And if he wants to bring Nerrick's son, Hedrek, along, that's quite alright as well."

• • • • • •

The Council convenes the following week. I'd planned to start inviting Geoffrey to the occasional meeting following his sixteenth birthday, but since the new trade route is such a vital issue for the kingdom, I think it's important he hear the arguments. And anyway, his birthday's in March, so I'm not getting too much ahead of plan.

Nevertheless, it's a bit startling to see him at the far end of the table, next to Rupert. How is it possible that my son is actually old enough to be sitting in this room? Wasn't it only yesterday that he was begging Osbert for pony rides? Or that he and his mates were squabbling with the girls over who could be part of a foot race?

Devereux's voice shakes me out of my musings. "Very well, gentlemen. Time to get back to the matter of trade – and the questions we set aside to deal with that unfortunate business with the Holy See. Lord Guyat . . . Lord Richard . . . I think maybe now you have our full attention."

"Curiously, gentlemen," Guyat begins, "that unfortunate business the first lord mentioned may have worked in our favor on this matter. Though our attention was diverted from it, we had a really robust trading season. That, combined with a better than average harvest, means the Treasury has made good strides in recovering from the costs of the campaign against the Teuton ambitions across the sea. Not a complete recovery, mind you, but we're in a much better position than when we were debating this matter last year. Absent another catastrophe, it now seems viable to fund a subsidy to the merchants ourselves rather than having to approach our allies about helping to finance it."

Knowing that our commercial interests would – as they always do – have strenuous objections to any increase in either their cost of goods or their taxes, I'd tasked Guyat and Richard with working out how to fund a temporary subsidy to ease them into what we expect will be the extra costs associated with trading through the Southern Nordics port. With our Treasury suffering from the expense of the last campaign – to the point Guyat was considering a rise in taxes – the notion they'd come up with was to have anyone who trades through our port participate in funding the extra costs. We'd dropped the discussion with everyone concerned about future, unforeseeable consequences of such an arrangement and with Guyat and Richard charged to return with a different proposal for doing it all on our own.

"That is," Guyat continues, "if we still believe a subsidy is necessary and if there aren't other perceived advantages for drawing our allies into being part of the solution."

"I can offer some insight on the first 'if,'" says Richard. "When the Assembly met in October, I floated the notion of new trade routes with them. Support for the idea was unanimous and enthusiastic. It seemed the disruptions arising from the Teuton campaign had really opened their eyes to the risk of heavy dependence on a single port." He pauses.

"Why do I think that's only half the story?" I ask, prompting quiet laughter all around the table.

"Because you're a wise and virtuous king who's had to put up with hours of my rants – and Thorssen's before me – about their obstinate belief that they have a God-given right to have absolutely *nothing* interfere with their profits." The laughter a bit louder this time. Richard gestures around the table. "Gentlemen, I would happily – nay, gleefully – step aside from this role if any of you would care to try your hand at coaxing them to reasonableness." Even louder laughter, accompanied by uniform shaking of heads all around the table. "Well, it was worth a try.

"But you *are* right, Sire," he continues. "It didn't take long for someone to bring up the fact that you'd offered the avoidance of more expensive trade routes as a major reason for sending our armies to hold the Teutons in check. And it took less time still for them to come up with the convoluted argument that, with that achieved, there was no reason for them to incur new costs for new routes. They simply can't see beyond the money that's on the table in the moment."

"Which means we have to show them a different path," I say.

"Actually," says Bauldry, "I'm getting pretty annoyed with their constant whining. They expect to be cockered at every turn but don't do a *thing* for the common good."

"Well," says Phillip, "they did build the woolen mill."

"And they damn well should build another one, now that it's supplying cloth to both our own people and the Territories. The whole point of that mill was for people with little means to have decent cloth at a price they could afford. But now that there's more demand, what do they do but raise their prices when what they *should* be doing is producing more cloth. Maybe you should ram *that* point home, Lord Richard, the next time they meet. Someone needs to make them see they have a duty to more than their own profit." Bauldry stops, his rant apparently finished.

But then he resumes. "I told Edward in private this whole thing was a bad idea – that it would serve nought but to make them puffed with their own importance. And that's exactly what's happened. You mark my words – the day's not far off when their whining turns into something far more threatening."

Where is all this anger coming from? Has it been simmering for years? Or is he just particularly grumpy today and the Assembly is a convenient target? Regardless, his tirade is distracting us from the matter at hand. Devereux relieves me of the need to intervene. "I think Edward's intent was to forestall that threat. But that's a different conversation we can consider on a different day. For now, I'd like to return to Lord Guyat's other point – whether there might be a reason we would *want* our allies to contribute."

"That was the big sticking point in our last discussion," says Montfort. "I, for one, see no reason to risk those unforeseeable consequences if we don't have to. I'm not ready to invite others to want a say in how we run our port unless it's completely unavoidable. And according to Lord Guyat, it's not."

Nodding heads accompanied by "Aye" and "Agreed" all around the table prompt Devereux to declare, "Then that, too, is a conversation for a different day."

Samuel's brow is furrowed, his head cocked sideways. "Something on your mind, de Courcy?" Devereux asks.

"Just thinking ahead, I suppose. This is meant to be a temporary subsidy, right?"

"My preference would be no more than a year," I reply.

"So what's to prevent the whining Bauldry abhors from resuming when the subsidy is withdrawn?"

"Anything that makes the new trade route attractive . . . which probably means goods they can't get elsewhere."

"And what might those goods be?" asks Phillip.

"I have absolutely no idea. All I know is that we have a year to figure it out. Or better still, for the merchants to figure it out so that everything's all their idea and they barely notice the withdrawal of the subsidy."

At the far end of the table, Geoffrey's been whispering to Rupert. I touch Devereux's arm and incline my head slightly in that direction.

"Lord Geoffrey," he says, startling Geoffrey from his side conversation. "Is there something you wish to discuss?"

My son hesitates. I'd told him his only role was to observe, so being addressed directly is completely unexpected. "Am I permitted, sir?" he asks.

"If you have something to contribute," says Devereux, "then we'd like to hear it."

"Go on," Rupert prompts.

"Well, sir, I was just wondering about the additional ships that would be needed, but I didn't know if maybe that had been discussed already."

"Additional ships?" Devereux.

"Well, sir, it seems to me that we wouldn't go to all the trouble of negotiating a new trade route and then not use it. And if we're still using the other trade routes, then those ships are busy, so it seems to me we would need at least one new ship – maybe two – for the new route."

I'd been waiting to see who would find their way to that little dilemma first. It takes all my self-control to keep my expression neutral and not beam with pride that it was my own son. The price of being king. Something I learned from my grandfather. My father too, though by the time I observed him as king, the lesson was pretty well engrained.

Bauldry goes on the attack immediately. "There. You see? Another example of what I'm talking about. Why should it be up to the Crown to provide the means of transport? The merchants and traders should commission their *own* ships. Just like they hire their own wagons and wagoners."

"And I can assure you, Bauldry," says Phillip, "that their argument will be the same one we faced when trying to rebuild after John's reign – that it's not good business practice to invest in advance of proven need."

What ensues is a lively discussion on whether we should provide the ships at all, what form the subsidy should take – ships only or ships and funding – giving the merchants a choice between ships and funding, or abandoning the idea of a subsidy altogether. Good questions, but missing several key points. Geoffrey looks a bit intimidated that his question should have triggered what is rapidly becoming a heated debate.

Time for me to intervene. "Gentlemen." It takes a moment, but eventually the room goes silent. "Bauldry has a legitimate point. So does Thorssen. And so does the notion of providing our subsidy in the form of the ships.

"But consider this. If the Crown commissions the ships, we own them. Should the good of the kingdom require it . . . if we should need ships for another campaign . . . then we have them at our disposal. No need to hire as many. Besides, Lord Laurence tells me our existing fleet is aging and replacements will be needed soon. If the Crown commissions these new ships, they can be built to *our* specifications.

"Here's how I envision this unfolding. We commission one ship straightaway, work to begin as soon as the weather permits, and another to be built as soon as practical after the first one is launched. We secure an agreement with the Southern Nordics for access to their port. Our goal should be to have that in place in time for this summer's trading season. Then we encourage use of the new trade route through the monetary subsidy, make one ship available for that purpose, and do whatever's necessary to help the merchants discover new goods that they can't get elsewhere. Next year, we withdraw the monetary subsidy. If needed, we continue to make one or two ships available. By the end of the second trading season, the people will have developed a liking for – or perhaps even a dependency on – the unique goods available from the new route, so the merchants and traders will be at pains to have those goods in their shops and warehouses. Then we start demanding a fee for the use of ships from the Crown's fleet to support trade. That will force the merchants to decide if they'd rather pay our fee, knowing the risk that we might pull the ships back at any moment, or if they'd rather make the investment to commission their own.

"It's a longer process, gentlemen, but perhaps better overall for the kingdom. We get the new trade route functioning while there's no emergency, we avoid a rebellion from our commercial interests, and we wind up, at the end, with two modern, larger ships. In fact, we'll probably also wind up with a bit of money in the coffers unless the merchants and traders get wise early to the need to own their own transport."

As I've been speaking, the expressions around the table have shifted from grumpy, angry, and exasperated to thoughtful – and in Geoffrey's case, to relief that his question is no longer the source of on-going contentiousness. No one says a word.

Samuel finally breaks the silence. "Now *that's* something that actually makes sense to me. A broader strategy for the good of the kingdom. And the monetary subsidy is just a short-term tactic to keep the merchants from raising the hue and cry for our heads on pikes."

"Agreed, de Courcy," says Montfort as other heads nod around the table – excepting Bauldry's.

"In that case," says Devereux, "it seems to me what we should be voting on is the commissioning of the first ship and a one-year subsidy to launch the new trade route." He looks around the table, his gaze pausing on each man, to give everyone a chance to offer any further commentary. When there is none, he begins the vote. All aye's until he comes to Bauldry.

"The king's vision has persuaded me not to vote nay. But neither can I vote aye, since I don't think we've yet solved the problem of compelling the merchants to contribute to the common good. So I shall refrain from voting."

Devereux finishes his poll. "Thank you, gentlemen. We seem to be mostly in agreement, Your Grace. Now if there's nothing further?" He pauses to glance around the table. "We're adjourned."

I rise in preparation for leaving the room. "Lord Guyat, Lord Richard . . . a word in my private reception room when you've finished here." I close the door behind me and make my way through the corridors, still musing on Bauldry's unaccustomed behavior. His fundamental point that the merchants continue to be part of the problem and not part of the solution has merit, but his outbursts . . .

Rapid footsteps behind me interrupt my thoughts, and I turn to see Geoffrey running to catch me up. "Something you wanted to talk about?" I ask when he falls into step with me.

"Aye, Papa. I just wanted to know if I did the wrong thing asking about the ships. The way it stirred everybody up and all . . ."

"Not at all, Son. In fact, I was very proud of you that you had the insight to recognize that issue. I just can't show that kind of reaction in the Council chamber."

"But it seemed like I caused so much trouble."

"All you did was prompt an important discussion. Truth be told, Geoffrey, I'm the one who made a dog's breakfast of the whole business. I just assumed we could resume where we'd left off last summer. What I overlooked was that, with the disruptions caused by Hugo and Patrasso and Peveril's abduction, I'd never actually done my job."

"Your job?"

"I never discussed with Guyat and Richard how they'd present the plan. I never spent any time with the lords talking about what we were trying to accomplish and how I saw things unfolding. They were only looking at bits and pieces, and when you brought up the ships, that was just one more straw in a wind that seemed to be blowing toward indulging every whim of the merchants.

"And I'll tell you something else, Geoffrey, in complete confidence. Until this morning, I'd never actually articulated the bigger picture and how each of the pieces fit into that picture. So you see, I have no one but myself to blame for that little descent into chaos."

"But Lord de Courcy was right. What you said made perfect sense."

"Samuel would say I was making it up as I went along and did a pretty fair job of it. I think, though, my grandfather would have said that one of the things that distinguishes a good king from a mediocre one is the ability to listen carefully in the moment and recognize what the real problem is – then find a way to impart that understanding to others. He was the master of that."

By now, we've arrived at my private reception room, but there's clearly more on my son's mind. "So how do I learn how to do that? Or even how to do the job right in advance?" he asks.

"I learned by observation. But in this case, observation means not just the surface facts, but the nuances as well – not just what people say, but how they say it – and what might really be behind their words. I'm not suggesting it's easy, but I'll give you as many opportunities as I can to see how it's done."

"I think I have a lot more to learn."

"But you have time and a sharp mind to learn it."

"Denis is having to learn a lot faster. Would it be alright if I write to him to ask how he's doing it?"

"I see no harm in that, so long as all you discuss is the process. It would be highly imprudent to discuss any of the specifics of our kingdom's business."

"I understand, Papa. Maybe I'll ask Uncle Rupert to read my letter and be sure I haven't said too much."

"A good idea. He'll be delighted you want his advice."

He still makes no move to leave. I've seen this before. He's trying to decide whether to bring up one more thing. Finally, he makes his decision. "Papa, why was Lord Bauldry so belligerent?"

"Well, some of his points do have merit. But I agree that the way he made them was completely out of character. It could be no more than frustration that I failed to consult him in advance. But just to be sure, I intend to ask Guyat if there's anything else troubling his father.

"Now, Guyat and Richard will be here any minute, and you need to be off to your training. I told Tobin you would be late today and why."

"So did I."

"A wise move. It shows him you know how to take responsibility for your actions, and he'll respect you for that. Now off you go."

Richard and Guyat arrive just as Geoffrey is about to close the door. "Anything interesting come up after I left?" I ask them.

"Not much," says Richard. "Mostly a bit of grousing that they hadn't been given the big picture from the outset."

"Can't say that I blame them. Grandfather would have been appalled at how badly I bungled this one."

"Oh, come on, Alfred," says Richard. "You can't be perfect. Makes the rest of us look really bad."

"And I'm afraid that's exactly what I did – made you and Guyat look really bad for bringing a piecemeal recommendation."

"Well, it came right in the end," Guyat attempts to mollify me.

"Which is why you're both here. We need to decide who handles the negotiations with the Southern Nordics. I can't do it because I haven't been invited to their court."

"Too bad we can't just send Guyat's wife," says Richard. "She'd be a tough negotiator and at the same time, charm them into giving us everything we want."

"And at a price our merchants would relish, no doubt," I chuckle.

"So send Guyat and Amelia both, and she can be his privy counsellor – whispering secret advice in the darkness of the bedchamber."

"Tempting as that is . . . and with no disrespect to either you or your wife, Guyat . . . I'm afraid the job falls to you, Richard. It has to be obvious to everyone – most especially our Assembly – that whoever's negotiating for us has firsthand knowledge of our merchants' interests."

"I was afraid you were going to say that," Richard hangs his head in what I take as mock dismay.

"And furthermore, I'm going to deny you the companionship of the lovely Lady Amelia." Richard shakes his head sadly and Guyat grins. "Your companion needs to be a member of the current Assembly."

"Oh, the deprivations a man must endure in the service of the Crown!" Richard heaves a sigh, and I can't help but smile.

"Surely there's *one* of them that can see beyond this week's profits."

"Well . . ." Richard adopts a studied pose of deep thought. "Well . . . I suppose . . . perhaps that Mister Ouistreham from Neukirk Market *might* do in a pinch. He's back in the current group of delegates."

"Wasn't he the one who proposed the woolen mill in the first place, back when my father was king?"

"The very one." Richard now grins, enjoying his bit of theater.

"Then I'd say your mission will hardly be unbearable." I laugh out loud.

"Except for the deprivation of whispered advice in the bedchamber."

"You'll survive," I admonish him.

"When do you want us to go, Alfred?" Richard is now serious. "After all, it's early January still."

"Not until the weather's suitable. You'll have to let Captain Thorvald be the judge of that." I fill him in on Brandr's generosity. "And that will give you and Guyat time to refine exactly how much of a subsidy we can afford so that you have your negotiating parameters. And, Guyat?"

"Sire?"

"Don't make his job too easy." They both laugh.

"Anything else, Alfred?" Richard asks.

"Nothing other than a private word with Guyat."

Richard takes his leave, closing the door on the two of us.

"What can I do for you, Sire?"

"Your father seemed particularly out of sorts this morning. I don't blame him for being frustrated with the merchants . . . or with me, for that matter . . . but I couldn't help but wonder if maybe something else was bothering him."

"He's worried about Mother. She's really quite ill. That's why she didn't return to court with him. We fetched the infirmerer from the western monastery to attend her, and he said there wasn't much that could be done. Gave us a tincture to help with the worst of her pain and another to help her sleep, but it's really only a matter of time.

"Father's completely devastated, but you know how he feels about duty – felt he had to be here. My sisters are with her . . . and I said my goodbyes before I left. For him though . . . I don't know if you've noticed, but he's been keeping to his room except for formal court functions. He sends her a letter every day. I just wish there were something I could do to help him."

"Thank you for telling me, Guyat. There *is* something *I* can do for him . . . something I'll do straightaway."

As soon as Guyat takes his leave, I go in search of Osbert, finding him, fortunately, in the first place I look – my dressing room. "Can you find out for me which room's been assigned to Lord Bauldry?" I ask.

"I already be knowing, m'lord. One floor down, along the north corridor. Fourth door on the right."

"How is it you're such a fountain of knowledge, Osbert?"

"That be me job, m'lord. In case ye be needing to know, see? And besides, I be hearing Lord Bauldry's squire moaning in the servants' hall how his master not be leaving his room and have to have everything brought up to him."

"So you think he'll be there now?"

"Fer certes, m'lord."

I make my way to Bauldry's room and knock softly. His squire opens the door a crack, then flings it wide open when he recognizes me, bowing all the while announcing, "M'lord, it be His Grace."

"May I come in, Bauldry?"

"Of course," comes from deep inside the room, followed by, "You may go, Tom." The squire leaves, closing the door behind him.

Bauldry is seated at a small writing table beside the hearth, his head bowed over his quill and paper. He lays down the quill and rises slowly as I cross the room. "Sire, I wasn't expecting . . ."

"Sit back down, Bauldry." I take the chair on the opposite side of the hearth. "I've only just learned how seriously ill your wife is. I wish you'd told me."

"It's not for me to burden you with my problems, Alfred."

"But it is for me to care about what might be troubling you."

He struggles to hold his emotions in check, but there are tears welling in his eyes. "The infirmerer said there's nothing more to be done but to try and keep her comfortable. I . . ." A couple of escaped tears roll down his cheeks, and he wipes them away with one hand. "She's been the very best wife a man could have. I . . ." And then the emotions break through in a flood. "I don't know what I'll do without her. I . . . I don't even know if I can go on without her."

I sit in silence, allowing him to express what is already grief, even before his wife's passing. When he finally retrieves a handkerchief to dry his eyes, I say softly, "I truly understand. I'd be lost without Gwen." He blows his nose and shoves the handkerchief to the back of the writing table. "Go home, Bauldry. There's no reason you have to be here."

"But—"

I'm sure he's about to offer some protest about duty, so I cut him off. "Go home and spend as much time as you can with your wife. Guyat can look after the family's interests here, should the need arise."

"Are you certain, Alfred?" His eyes brim with tears once again.

"As certain as I've ever been in my life."

He rises and I stand to embrace him, any thought of royal protocol drowned in the tears of his pain.

I've always been fascinated by how quiet the world becomes when snow is falling. It's as if the descending flakes muffle all sounds of life as they wrap the earth in a blanket of white. Perhaps it's because life does take a pause, humans and animals alike sheltering close together for warmth in their homes or dens or burrows until the snow clouds have moved on.

The snowfall began a few days after Bauldry's departure, barely enough time for him to have made the journey, though I've no doubt he urged his coachman to press the horses somewhat harder than usual. It snowed all day, through the night, and into the next morning before taking a pause. Not a winter storm with blowing snow making drifts against walls and hedges, but a slow and constant fall of flakes covering everything on earth with an even layer of white. Absent any wind, the snow clouds remained . . . and kept adding to the accumulation day after day after day.

Every few days the stable boys would drag out their ladders and climb to the roof to sweep off the snow so the roof wouldn't collapse. Anyone venturing outside in the courtyards gave the castle walls a wide berth, to avoid being the victim of a miniature avalanche when snow masses on the steep roofs inevitably slid off.

Candlemas has come and gone and still the snow clouds linger, adding a bit each day to the already thick blanket covering the earth.

Any man venturing outside risks his boots being inundated with cold and wet if he deviates even a single step off the well-trodden paths made by the servants and guards going about their business. Our payback, it seems, for the mild winter we enjoyed last year.

One afternoon, when I've grown tired of reading and pacing the corridors for a bit of exercise, I invite Samuel and Geoffrey to join me in the old library – as close as one can get, within the castle walls, to the absolute privacy of the hut in the woods. I'm curious how the lads are progressing on the question of cannons at Peveril Castle. It's unlike them to take so long on something like this. "I know it's been a long time, Papa," says Geoffrey when we settle in front of the fire Osbert had ordered lit as soon as he heard where I wanted to meet. "It's just that we can't seem to come to an agreement – at least, not on everything."

"What do you agree on?" Samuel asks.

"Well, there's no disagreement about what the armorers and engineers can prove with their calculations and experiments. Even with the extra elevation required for the firing angle, a cannon shot from an invader in the valley could reach the walls of the castle." He pauses, as if waiting for some confirmation or approval from one of us.

"Go on," Samuel prompts.

"We're pretty sure the defenders could take out those manning the cannons and the horses hauling them."

"Anything else you agree on?" I ask.

"Two things. The first is that cannons at the top of the hill could definitely disrupt an invader. The invader would have two choices. Either set up their own positions far enough away from the hill, which means their own range might not be sufficient to inflict much damage – or try to attack from really close, at a point where the castle cannons couldn't be effectively aimed downward, but that option is no different from the traditional problem of assaulting Peveril Castle, with all the advantage going to the defenders."

"And the second thing?" I ask.

"That their greatest vulnerability lies in their escape route. An invader with the audacity to try to attack uphill through the woods – where the slope is far gentler than the north-facing one – might be able to get some cannons in place to bombard the west wall and to either breach it or force the defenders to divert attention from an attack on the north wall. So we're all in agreement that there should be two or three cannon positions set up near the western side of the ravine to thwart any ascent up that hill from below. And those positions could be supported by longbowmen in the keep to suppress the attempted ascent."

"That's good strategic thinking, Geoffrey," says Samuel, "and exactly what I told Peveril he should consider when he asked for my advice before he left to return to Denis's court." Geoffrey sits up a bit straighter in his chair – something I recognize as pride in knowing he came to the same conclusion as the man he considers something of a military legend.

"So what don't you agree on?" I ask.

"The answer to the fundamental question. Are cannons necessary at Peveril Castle?"

"Is there a consensus developing?" I'm surprised when that question puts my son into a dejected slump.

"From everybody but me." When neither of us offers a comment, he goes on. "They all think it's inevitable that we have to have cannons there since it's the first stronghold we have against an attack from the east. They say there's an obligation to stop an invader before they can get deeper into the kingdom."

"That's one line of reasoning," says Samuel. "But you must have a different one if you disagree."

"I keep remembering something Lord Peveril said. He's convinced that having cannons on the ramparts will make the castle more vulnerable – not safer. And if our objective is to stop an enemy before they get too deep into the kingdom, shouldn't we do that well before they reach Peveril Castle? I've talked to Sir Evrouin a lot about the strategy when King Charles invaded – meet the opposition in the field father east and keep Peveril Castle as a stronghold to retreat to should that become necessary."

"That's exactly how we thought about it. It gave us another advantage too."

"What's that, sir?"

"By meeting their advance farther east, we made it much harder for their scouts and spies to get past us to assess the defenses at the castle."

"That makes sense, sir. Sir Tobin keeps reminding us not to forget the role of scouts in any clash of arms." Geoffrey pauses for a moment. I'm enjoying watching Samuel guide his thinking. "There's another thing, sir. The castle isn't well suited for cannons on the north wall. The kitchens and the stable would have to be moved to the south wall, which wouldn't be as safe or pleasant for the family. Either that, or a new curtain wall would have to be added down the hill to accommodate firing positions – and that would just put the new wall within easier range of enemy cannons in the valley."

"So you've had no luck persuading the others to your point of view?" asks Samuel.

"Well, I've had Barat almost convinced a couple of times. But then Ancel and William come back with their argument that if it's inevitable, why not just go ahead and do it . . . and Barat vacillates. I'm not criticizing him, sir," Geoffrey hurries to add. "I just think he's trying to see all sides."

"Well, from the questions he's asked me," Samuel chuckles, "I'd say you're reading his motives perfectly."

"I've just run out of ideas for how to change their minds."

"So what if you were to change the conversation?" I ask.

"I don't know what you mean, Papa." Geoffrey looks puzzled.

"What I'm suggesting is that it's possible William and Ancel have taken their positions for long enough that they might see it as weakness if they changed their minds. So instead of backing them into a corner, reframe the debate. How much would all this cost? Could they convince the Council to pay for it? Could they convince me to go along with it? Maybe it isn't a question of 'if' but of 'when.'"

"Another approach," says Samuel, "might be to get them to thinking about their own homes and whether they'd want cannons there."

"I think, sir, they might say that's not the problem that's been set for us."

"In which case, I think they're being short-sighted. Not that I'm suggesting you tell *them* that," Samuel is quick to add, "but that you help them see it. All our defenses are interlinked. Strengthen one, and the enemy will seek out a different one as an easier target."

I can almost see the thoughts turning in Geoffrey's mind as he takes all this in. "This is hard."

Samuel chuckles. "The first time *is* hard. But you learn. The hardest thing is when you really *are* the commander. And the very hardest of all is when you know in your heart and mind that the right decision isn't necessarily the most popular one."

"Can I ask you something, Sir Samuel?"

"Of course."

"What do *you* think?"

Samuel pauses for a moment. "I won't answer that right now, Geoffrey. It seems to me there's a bit more discussion for you lads to have among yourselves. But ask me again when you've reached your decision – before you talk to your father. I do have an opinion, and you deserve to hear it."

"I'll do that, sir. Can I go now, Papa? I promised Edward I'd go to the stable with him to check on the colts."

"Best be on your way then." Neither Samuel nor I make a move to leave. "Guess it takes more than a bit of snow to come between a lad and his horse," I chuckle as Geoffrey closes the door behind him.

"Something I sort of remember, but at the moment I see no reason to waste a perfectly good fire."

"So what *do* you think, Samuel?"

"That Geoffrey's got the right end of the stick. The strategic position in that part of the kingdom hasn't changed . . . and won't for quite some time. Peveril Castle is a good stronghold, but one we should keep for ourselves, although I do think the plan for a couple of weapon positions on the western side of the ravine is sound. They'd come as a real surprise to an enemy who thought he'd found a stealthy way to mount an assault.

"What makes far more sense to me than trying to arm a place that's ill-suited to cannons is to establish new defenses farther east. A different style of fort designed to stop an invader in their tracks. I don't expect the boys to get all the way to that notion on their own, but it's the seed I intend to plant in Geoffrey's ear the next time he asks my opinion."

It's been far too long since Samuel and I have had a conversation like this. Don't let so much time pass before the next one, Alfred, I chide myself. This is just as important as trade routes. "And what does Jasper think?" I ask.

"Didn't take him long to come around to my way of thinking. Trying to work out how to adapt old fortifications to new weapons was giving him a real headache. All he needed was the spark of an idea. He's got Evrouin, the captain of the armory, and a couple of his other senior captains working on it now. When he's ready to bring his plan to the Council, it will be vastly different from what you thought you were going to see."

"So what did you tell Peveril?"

"Pretty much what I told you and Geoffrey – and that he needn't worry for now about his home being disrupted."

The fire is starting to die down a bit, but I don't want to add another log, so I change the topic to the other matter I've been wanting Samuel's opinion on. "While we're talking about threats from the east . . . have you ever seen any of the eastern border south of the main crossing?"

"Not in person. And that's been by design."

"Aye, Evrouin told me secrecy has always been the strategy for protecting that area. I saw it for myself on that patrol last autumn, and ever since then, I've had this nagging feeling that we might just be closing our eyes and pretending we're safe."

"And you want me to have a look for myself?"

"Actually, I want us to have a look together. Just you and me . . . and maybe Carew."

•　•　•　•　•　•

Finally, on the eve of St. Valentine's Day, a gentle wind begins to blow from the southwest, and we wake the following morning to a brilliant sun in the bluest sky I ever remember. The sun's reflection from the snow creates an ever-present glare for anyone outdoors. But after weeks of confinement inside four walls, it seems everyone is eager to enjoy the fresh air and sunshine even if only for a few minutes.

And just like the snow clouds that came before, the blue skies seem determined to stay. Over the next two weeks, the warmth of the sun turns the pristine white blanket into a slushy, muddy mess in all but the most densely shaded spots. Though getting around is treacherous, the farmers will be grateful for the slow, deep soaking of their fields; and the spring snowmelt from the high peaks will exceed the capacity of the reservoir, meaning the canals will be full when their bounty is needed to nurture young crops and pastures.

As February draws to a close, we get word of Lady Bauldry's passing into the next world. "I'm taking Amelia and the children home for the burial," Guyat says when he brings me the news. "We'll be back as soon as we can."

"Take some time, Guyat. Your father's going to need you."

"What he'll need most, I think, is his grandchildren. But I don't know if even they will be enough. I'll have to see what state he's in when we get there. Everything's in order, Sire, and my clerks know what's expected of them. I'll try not to be away too long."

Ten days later, Captain Thorvald declares he's ready to sail whenever Richard wants to begin his mission. "If we go now," Richard tells me, "I should be back before Easter, even if we have weather delays. So I've sent word to Ouistreham to meet me at the port."

That same evening, Mother and Devereux announce their intentions to travel to Devereux Castle. "Someone needs to check in with the estate manager on the lambing and the spring planting," says Devereux. "And since my heir will be sailing the high seas for his king, it seems the duty falls to me." He chuckles.

"We'll go with Richard as far as the port and be back here in time for Easter," Mother adds.

Two nights later, it begins to feel like some sort of mass exodus from the castle is underway. With Catherine and Rupert off at the country manor and Mother and Devereux en route to their estate, Juliana and Rainard are the only family here to gather in my private reception room before the court dinner. Juliana is brimming with excitement. "I had a letter from Richenda yesterday," she says. "You remember, Mama, when Richenda and I came back from that visit when she was first betrothed to Denis? The stories we told about the paintings in the castle there and the artists who came from all over . . . and the court musicians?"

"I do indeed," Gwen replies.

"It seems all that collapsed while Charles was king. Oh, the paintings are still there. But during the war and the unrest that followed, no one paid the artists or the musicians so they all drifted away, looking for somewhere they could find the means to live and work. Well, Richenda's decided she wants to restore things to the way they were in Goscelin's time, and Aunt Petronilla thinks it's a good idea.

"Word is that some of the artists went as far as Rome and even Lucia's homeland, while some of them found patrons in the smaller principalities north and west of Rome. In any event, Richenda's going there to find and hire some people for Denis's court, and Lucia's going with her to help with the language and with introductions to some of the courts and noble houses. And they've asked me to go with them." She takes Rainard's hand. "We've talked about it, and I'm leaving on Monday."

Over brandy later, I ask Rainard, "I know Juliana's excited about the journey, but what do *you* think?"

He laughs. "That I'd be foolish to try to rein in her enthusiasm. You said yourself, sir, that we might need something new to capture her imagination, and it looks as if we may have been handed a gift."

"Perhaps we have at that. But are you concerned about such a long journey on her own . . . and just at this time?"

"She won't be on her own. I'll go with her as far as Denis's castle. Then she'll be with Richenda and Lucia, and Juliana assures me they'll have guards accompanying them." When I don't comment straightaway, he looks at his feet a bit sheepishly before addressing my second point. "As for the other, I'm content to be patient. Constraining her until after we've produced an heir just doesn't seem right. What if that never happens?"

"Oh, it will. I rather think much of the court was beginning to despair of Gwen and me before Juliana finally came into the world. It seemed to bother everyone else far more than it did us," I chuckle.

Thus it is that, for the first time since those days in exile at the cottage, private family suppers have become only Gwen and me and the children. Rainard puts in an appearance now and then but spends most evenings keeping his father company.

As the equinox comes and goes, spring is in the air. Watching Geoffrey and Edward begin seriously training their yearling colts, I find myself longing to do the same. It's been too long since I've enjoyed the deep sense of contentment I get from working closely with one of these magnificent creatures. One morning after my ride, I pause to survey the yearlings in the paddock. Elvin comes up quietly behind me. "Which one ye be liking?"

"You know, Elvin, I keep coming back to that bay over there . . . the one that looks so much like Star Dancer . . . the one I considered giving Geoffrey before deciding on the grey."

"I be wondering when ye get yer mind around to that," he chuckles.

"You like him too?"

"Aye. Look like mayhap he turn out to be Star Dancer made over."

The colt my grandfather gave me . . . the horse who became a legend for saving the future king's life while the sickness raged . . . the grandsire of my current mount, Altair . . . Star Dancer breathed his last on the eve of the new year. Elvin found him collapsed in his stall, and within a few hours, he was gone. At least I got to say goodbye. But that doesn't mean there's not a little piece of my heart gone with him.

We walk across the paddock to where the youngster has his head between the rails of the fence, sampling the grass at the very limit of his reach, having already mowed down the turf closer by. He ignores us completely until Elvin touches his shoulder to get his attention. When he raises his head, the resemblance is undeniable – not just his markings, but the slope of his shoulder and the way he holds himself. When I reach up to stroke his cheek, he lowers his head and nuzzles my chest, just like Star Dancer always did.

"Methinks ye best be deciding on a name fer him," says Elvin.

I don't know how, but from somewhere, he's come up with an apple that he passes to me, and I offer it to the horse . . . who takes it as gently as Star Dancer would and munches contentedly, his head still resting against my chest. "What do you think of Regulus?"

"Seem fitting fer a king's horse. Seem fitting, too, ye be training yer own mount alongside yer sons." Elvin retrieves a lead rope from one of the nearby fence posts and slips it over the head of the colt, who follows us willingly back to the stable.

"You have a good stall for him?" I ask as we pass through the door.

He doesn't answer – just leads the horse to the empty stall where I'd said goodbye to my old friend. "I be saving this fer when ye make up yer mind." Regulus nickers softly, flicks his tail, then walks in as if he knows this is his home.

It's not unusual to have a late snow sometime around Easter. This year, winter decides to give us one last great swipe of the bear's paw in the form of a raging blizzard with so much snow blown about in the wind that a man can barely make out what's just two feet in front of his nose. It lasts most of a day then vanishes overnight, leaving tall drifts in its wake that melt rather quickly under the onslaught of the brilliant sunshine.

Richard should be back any day now, and I'm eager to learn what he's managed to negotiate. Be patient, Alfred. If that snowstorm went east, Thorvald would have insisted they wait in port rather than get caught in something like that at sea. They'll be back soon enough and a few extra days isn't going to change the outcome.

When Holy Tuesday arrives with no sign of Mother and Lord Devereux – and no word from them – my eagerness is replaced by an odd foreboding. "I doubt there's really any reason to worry," says Gwen when I bring it up in our bedtime conversation. "If something delayed their departure a day or two, they likely wouldn't have bothered sending a messenger, since he wouldn't arrive much before them anyway."

"You're probably right," I acquiesce to her logic.

But when morning comes and I still can't shake the feeling, I ask Jasper to send a couple of men to check on them. Good Friday comes and goes without any word. Easter is somber, the entire court now infected by my sense of dread. When Alicia asks plaintively why Grandmama didn't come back to celebrate Easter with her, it takes every ounce of self-control I possess to remind her that lords and ladies sometimes need to celebrate holidays on their estates.

As the sun is lowering in the western sky on Easter Monday, one of Jasper's men returns. "It seems they left Devereux Castle in time to have arrived here a week ago, Sire. Last Tuesday at the latest. They spent a night at the inn in Neukirk Market and left the following morning. That's the last time they were seen. The sheriff of Neukirk organized a search straightaway when we told him they were missing. Sir Nigel stayed behind to help with the search while I rushed back to tell you, Sire."

"Did they have their guards with them?"

"Aye, Sire. Both the steward at Devereux Castle and the innkeeper in Neukirk confirmed that both guards were with them. Lady Devereux's maid and the lord's squire were riding in the carriage."

"And the coachman?"

"Lord Devereux's trusted man. The same one who drove them from here."

"Alright. Report to Jasper and see what he and Carew want you to do."

For the next three days and nights, worry mounts. And though she does her best to try to provide some sort of comfort and reassurance, I can tell Gwen is no less anxious than I am. My eagerness for Richard's return becomes something of an obsession.

On the morning of the fourth day, when Laurence walks through the door of my private reception room, my heart sinks. "They've been found, Alfred."

Still desperately trying to cling to hope, I ask, "And?"

Laurence shakes his head slowly, his expression grim. "You'd best sit down." Hope now completely shattered, I do as he says. "They were found in the rubble of a collapsed barn about halfway between Neukirk Market and the ferry crossing. From what we've been able to piece together, they were on the road when that blizzard closed in and they must have decided to take shelter in the barn. It seems the farmer had built a new barn last summer and was planning to pull the old one down once he finished with calving season. He said the January snows weakened the structure badly – particularly the roof – but everyone thereabouts knew it wasn't safe and knew to stay out of it. When he saw it had collapsed in the blizzard, his only thought was that the storm had done most of his work for him. Poor man was completely distraught when he learned what had happened."

"And they were all there?"

"All of them – guards, carriage, coachman, horses, and, of course . . . The whole weight of the barn came down on top of them." He stops, as if unsure how much more to say.

"Tell me the rest, Laurence."

"A huge beam fell squarely onto the carriage. Your mother and Lord Devereux were found in each other's arms in the broken carriage." He stops again to let me come to grips with the sad, awful truth. "If it's any comfort, Alfred, I'm told it would have been quick – that they wouldn't have suffered."

"But . . . why were they in the barn in the first place?" is all I can think to say.

"You saw how fierce that storm was, Alfred – a man could barely see his hand in front of his face. I'm sure the guards – everyone for that matter – thought it would be wiser to wait it out in the shelter of the barn rather than risk going off the road into a ditch and freezing to death in the blizzard. They had no way of knowing the structure was unsound."

I bury my head in my hands, struggling to hold my emotions in check. I'm vaguely aware of the click of a door latch, and then Gwen is beside me, her arm around my shoulders. At long last, I feel able to deal with the mundane. "Where are they taking them, Laurence?"

"They're taking the coachman back to Devereux Castle – his family's in the village there. Everyone else, they're bringing here. The wagons should arrive late tomorrow or early the following day." He pauses. "Alfred, I can't tell you how sorry I am. We all loved her."

"I know, Laurence. And thank you for bringing the news yourself." As my mind tries to make sense of everything, I'm struck by a sudden thought. "That farmer, Laurence. The one who hadn't demolished the barn yet. What's happening with him?"

"The sheriff took him to the magistrate, uncertain if he should be charged with negligence for not tearing down the barn sooner or if he was perhaps in some way culpable in the deaths. The magistrate considered it for a day then ruled that what happened was an act of God and that the farmer had no intention of causing harm."

"I'm glad to hear that."

"There's one other thing, Alfred, though I don't quite know what to make of it. There was another body found in the barn. As yet, no one's been able to figure out who he was. His clothes were ordinary, and his cloak wasn't new, but neither was it threadbare."

"I wonder what he was doing alone on the road in the middle of a blizzard."

"Likely caught by surprise, just like the Devereux party was."

"Any other clues? No horse?"

"No horse. He was carrying a small satchel, but the only things in it were a clean shirt and stockings. The only other possible clue was that he had some sort of amulet on a chain around his neck. Not a cross exactly." Laurence pauses, musing. "But now that I think about it, it did sort of remind me of those Maltese crosses from the Crusades. In any event, it was far finer than his clothing."

"Maybe given to him by some rich person he used to work for? Or did something special for?"

"More likely it was stolen. It was hidden inside his shirt. In any event, the sheriff's still trying to figure out who he might have been. Until he does, it's all something of a mystery."

My mind is full of questions. Was he already in the barn when Mother's party got there? If he came later, I've no doubt my kind-hearted mother would have told the guards to allow him to come in out of the storm. Was he traveling north or south? If no one in Neukirk Market knows who he is, then where did he come from and where was he going? For that matter, was he the one who showed the Devereux party to the barn as a shelter?

"Is there anything else, Alfred?" Laurence interrupts my thoughts. "I . . . I need to find Avelina and William and tell them. Then I need to get back to the port. I don't want anyone but me meeting Richard's ship."

"Bring him here straightaway, Laurence. And I think I should be the one to tell him."

"If that's what you want."

"And, Laurence," says Gwen, "tell Avelina to come to us now. We have to tell the children first, then we'll all be in my sitting room."

• • • • • •

There's a strange kind of calm that comes with finally knowing what's happened – even if it's the worst that could have been. Though my dreams are strange and confused, I manage a full night's sleep for the first time in many days. Someone must have sent word to the monastery. Abbot Warin and Prior Frery arrive just before the midday meal, bringing with them that sense of peace I always find in their company.

As Laurence predicted, the wagons arrive in late afternoon. As they pull into the inner courtyard, Carew takes charge, quietly issuing orders to the phalanx of guards he's assembled there. Three wagons, each bearing two coffins. In groups of twelve, the guards assemble behind each wagon. Six guards to a coffin, they begin unloading and carrying them inside. "We're taking them to the chapel, Sire," says Carew. "I'll have men on duty there day and night." We watch in silence as the guards go about their business. Even Alicia is subdued.

When the wagons start to leave, we turn to go inside and make our way to the chapel. Seeing all six coffins side by side in front of the altar instantly brings all the emotions back to the surface. Someone took the trouble to carefully carve a name on the top of each coffin. Lord Devereux. Queen Alice. Nona. Rodge. Sir Giles. Sir Bertram. Tears well in my eyes and I let them fall as I trace my fingers slowly over my mother's name. The gentle woman with the irrepressible spirit who buried one son so the other could survive and who ultimately found happiness twice in marriage. Turning to Lord Devereux's coffin, I once again trace the letters. My father's best friend. The man who's guided this kingdom through turmoil and triumph. Oh, how they will both be missed!

Alicia starts to ask a question. "Mama, why—"

"Shhh," Gwen interrupts her then whispers, "Let's just give your father a moment of quiet. You can ask me later."

But in that moment, my daughter reminds me that life goes on. I turn and offer Gwen my arm. Carew is waiting with Warin and Frery at the back of the chapel. "Be sure the guards know, Carew, that they're welcome to pay their respects to their fallen comrades at any time. Any of the other knights, for that matter, who want to do so."

"I'll see to it, sir," he replies.

• • • • • • • •

The next morning, a fast courier arrives with a message from Laurence.

Thorvald's ship arriving on the morning tide. We should be with you by midafternoon.

Richard is railing at me as he walks through the door to my private reception room. "My God, Alfred, I know you're eager to hear the news, but can't a man at least shed—" He stops short the minute he realizes there are others in the room. Gwen, Geoffrey, and Edward. His wife, Avelina, and their two sons. Samuel. Phillip. Laurence follows him in and finds a place to sit as Avelina beckons to her husband to join her on the couch. "This can't be good," says Richard, sitting down and taking his wife's hand.

"It's about your father, dear," Avelina says softly.

"I didn't want you to hear it in the corridors or from the servants, Richard," I tell him. "Your father and my mother . . . they died in the pre-Easter blizzard."

His face goes pale. Avelina tries to put an arm around his shoulders, but he shrugs it off, clearly in shock. "What happened?"

Perhaps it's just as well I've had a couple of days to absorb the enormity of it all. It makes the telling just a little easier. As he listens, Richard's shoulders slump, and this time, he accepts Avelina's comforting arm as he tries to take it all in. I end with, "We brought them here to await your return. The coffins are in the chapel."

No one says a word as he tries to come to grips with what he's just heard. My friend's pain weighs as heavily on me as my own. At long last, Richard breaks the silence. "I . . . can I . . . I want to see him."

"Go. Then refresh yourself from your travels. We'll all be right here for a quiet supper this evening."

Avelina rises and reaches for her husband's hand. "Come with me," she says softly.

When everyone returns for supper, Richard is refreshed in body but hardly in spirit. That will take time. He embraces Samuel, Phillip, and Laurence in turn, then hesitates. "There's something I forgot to do earlier." He walks to me, drops to one knee, and recites the lord's pledge. I raise him up in acceptance and we embrace in shared sorrow.

The food Matthias has left on the sideboard is simple fare. It's comforting, but no one seems to have much of an appetite for food or conversation. "We've made no arrangements yet," I tell Richard. "It didn't seem right until you could be part of it. I'd be pleased if you wanted to bury your father alongside Mother in our family crypt."

"That's generous, Alfred," he replies, "but the Lords Devereux have been buried in our family cemetery since long before there was ever a kingdom in this land. He didn't want to disrupt that tradition, so I'll take him home to rest with his ancestors."

"Of course."

"Your mother knew his wishes, Alfred, and also that he wanted her to be laid to rest beside your father. She was content with that."

We hold a single funeral mass for Mother, her maid, and the two guards. The following morning, the remaining two coffins are loaded into a wagon, and Richard and his family set out for Devereux Castle. Samuel, Phillip, Laurence, and I will follow on the morrow to pay our respects as the new First Lord of the Realm commits his father's soul to God.

"There was something rather strange on market day while you were away, Alfred," says Gwen as she climbs into bed on the night of my return. "A woman begging in the square, mostly near the steps of the church, but occasionally she'd venture toward the nearest stalls."

"Not all *that* unusual. I presume the sheriff made sure she didn't cause any trouble."

"The odd thing was . . . I swear, I think it was Gunhild. I wasn't that close, and I didn't want to show any particular interest by getting closer, but . . ."

Gunhild. The younger sister of my brother's wife, Gundrea, who came with her father, Lord Erik of the Eastern Kingdom, for John's coronation. Who John took to his bed and left with a child that twice became an instrument to try to deny me the throne. "What on earth would she be doing here?" I ask. "Surely it was just some poor woman whose looks dredged up that memory."

"If she was, then the resemblance was uncanny. She looked exactly like Gundrea and she was dressed in one of those severe frocks that both sisters always wore. From a distance, it seemed like people couldn't make out whatever she was trying to say to them."

"Maybe they were just trying to ignore her so she'd leave them alone."

"Perhaps. But it was more than just a little unnerving."

"I'll wager whoever she was, she'll be nowhere to be seen next market day."

"I hope you're right."

"Any other news before I show you how much I missed you while I was away?"

"Only a letter from Juliana. They seem to be having a delightful time, and she says she'll be home before Whitsuntide. You can read it tomorrow." She snuggles close and plants a soft kiss on my lips.

• • • • •

Any thought of beggars in the market square is banished when Richard returns a week later and I can finally learn the outcome of his mission. "Travel with Captain Thorvald is really quite enlightening," he begins when I find him waiting for me after my morning ride.

"Samuel said the same thing."

"I'm convinced he's far more important to King Brandr than just a ship captain."

"I've been coming to a similar conclusion."

"Anyway, when we arrived, there was no doubt he was known there. He was given one of the best berths, a bit more sheltered from the sea than most, and quite a warm welcome when we disembarked. It took a couple of days to reach the king's castle, and we arrived to find him away on a hunt, not expected back for at least a week. Thorvald took advantage of that time to show me the land border with the principalities of the great weaving houses. It's a pretty narrow border – less than a full day's ride in length. Most of their land adjoins the Teuton Kingdom. But they seem to do enough trade with those principalities that there's a good main road leading to and beyond that border crossing. That turned out to be part of the negotiations, so it was rather fortunate we'd had the time to see it in advance.

"Once we were back at the castle, there was another three-day wait for the king's return and then two days before he was ready to receive us. It was the waiting that took so long, Alfred, and then the stormy seas that delayed our departure."

I hold my impatience in check, since I know that storm now has a whole different meaning for my friend. "Tell me what he was like."

"The king?"

"Aye."

"Puzzled at first, even though he'd read Brandr's letter, but his interest grew as I explained our purpose in being there. I rather think," he adds with a grin, "that the moment he decided to actually listen was when I assured him we had no interest in fishing.

"Not much progress on the first day, but the next day he was more forthcoming. I could be wrong, but my instincts tell me he had a conversation with Thorvald overnight. It turns out he has a dependency on the Teutons for grain to supplement what they can grow themselves. That trade is part of the delicate dance they do to keep the Teuton threat in check. And it's something of a vulnerability in their strategy. When the Teuton harvest is poor, his cost of grain is quite high, but he dare not quibble much lest he upset the strategic balance and his people go hungry. The greater risk, though, is if the Teutons simply cut off the supply. So he's been thinking about how to mitigate that risk, and the opportunity to buy grain from us would do just that."

"Although it would be costlier because of the sea voyage."

"That's where we found a basis for negotiation. His initial demand was for tariffs of ten percent of the value of any goods that pass through his port."

"Ouch!"

"Pretty much what Ouistreham said. Actually, what he said was there was no way our merchants would ever accept such a big increase in their costs, so we might as well just go home."

I chuckle. "Damn good thing it was Ouistreham with you. One of the more rabid ones might have given the king a piece of their mind right then and there."

"Actually, Ouistreham's a pretty shrewd trader and knew he was there to play the game. The king didn't want to back down on tariffs at all. His argument was that they were needed to support maintenance of the road to the principalities for all the extra traffic we'd be creating. Ours was that we already had a longer voyage and greater risk at sea. We eventually were able to link our needs to his.

"We both want to start slowly, and neither of us wants the Teutons to get wind of what we're doing. We'll sell him small amounts of grain at the same price we do for the larger traders in return for a tariff rate on all goods of seven percent. When he buys more grain, our tariffs go down, and they can come down even more if we buy goods from him rather than just use their port. The details are in the documents I gave Guyat to review, but it all seems financially sound to me. And Ouistreham's pretty sure he can convince his colleagues on the Assembly to see the sense of it."

"Plus, it fits with our plan to make the subsidy temporary," I comment. "Are you planning to have Guyat bring it to the Council?"

He looks at me quizzically . . . and then recognition dawns. "Dear God in Heaven. I'm really going to be sitting in that chair. You're going to have to be patient with me, Alfred, while I figure this out. I've watched my father for years, but somehow that's not the same as actually doing it."

When the Council convenes two days later, I watch through the open door as Richard stops behind the first lord's chair. Utter silence prevails as he runs his hands over the carving and grasps the uprights in preparation for pulling it out from the table. "I rather think, gentlemen, that it might be some time before I have the wisdom and skill of the man who used to sit here. And for that I ask your forbearance."

"I won't deny the sense of loss that comes with not seeing him in that chair," says Montfort. "But you can count on us to persevere as always."

"Thank you, Montfort," says Richard. But he still hesitates, and no one makes a move to hurry him.

Finally, Phillip breaks the mood. "Oh, for God's sake, Devereux, put your arse in the chair and get on with it. You can't possibly muck it up any worse than the rest of us would."

In the laughter that follows, Richard takes his seat – my cue to join them. "Very well, gentlemen," says Richard, "pursuant to Lord Thorssen's most eloquent invitation, let's get straight to the business that brings us here. Lord Guyat?"

Guyat takes them through every detail of the proposed agreement, ending with, "And I think if my father were here, he'd be satisfied that this provides some incentive to push the merchants in the right direction."

"But does it put too much pressure on our grain harvest?" asks Samuel.

Richard opens his mouth then shuts it quickly – visibly restraining himself from answering as he makes the transition from contributor to arbiter of these discussions. "A risk to be aware of, certainly," says Guyat, "but don't forget the Territories. Nerrick's wheat. Boskren's oats. We can buy from them and trade onward – or even expand the agreement to include them once we have everything on a sound footing with the Southern Nordics."

A bit more discussion follows, delving into the details of how the tariff reductions are expected to work in practice. When the conversation wanes, Richard calls for a vote. After Montfort's "aye," Richard turns to me. "It seems the Council's in agreement with the deal, Your Grace. And that you and I now have to figure out which of these lucky gentlemen," he gestures around the table, "gets to break the news to the Assembly."

Oh, dear . . . something I'd forgotten. Richard can no longer serve as Council liaison to the Assembly. Yet another conundrum to sort out. With the elder Devereux gone, Simon Meriden not yet of age, and Bauldry still in mourning, my options are increasingly constrained.

Richard's "Is there anything else, gentlemen?" jars me out of my thoughts. "Very well," he says after a brief silence, "we're adjourned." My cue to leave . . . with a big smile on my face as I hear, from the corridor, the words of congratulations being offered to my friend for his first steps as first lord.

An hour later, he finds me in the library. "Well done," I tell him.

"I have to admit it was a bit daunting taking that seat for the first time. Thank God for Phillip." We both chuckle. "And for the fact that there was no real controversy. I hope this gets easier with time."

"I wouldn't necessarily say easier . . . just more familiar. But that doesn't mean you won't bungle something eventually. I've learned that just comes with the territory."

"I saw the expression on your face when I mentioned a new liaison for the Assembly. One of your 'bungles'?"

"Well, certainly one of my 'haven't given it the thought it deserves.'"

"Then you're in luck, because I have . . . given it some thought, that is. And it's occurred to me we might have been overlooking the obvious choice for years."

"Oh?"

"Ademar. He's the only heir that's not somehow engaged in the running of the kingdom. Well, if you don't count the ones that aren't of age. And he's rather a wizard at managing scarce resources for a reliable profit. The Assembly members might actually think he has more in common with them than any of the rest of us do."

"They might at that. Do you think he'd be willing?"

"We won't know until you ask him. Or order him." He pauses, then adds with a mischievous grin, "Or take a page from Phillip's book and embarrass him into it."

"There's just one thing. That would put three Peverils in the Crown's service. Does that look like too much power in one family's hands?"

"Well, only Ademar would be on the Council. And, in point of fact, there are three Ernles. We all know you'll continue to consult Rainard's father, and Samuel is still an Ernle despite the new title. I think Father would have said you can't always have perfect balance, especially in times like this when Meriden is still not of age and Bauldry's health is in question."

"I suppose you're right. It's rather a shame I can't just put Mary on the Council until Simon's ready. And probably just as well that Juliana's away for now, since she'd no doubt be pressing me to do just that."

He nods in acknowledgement, but offers no comment. "So you'll talk to Ademar?" he asks.

"I think we both should. Send for him and we'll have that little chat. The more I think about your idea, the more I like it."

"Shouldn't you be the one to send—" Seeing my grin, he stops short. "Damn. I guess I *do* have that privilege now."

When Coliar announces, "Lord Laurence, Sire," my heart skips a beat. Calm down, Alfred. Laurence can visit without bringing bad news. But when the first thing out of his mouth is "What do you say to going riding?", my stomach does its own little somersault. That's completely out of character for Laurence. Usually, he complains that he's already spent too much time in the saddle just getting here from the port.

"Why do I suspect you want to go to the hut?"

"Don't fret, Alfred. It's not dire. Just something I need to talk over with you."

"Then lead the way."

Laurence offers nothing further until we're inside the hut, certain no one else is anywhere near. "That instant of anxiety I saw on your face earlier might actually have been prescient, Alfred. Truth be told, I'm not really sure what you're going to think of this, but I've decided I have no choice but to discuss it with you."

"Then don't keep me on tenterhooks."

"There's a rather unexpected person being held in custody by the sheriff in the port at the moment. She was dragged out of one of the brothels where she was causing a rash of trouble and no one could make head nor tail of what the to-do was all about. When he couldn't make any sense of her carrying-on, the sheriff sent for me. Alfred, it's Gunhild."

"Oh, come on, Laurence, you must be mistaken. Why on earth would she be here in this kingdom? She hates everything I stand for."

"No mistake. I was pretty sure, but to remove any doubt, I sent for Brother Nicholas and he confirmed it. Her father died last autumn and her brother, Gunnvor, is now the lord. At the first sign of spring, he threw her out. Told her she was a complete waste of food and space that no man would ever agree to take off his hands. Gave her two days to pack up whatever she could carry and get out of his sight.

"Turns out she may be more cunning than we've given her credit for. She claims to have convinced Gunnvor that she could spy on us and bring him information he couldn't get otherwise. Told him that would be her revenge on us for ruining her, and she'd make it worth his while to keep her fed and a roof over her head. She says he agreed to let her try, and then he'd make his decision."

"Is he really that naïve to think she could learn anything useful when she barely has two words of our language?"

Laurence chuckles. "Somehow I doubt that. But this got her out of his hair straightaway. And I'd wager he just plans to throw her out permanently when she returns with nothing that's of any value to him."

"Well, that does explain one thing."

"Oh?"

"A couple of weeks ago – would have been three weeks or more since the actual event – Gwen told me she'd seen a woman begging in the market square who looked remarkably like Gunhild. I dismissed it as just a striking similarity, but now I need to tell her she was probably right."

"You may want to hold off on that."

"Why would I do that?"

He rises, makes a full circuit of the hut, then returns to his stool. "I'm about to break with precedent . . . bring you into some operational details. I've given this a lot of thought, Alfred . . . barely slept at all the last two nights. But given what that girl's tried to do to you and to this kingdom, I don't think it would be right to proceed without asking your permission.

"Alfred, I want to turn her. Get her to spy for us. It means we'd have to give her some tidbits for Gunnvor that tantalize him enough to send her back for more. But this seems like a gift that's fallen into our hands to be able to get some insight into the Eastern Kingdom. We might never get another chance like this."

"I don't know, Laurence. She seems so easily manipulated. First by her father – or maybe that was Gunnvor – and then by Charles and Isabella. Who's to say her whole story now isn't just Gunnvor manipulating her again?"

"Quite likely it is. But that's what makes this so attractive. By turning her, we can control what information she supplies to Gunnvor, and if we reward her just enough to keep her loyal to us, then we might be able to develop her into an agent with access to their nobility or even their king . . . and do it much more quickly than if we had to find a suitable candidate and insert them into the right places."

"And how do you overcome her lack of our language?"

"That's my biggest stumbling block. We can teach her stealth . . . how to observe without attracting attention . . . how to get people to reveal things. But we can't do any of that if we can't talk to her. The only option I have is to use Brother Nicholas. So that's another thing I need your permission for."

"And that's permission I have no authority to give. Only Warin can do that." Like our hereditary lords, the Abbot is privy to the knowledge of Laurence's role as spymaster. But I wouldn't dare speculate how he might react to one of his brethren playing a part in the world of secrets.

"I know," says Laurence. "And I hope I can persuade you to go with me to speak with him. But there's no point in even contemplating that if you object to Nicholas's involvement."

"Let me think about it. Why don't you start with how you propose to go about this? How do you intend to persuade *her*?"

"One step at a time. First, I offer to free her from jail if she'll work for me. Chances are, she'll jump at that. But as soon as she's out of jail, she'll figure out quickly that she should've demanded more, so the next step is a roof over her head and food without having to work in the brothel . . . and what that gives me is control over where she is and what she gets up to because she'll be living with one of my most trusted agents.

"We'll test her with something fairly easy. Take her to the port defenses and let her see them for herself. Nothing more than what anyone could see just passing by on land or by ship. But I'm fairly confident that, even if Gunnvor has an inkling we might have new defenses, he'll salivate over getting some details and send her back for more. What I'll ask her to bring back to us is how much Gunnvor knows about cannons and if he knows how to make black powder. She should be able to use a description of our defenses as a way to get him to reveal something of what he knows. We'll give her a few hints on how to get him talking – and, of course, best of all would be if she can eavesdrop while he's bragging to his retainers.

"Then, when she comes back, her room will be a bit nicer and her minder will take her to the dressmaker for a new frock. That's when we begin teaching her some of our language . . . not too much at first . . . just some basics. Gunnvor would be a fool to think she can get much information without learning the language, but equally, he'd never believe she'd learn very quickly just picking it up on the streets. He'll be testing her when he sends her back, but we can handle that."

"And what if he doesn't send her back? What if he threatens her or beats her and gets the truth out of her? He'll know what we're up to then."

"A risk we take anytime we send an agent into a situation like this. Which is why I prefer more subtle methods. But I don't think we can pass this up. Before we send her back, we'll paint a picture of the pleasant things she'll be coming back to. Our last instructions will be that if she thinks she's in danger, she's to flee back here and we'll protect her."

"And how do you intend to do that?"

"Depends on how we assess the danger she thought she faced. If we think it poses a risk to us, she disappears . . . forced to take the veil in a cloistered order with strict rules of silence."

"That's pretty extreme."

"Spying's an extreme business, Alfred. When an error in judgment or an avoidable mistake can cost lives, there's no room for the benefit of the doubt. But it's a subtle business too. That's what makes it so hard."

"Have you asked Rupert what he thinks?"

"No . . . but only because I already know. We talked frequently last summer, when I was so frustrated at being unable to uncover who was behind that business with the papal legate. He told me then that he'd thought more than once about trying to use her but the circumstances were never right . . . and there was no way to get to her last summer. That's why I'm convinced we should take this chance while we have it."

"Can I think about it overnight?"

"Yes. But no longer. Time is of the essence. If this is going to work, I have to spring her from jail while she'll still be grateful. I can't wait until she's been in there so long that she comes out mad and ready to lash out at anyone and everyone. Nicholas told her it would take two or three days to arrange things so she wouldn't be charged with a crime. So if you give me your blessing, I want to see Warin tomorrow and get back home in time to get her released before sundown.

"Sleep on it, Alfred. But if you decide to approve, I want to go to the monastery in time to catch Warin before Terce. I don't have that extra hour to lose."

Long after Gwen's fallen asleep, I lie awake thinking about what Laurence wants to do. Finally, in a moment of clarity, I remember Abbot André's words when helping me to make peace with what I'd finally recognized about the death of Gunhild's son. "A king must peer into the shadows, Alfred, for it's there that discontent festers and rebellions take root. But at times, perhaps, it's best not to peer too deeply." Were the person Laurence wanted to use anyone other than Gunhild, he'd never have brought this to my attention. He'd have simply launched the operation and brought me any result he thought I should know. I trust Laurence's judgment for that. I should trust him now.

Though I rise at dawn and dress quickly, Laurence is already waiting for me, his carriage ready, when I arrive at the stable. "So *that's* why you were so willing to go riding when you arrived yesterday!" I tease him.

He grins. "Well, I had to be prepared in case I had passengers today."

Warin is taken aback at the timing of our arrival at the monastery. "You're most welcome, as always, Alfred, but what brings you here so early? It's almost time for Terce."

"Laurence's business," I tell him. "You'll understand once you've heard him out. Is it permissible for Frery to take the service?"

Still quite perplexed, Warin asks, "Is it truly so urgent?"

"Please forgive my imposing, Abbot," says Laurence, "but time is rather of the essence."

"Very well. Allow me to go speak with him. I'll be back momentarily."

When he returns, I leave the explanations to Laurence. Warin looks increasingly thoughtful, his chin resting on steepled fingers as he listens, but offers no immediate response. Laurence doesn't press. Eventually, Warin addresses Laurence directly, "Nicholas told me, of course, why you'd asked for his help a few days past. So when you arrived here, I surmised the fundamental nature of your request, but not its depth. Ours is a life of service, my son, but the service you desire goes into a realm beyond what we're accustomed to. Yes, we often help with overcoming the barriers different languages create, and Brother Nicholas has done so many times. But making him part of these shadowy operations is a bit more troubling. I don't know if it's right to ask one of our brothers to expose himself to the dangers that might be involved. Nor can I think of any plausible reason for him to be seen so much in the port town. That, in itself, might actually draw attention to your activities in a way that would be completely undesirable and perhaps expose Nicholas to even further danger."

"I think I can put some of your concerns to rest, Abbot," says Laurence. "There's no need for Brother Nicholas to be seen about the port. There's a place – where, I won't say – that I hold clandestine meetings and that I also use when an agent needs a safe place to stay out of sight for a time. I intend to install Gunhild and her minder there. It's quite comfortable and sufficiently large that Brother Nicholas would have his own room. His only job would be translation and, in time, tutoring her in enough of our language to do her work credibly . . . much as he helped Gundrea."

"But in the course of translating," says Warin, "he would learn secrets that he must keep in perpetuity."

"That's true. And yet, how different is that from the sanctity of the confessional?"

"I can't argue with that, but Brother Nicholas is not yet anyone's confessor nor do I know if he ever will be. So he has no experience of this." He pauses. "And what about any dangers to his person? You can't possibly know yet if Gunhild is prone to violence of any sort."

"And I can't argue with that," says Laurence. "But know this. There will be no weapons permitted in the cottage. Only my trusted agent – Gunhild's minder – will be allowed to prepare food. Gunhild will eat the same food from the same dishes as everyone else. Kitchen knives will be locked up when not in use. And the wine and ale will come directly from my cellar and be kept in a locked cupboard except when being served. We have no intention of trusting her until she earns it. And by that time, I suspect Brother Nicholas's service will no longer be required."

Warin stares off into the distance for a bit before asking, "And when do you need an answer, my son?"

"As I told Alfred yesterday, for this to succeed, I have to get her out of jail while she'll still be grateful – before there's time for her anger to build to the point that she's in a rage about everything."

"I need some time to think and to pray. Meet me in my dining room for the midday meal. Until then, entertain yourselves as you please within our grounds." Laurence and I make our way to the door and, just as Laurence steps out, Warin adds, "A word, Alfred?"

"I'll catch you up, Laurence."

Once I close the door, Warin resumes his seat and gestures for me to do the same. "You've said nothing this morning, Alfred, and yet you came. Should I draw the conclusion that you hope to sway my decision?"

"The only conclusion you should draw, Warin, is that I want you to reach your own conclusion . . . from your own perspective."

He sighs. "I only hope that perspective isn't colored by my experience at the hands of Prior Dunstan." Realizing I'm likely to try to offer reassurances, he quickly adds, "Oh, Frery has been quite successful in restoring my faith in my own judgment. But until this morning, I've never contemplated the implications of involving one of our own in the dark underbelly of espionage."

"Perhaps it's better to think of it as André expressed it – 'toiling in the shadows.' Sounds less ominous that way."

"I remember that day well. And I remember he cautioned you not to involve yourself directly in that shadowy world. So why are you now doing just that?"

"It's not by choice. Laurence felt obligated to get my permission because of Gunhild's history with my family. But in the small hours this morning, I came to realize that André's counsel still applied – that I should trust Laurence and not be tempted to meddle in how he gets results." I pause. "It also didn't hurt to know this was an idea Rupert had long sought an opportunity to act on."

"A bit of insight I find helpful as well. Now, go find Laurence and busy yourselves for a bit. There's something I want to refresh my memory on."

I find Laurence sitting on a fence rail laughing as two very young dogs try to get a group of chickens into the coop while Brother Adam looks on. "They don't look much like herders to me," Laurence says when I join him on the rail. "Every time they get the hens more or less pointed in the right direction, one or two escape, and while the dogs go after the escapees the rest of the flock scatters hither and yon."

"Have *you* ever tried herding chickens?"

"Can't say that I have," he chuckles.

"All part of their training."

"Chickens?"

"They start on chickens before moving up to geese then sheep and cattle. Adam says if they know a bit about what they're doing, they're less likely to get hurt with the bigger animals. He's got a couple of cranky geese that teach the youngsters to stay out of the way and still get their job done." The young dogs are enthusiastic, but getting frustrated. I know what's coming next. "Now watch," I tell Laurence.

"Tilda! Joppa!" Adam calls, and two adult dogs come running from where they'd been waiting inside the kennel building. "Tilda. Joppa. Coop!" The adults get to work as the young ones do their best to help, trying to imitate what their elders are doing. In little time at all, the hens are all in their pen, and Adam closes the gate before coming to join us at the fence.

"That was quite a display," says Laurence.

Adam chuckles. "Well, the youngsters have the instinct for what they're supposed to do. They just don't quite know how to do it yet. But they'll catch on. And Alfred – what a joy to see you! How's that adorable daughter of yours getting on with her dogs?"

"She's quite full of herself at the moment. While Juliana's away, she has charge of all four dogs once again and is utterly convinced no one could do it better."

"Perhaps I should pay her a visit and see if she needs any hints."

"She'd be over the moon."

"Well, Brother Kitchener is planning to come down in a day or two to see if he can wheedle some supplies from your cook, so I'll join him on the wagon."

"I should drop in on him while we're here. If he can give me a list of what he wants, I'll ask Cook to have things ready and spare him the wheedling."

By the time we finish in the kitchen and have a quick look at the orchards where the trees are just starting to bloom, it's time to rejoin Warin. Nicholas's presence reveals Warin's decision straightaway.

"Father Abbot explained what you want, Lord Laurence," says Nicholas. "If I can be of service, then I'm pleased to do so."

"He explained, I trust, that it might involve keeping more than a few secrets?" asks Laurence.

"That he did. And you can put your mind at rest on that score. While Prior Dunstan was here, we all became quite adept at keeping our own counsel. Nothing I learn while translating will pass my lips without your explicit permission."

His eyebrows raised in the unspoken question, Laurence looks to Warin, who nods slowly in unspoken reply.

"In that case, Brother Nicholas," says Laurence, "are you agreeable to gathering what you need and coming with us straightaway? I'd like to be back at the port before nightfall."

"I've already prepared, sir."

"Then let's go collect your things and get settled in the carriage." Before he turns to follow Nicholas through the door, Laurence offers Warin a small bow of the head and a quiet "Thank you."

When they've left, I ask Warin, "Is it permissible to ask how you came to your decision?"

"Something few people know, Alfred, is that, in addition to chronicling your grandfather's reign, Francis kept a personal chronicle of his time as abbot. That's what I wanted to consult. And I found there what I thought I remembered."

I rise to leave and he follows suit, but before I get to the door, he asks, "Aren't you curious what I found?"

"Curious? Of course. But it's enough for me to know you were satisfied."

"Perhaps you haven't reached this point in your grandfather's chronicle yet . . . or perhaps it's purposefully omitted from that record . . . but Francis himself actually undertook a clandestine mission for your grandfather once. Brother Nicholas will be walking in hallowed footsteps."

The coming weeks pass in a flurry of activity that serves to further postpone my scouting trip to the eastern border with Samuel. At the beginning of May, we play host to the King of Peaks and his entourage as they take a two-day break in their journey to Denis's court for the state visit. His heir, Dafydd, once one of Juliana's suitors, is now betrothed to a princess from the Kingdom of Lakes, a distant cousin of Gwen's. This summer, it seems, is to be the Season of Royal Weddings.

"It's a good alliance," the king tells me as we enjoy a midday meal on the lawns, the day being particularly warm for early May. "But I've not abandoned the idea of one between us." He inclines his head to the left where Geoffrey and his daughter, Eirwen, are sharing a blanket spread on the ground to enjoy their food.

Like her brother, Eirwen has the dark looks of the Peaks highlanders. But rather than Dafydd's somewhat brooding affect, she radiates joy and good spirits . . . and perhaps just a hint of highland magic. Geoffrey's eyes lit up when they were first introduced, and he didn't waste a moment in offering to show her around the grounds.

It's not long before Richard's son, William, shows up, claims a spot on Eirwen's left, opposite Geoffrey, and joins in the conversation. "It seems my son is not the only one to take an interest in your daughter," I chuckle as my fellow monarch and I resume our own conversation.

When our wine glasses are empty, I look around for a servant and discover that Ancel Thorssen and Barat de Courcy have dragged another blanket up to join the group. Instead of the usual bevy of young ladies, Eirwen is now holding court to a bevy of young men vying for her attention. Who'd have guessed, years ago, when Geoffrey and his mates decided to learn the language of the Peaks as a competition with Juliana and Richenda, that they'd now be using that skill as romantic rivals for a beautiful princess?

The King of Peaks laughs as a servant hurries over to fill our glasses. "Well, it looks as if we will have our alliance one way or another," he says, "though it would be my preference if we could steer her affections toward your son."

That will be up to him. My conversation with Geoffrey will be just as challenging, though, since I have absolutely no experience of how to attract a woman when others – in particular, your best mates – are on the same mission.

Gwen laughs when I mention it in our bedtime conversation. "As I remember it, you were quite adept at courtship."

"Yes, but I didn't have to compete with other suitors."

"True. But you had to overcome your brother's attempt to drive us apart."

"Be that as it may . . ." I let the thought hang in the air.

"You could always just make the agreement with your fellow monarch and tell Geoffrey his future's been decided." Her tone is . . . what? . . . coy? . . . teasing? . . . a match for the expression on her face.

"I could."

"But you know that would be the easy way out."

Now I'm sure she's toying with me. Two can play this game. "And why shouldn't I get something easy now and then when responsibility weighs so heavily most times?"

She giggles and dances her fingers up my chest. "Because you're a good father who wants his son to look forward to all the delights of the night that you've enjoyed." And then she reaches for my crotch in that familiar way that still comes as a surprise in the middle of a conversation and that still makes my body respond in an instant, banishing Geoffrey's problems to some other time and place.

•   •   •   •   •

When Geoffrey finally tells me his conclusion about defenses at Peveril Castle – which haven't changed from what he told Samuel and me earlier – he seems rather morose. "And did you ask Samuel's opinion?"

"He agreed with me."

"And that didn't please you?"

"In a way. But . . . ." He sits slumped in a chair in my private reception room, his expression somewhere between sadness and frustration and something I can't quite put my finger on.

"But something's still troubling you."

"I just don't know why I couldn't convince all of them. Barat's mostly come around to my view, but not William or Ancel. I remember what you said after that Council meeting, Papa. About how the discord was because you didn't do your job – didn't discuss things with people beforehand and explain your thinking to them. But I've done all that, Papa, and I've still mucked it up."

"Did you ask Samuel about that?"

"Aye."

"And what did he have to say?"

"He said the reason it's so hard for a commander to make a decision that goes against the advice he's received is because he knows that, if he's wrong, the consequences will be terrible for so many people in so many ways."

"Is that how you're feeling right now?"

"Maybe." He looks down at his feet, a sure sign he's thinking through what he wants to say next. "Or maybe I'm just not cut out to be a king."

I pull my chair over to sit directly opposite him, our knees almost touching. When I set him the challenge, I never imagined it would become such an intense lesson in the art of kingship.

"Or maybe," I tell him, "you're just getting your first taste of the weight of the crown." He looks up at me quizzically. "I'm actually rather pleased that all your mates didn't agree with you. It tells me they aren't sycophants who'll go along with anything just to please you. Not that I ever thought they would be, but the proof of that is really quite reassuring. And it should be to you as well."

"I suppose." He's not entirely convinced.

"I'm just as pleased with *you* that you've listened to them and thought about their perspective and found your way to your own conclusion. Samuel's right. That takes courage. And it weighs most heavily on those who care the most. The turmoil you're feeling right now comes with the role from time to time, Son. But the lesson to learn is not to let it overpower you, because that can impair your judgment just as much as failing to seek advice in the first place." Enough for now, I think. There'll be other opportunities to teach him vigilance on the outcomes of his decisions and the importance of changing course if events should prove him wrong.

"So what do *you* think, Papa? About the defenses at Peveril Castle."

"I'm not sure what to think yet. Only two of my advisors have weighed in so far."

"Two?"

"You and Samuel." Geoffrey smiles and sits up straighter in his chair, his confidence returning. "I haven't heard from my military advisors yet."

"Why is it taking Sir Jasper so long, Papa? We went on that patrol last autumn. And why haven't you pressed for an answer sooner?"

"We're under no immediate threat at the moment. So I can give them some time to really think through what modern warfare means and how we need to prepare."

"But you'll have an opinion before they come to the Council, right?"

I clap him on the shoulder. "See? You're thinking like a king already."

• • • •

Three days later, Coliar informs me that Sir Jasper wants a meeting but would prefer to do it in his office, since they have all their maps and materials spread out there. I've been looking forward to this ever since Samuel mentioned his idea about a different style of defenses. And it sparks an idea for giving Geoffrey and his mates more understanding of their recent experience.

Returning from my morning ride, I seek Tobin out before heading to Jasper's office. "I want to steal the lads from you this morning, Tobin. After what I asked them to do, I think it would be good for them to hear what experienced men came up with and why."

"I couldn't agree more, sir. The lads did a good job for their very first effort, but in the end, youthful enthusiasm for the new held sway for a couple of them. It'll be most interesting to hear their views after they listen to what Jasper and the others have to say. I've been keeping up with their progress as I've had the time. I think you'll be intrigued."

"Then send the lads to Jasper's office once they're all here. I'm headed there now to tell him what I have in mind."

"Of course, sir."

"By the way, Tobin, I haven't asked recently. How's your lovely wife?"

He beams. "Sarah's quite well, sir, if a bit uncomfortable. We'll be welcoming the wails of a newborn in about six weeks."

"Congratulations, Tobin! To both of you."

"Truth be told, sir, I've wondered if I have any idea at all how to be a father. But I've come to the conclusion of late that I can't go far wrong if I look to you and Lord de Courcy as role models."

Jasper, Evrouin, and several senior captains have gathered in the commander's office and jump to their feet when I arrive. "As you were, gentlemen." There are maps, diagrams, charts, documents, Evrouin's drawings . . . all manner of things spread on tables and affixed to the walls. There's even a model of a castle on a hill set on a campaign desk in the corner of the room. Looking around as Samuel comes through the door to join us, the only thing I can think to say is, "If I didn't know better, I'd think you were making war plans."

They all smile and Jasper actually laughs. "In a peculiar way, Sire," he says, "I think that's precisely what we've been doing." I look around the room again, trying to take it all in. "Don't worry," Jasper adds, "we'll take you through everything."

"In detail, if you will Jasper, including how you reached your decisions. That's less for me than for the lads. They struggled a bit with the exercise I set for them and never reached a consensus. Geoffrey was pretty dismayed by that, and I think the others were frustrated too. So I've taken them away from this morning's training to get some insight into how you and your men go about this. They'll be here any minute. And don't gloss over any disagreements you may have had along the way. Learning that there *were* disagreements will allow them to see there was nothing wrong with their own."

"Our pleasure, Sire. It will take a bit longer, but—"

"Don't concern yourself, Jasper. I've nothing else pressing today, so my time is yours . . . and the lads'."

As if on cue, the door opens and Geoffrey pokes his head in. "You sent for us, Sir Jasper?"

"Come in, young lords. Sir Evrouin and Sir Gilbert are just stepping out to fetch a few more chairs."

Once everyone is seated, Jasper begins with Evrouin's drawings. "We started at the same place the young lords did, Sire, since the mission of last autumn's patrol was to assess the defense of Peveril Castle should we face an attack from the east." He goes through all their considerations, offering diagrams of cannon positions, firing angles, and expected results, both from the valley and from the castle.

"In the end, Sire, we came to the conclusion that the strategic situation was no different from when King Charles invaded. We need to be prepared to stop an invader before they get that deep into the kingdom. And that led us to the further conclusion that the money required for the modifications that would be necessary to accommodate cannons at Peveril Castle would better be spent on defenses farther east. Keep that in mind, as I'll come back to it later."

I glance at the boys. Geoffrey's trying hard not to look smug as Barat elbows him in the ribs.

"What we learned studying Peveril Castle," Jasper continues, "made us take a good look at our other castles. Devereux Castle has precisely the same issues, even if the terrain isn't quite as extreme. Fortifications designed for archers at the top of a high point in the landscape with a village close in at the base of the hill. And in that case, there's not enough territory between there and the border to realistically expect to stop an invader farther north – and what territory there is, is woodland. Even here – your own castle, Sire – the defenses are based on archers on the high walls on high ground. And the town below the castle is much larger than the villages below the other two. The approach to Thorssen's is up a gentler slope, but that means they're just that much more vulnerable. Every one of those locations has its own unique problems that would require extensive changes to make it suitable for warfare with cannons. Nevertheless, we went about trying to work out some common modifications to recommend for all those sites."

"Sir Gilbert?" Jasper invites one of the captains to pick up the narrative.

"I was pretty convinced, Sire, that it was just a matter of engineering. Most issues with structures come down to that in the end. So my engineers built our model and tried to incorporate as many of the aspects of all three castles into it as they could. And yes, lads, it can be done. This would be just another in a long history of changes, expansions, or updates in the lives of these castles."

Ancel nudges Geoffrey and, though he keeps his voice low, no one misses his, "See? What did I tell you?" And William is now the one trying not to look smug.

"Once I had Gilbert's preliminary report on what would be required," Jasper resumes, "I sat down with Lord Guyat to look at the costs. Suffice it to say, I was pretty taken aback."

"But *I* was confident that, once we worked out detailed plans for each site," says Gilbert, "those costs would come down."

"*My* concern," Evrouin chimes in, "was time. If you recall, Sire, my father worked for builders. And one thing I learned about building is that it always takes longer than you plan for. Weather doesn't cooperate; materials don't arrive on time; tools wear out and have to be replaced; accidents happen. Anything that *can* go wrong, will."

"So what am I supposed to do as commander?" Jasper asks the lads directly. "I've got my captain of engineers telling me the work is completely doable, the Crown treasurer telling me it might bankrupt the kingdom, my deputy commander telling me he's worried about how long it will take, the engineers convinced they can find ways to save time and money . . . And in my own mind, I'm worried that even if we decide to move forward and spend the money, we still might not be ready before the need presents itself."

Jasper waits as the boys look at each other, uncertain if he really expects them to answer. Finally Geoffrey ventures, "So what *did* you do, sir?"

"I instructed Sir Gilbert to have his engineers start drawing up plans for modifications to the castle here. And then I went to someone I knew had been in this situation before. Not precisely the same situation, but a real strategic dilemma nevertheless. I had a long talk with Sir Samuel. Or rather, Lord de Courcy. Sorry, sir," Jasper inclines his head toward Samuel, "but to those of us of a military calling, you'll always be Sir Samuel."

"And I can think of no greater honor, Sir Jasper," Samuel replies.

"Anyway," Jasper turns his attention back to the boys, "Sir Samuel helped me see what I was overlooking. It can happen like that sometimes, lads, that you get so immersed in a problem that it actually colors your thinking and it's hard to see a different way. What Samuel said to me broke through that barrier."

"And what was that, sir?" William asks.

"He said, 'Maybe the problem is that you're asking the wrong question. Maybe instead of asking how to use what you already have, you should be asking what it is that you really need.' We talked at length about the idea that fortifications designed for one type of warfare might be completely unsuitable for what we now face. And the more we looked at it from that point of view, the more it began to appear he was right."

"Interestingly," says Gilbert, "once my engineers started drawing diagrams for the modifications they thought were needed, they started finding more problems. Blind spots, that neither archers nor cannons from inside the castle could cover. Firing angles that would work for certain distances but couldn't be adjusted quickly enough – or enough at all – as an opposing army advanced up the slope toward the castle.

"Parapets would have to be reconfigured. In some cases, the merlons, where archers hide when not firing, would need to be widened to protect those manning a cannon position, since it takes more men to operate a cannon than to loose an arrow or fire a bolt. That would mean closing off some cornels, resulting in fewer openings for archers or crossbowmen to operate. And the machicolations in proximity to the cannon positions would become unusable, leaving more places where men could get close in to the castle walls without fear of hot oil or boiling water being poured down on them.

"The more we delved into the details, the more we could see that the problem was bigger than what we'd originally thought. In the end, my contention that it was a simple matter of engineering had to be abandoned."

"But wasn't that embarrassing, sir?" William asks. "Having to go to the commander and say your first assessment had been wrong."

"Not at all," Gilbert doesn't hesitate. "What I was taking to the commander was new understanding. Maybe it meant we had to rethink things, but better to rethink and come up with something that works than to spend a king's ransom only to discover what we'd done was inadequate at best or an abject failure at worst."

Jasper catches my eye, his eyebrows raised in question. I nod. The boys are taking in the lesson. Time for him to move on to his recommendations.

"We've reached the conclusion, Sire, that a different type of fortification is needed. And that's what we want to turn our attention to. Which brings me back to the point about our defenses in the east. We've never had a garrison there, though why, I really couldn't say. Presumably, your predecessors and mine thought the greater threat was in the west. That assessment's no longer valid. Plus, we understand from experience how the river impedes our ability to react swiftly to a threat from the east. So we want to install a permanent garrison there, somewhere east of Peveril Castle. And we want to use the construction of that garrison to learn and experiment with a new type of fortress – something better suited to cannon warfare."

"What about defense of our current strongholds?" I ask.

"I know it seems contrary to conventional wisdom, Sire, but we think it's better to put our attention and the Crown's money toward stopping an invader before those positions come under threat." Anticipating my next question, he rushes to add, "Don't worry – we'll have plans for their defense that don't involve major reconstruction. But what we have to prepare for now is something the architects of those defenses could never have imagined. We . . . all of us . . ." he gestures around the room to his captains and all of them nod in agreement. "We're convinced Sir Samuel was right. We need to put our energy into what we need now. And to that end, I've already tasked Sir Gilbert and Sir Evrouin to begin working on designs for a new type of fortress."

I don't answer straightaway, instead, making a circuit of the room to look at the drawings and diagrams on the walls that clearly illustrate all the issues Sir Gilbert described. No one says a word. The silence is so intense, I wonder if they're actually breathing. They know how much is at stake. When I return to my seat, all eyes are on me – even those of the lads. "I'm impressed, Sir Jasper." There's a collective exhalation as smiles appear on faces all around the room and postures relax. Samuel beams like a proud father. "My son asked me a few days ago," I continue, "if I was concerned that it was taking you so long to make your recommendation. I won't deny I was getting curious." Some suppressed chuckles around the room. "Your time was well spent, so I'm really glad I kept that curiosity in check. How close are you to being ready to take this to the Council?"

"Whenever you wish, Sire."

"As soon as we can, because I think we need to get started. But if you'll indulge me, I'd like to ask each of the Councillors to come here and see and hear all this for themselves. I know it puts an extra burden on you, gentlemen, but it will save you having to drag all this stuff to the Council chamber and try to get them to take it in all in one gulp."

"I like that idea, Sire," says Jasper. "Far easier to understand when it's all spread out here."

"I may have a few more questions as I give it more thought, but I'm pretty sure I know where to come for answers." Finally, they're all relaxed enough to laugh. "Is there anything else?"

"Just one thing, Sire." Jasper turns his attention to the boys. "I know this is far grander than the recommendation you young lords delivered to the king. But you can take pride in the work you did. With more experience, you'll learn how to take your thinking from the simple task to a broader understanding of the defense of the realm. And you're well on your way."

As I rise to take my leave, William raises his hand somewhat tentatively. "Yes, lad?" Jasper asks.

"Could we stay and look at the drawings?"

"What say you, Gilbert? Want to give the young lords a lesson in fortifications?"

"It would be my pleasure, Commander."

Jasper and Evrouin follow Samuel and me out the door as Gilbert takes the boys under his wing. "Well done, Jasper," I tell him. "Not just all your hard work, but the way you handled the lads as well."

The sounds of their voices questioning Sir Gilbert drift through the half-open doorway.

"I was a young trainee once myself, Your Grace," Jasper chuckles.

I wander back into the inner courtyard to find all the commotion of new arrivals – a carriage, two wagons laden with all manner of trunks and crates and boxes, and servants bustling about. Juliana is home. "All this?" I gesture to the wagons where the servants have begun unloading. "Looks like you may have bankrupted the Ernle estate."

"Hardly, Papa. And I'll tell you all about it over supper. Right now, I just want to get settled in and let Sela start unpacking."

We have most of our private suppers now in Gwen's sitting room. In the weeks since Mother's passing, I've begun to come to grips with her absence, but this is the first time for Juliana. As she and Rainard take their seats, I watch her eyes scan the room in what I can only describe as a sense of reverence. When Matthias finishes serving and takes his leave, Juliana says quietly, "I'm going to miss Grandmama."

We eat in silence for a few moments until, predictably, Alicia breaks the mood. "You promised if I'd be patient you'd tell us all about your trip over supper, Juliana. So when do I get to stop being patient?"

"What do you think, Rainard? Has she been patient long enough?"

Alicia can't help looking a bit perturbed, but she holds her tongue in check.

"I think you've kept them all on tenterhooks long enough, dear," Rainard chuckles.

"Very well." And with that, Juliana's delight from earlier in the day returns in an instant. "It was nothing short of amazing. Lucia took us to remarkable places and introduced us into so many of the noble houses. The art there was like nothing I've ever seen. The protraits, Papa, look just like the person does in life. Not just a flat drawing of the outlines of a face or body or clothing. They paint the curve of a cheek or the folds of fabric with such realism. Richenda hired a painter for Denis's court, and Lucia gave one a commission to come to Lamoreaux for the summer to do some new paintings for the manor there.

"I bought some paintings for us – for Ernle Manor – and one for you, Papa, for the library. That's what's in the crates. We'll get everything uncrated tomorrow so you can see."

"Sounds expensive," I venture.

Juliana laughs. "It might have been, Papa, but I made a bargain with the artist. In return for a good price, I'll display his paintings here for people to see and then he'll visit for a couple of months this summer in hopes of getting some commissions."

"That's ambitious," says Gwen.

"Wait until you see the paintings, Mama."

"Did you bring me something?" asks Alicia.

"You don't think I'd forget that, do you?"

Alicia swings her feet back and forth in anticipation. "Is it in a crate too? When do I get to see?"

"Not in a crate, but it's in a safe place in one of my trunks, and you can have it as soon as Sela gets everything unpacked."

Alicia tries not to whine. "How long do I have to be patient for that?"

"Just until tomorrow morning. But would you like to know what it is?"

"Yes."

"Manners," Gwen chides.

"Yes, please, Juliana."

"So, I tried to describe Dog to one of the artists, to see if he could paint her from my description. He did a silverpoint drawing, but it's not quite right. That's what I have for you now."

"Oh." Alicia's definitely disappointed.

"Don't you want to hear the rest?" Alicia nods. "He's the artist who's coming this summer. And if you'll keep his drawing safe, he'll finish it when he can actually see Dog in person, and he'll turn it into a painting for you." Alicia lets out a little squeal of delight, jumps up to go hug Juliana, then returns to her seat and tries to sit quietly.

"What else, dear?" asks Gwen. "Before you left, you mentioned musicians as well."

"Oh, Richenda also hired a court composer. What he writes is very modern. We could have spent another entire month exploring. And oh, Mama, such beautiful new fashions! I bought three new gowns so our dressmakers will have something to copy.

"Anyway, we couldn't linger. Richenda needed to get home for the state visit with the Peaks – which is turning out to be a huge success, by the way, Papa. They extended it an extra week, but the entourage should be passing back through here in a week or so, depending on the weather for the sea crossing.

"Oh, and guess who took me aside to talk about their stayover here?" She gazes pointedly at Geoffrey, who turns bright red and looks as if he'd like to crawl under the furniture. The twinkle in his sister's eye says he's in for some teasing. "Eirwen seems to have been quite taken with someone she met here. I wonder who that might have been?" She puts a finger to her chin as if trying to recall. "I think she did mention someone named William." Geoffrey bristles. "Or was it . . .?" She pauses again. "Oh, it'll come to me eventually."

• • • • • •

Two days later, Juliana's waiting in my private reception room when I return from my morning ride. "Well, this is a nice surprise."

"I wanted to have a serious talk with you, Papa."

"What about?"

"This journey was a real eye-opener for me. I was too young when I first saw the art and music at Goscelin's court to really grasp how important it was. But now that I have more insight, I'm convinced it's something we're lacking here. You've always embraced new ideas, Papa, just like your grandfather did. But what I saw in Rome and the surrounding kingdoms and principalities . . . Papa, we're in danger of falling behind, and I want to keep that from happening."

"And how do you propose to do that?"

"I think we should follow Richenda's example and bring artists and musicians to our court. Perhaps even some scholars who aren't churchmen."

"That sounds like it costs money."

"Well, I've never seen you hesitate to invest in books for the library. Expanding people's minds isn't just about reading, you know."

"Buying books is a one-time investment. Rather different from committing to providing a livelihood for whatever number of people you'd like to bring here."

"But we already provide livelihoods for *dozens* of people. Would you be so reluctant if Cook asked for another kitchen maid or Elvin wanted to take on a couple more stable boys?"

"Maybe. I don't know. In any event, there are other things I have to think about at the moment. We're going to have to invest in entirely new defenses and build new fortresses now that we have to assume anyone who comes against us will have cannons. And that's going to be expensive."

"We're not under any particular threat at the moment, are we?"

"Not today. But Denis comes of age in just over a year, and we've no idea what might happen then. We have to prepare. We're committed to supporting him. And that costs money too."

"Very well. All I'm asking is that you give it some thought."

"That, I can agree to."

She gives me a quick kiss on the cheek before hurrying out.

Well, Alfred, I admonish myself. You wanted her to find something new to capture her interest. Seems you've gotten your wish. Now what are you going to do about it?

There's just enough time before we have to depart for Thorbrand's wedding to return to the eastern border. "We'll travel as ordinary folk," I tell Samuel and Carew. We're walking our horses through the woods on the way back to the stable after giving them some vigorous exercise in the meadow. "Just the three of us – unassuming peasants going about our business. So get yourselves some servants' clothing and a plain pack that doesn't look military. And get with Elvin and choose a nondescript-looking horse."

"Really, Alfred?" Samuel whines. "After all these years, I finally have a horse with a smooth trot, and you want me to leave him behind?"

"You'll survive," I chuckle. "Just think of it as more of that extraordinary service to the Crown that got you your title."

"Well, when you put it that way . . ." He grins.

"I don't want to risk being recognized in a chance encounter with anyone in Peveril's domain. The horse doesn't have to be a nag. Just unremarkable. And we go unarmed."

It's Carew's turn to be dismayed. "Surely you don't mean that, sir."

"Oh, he means it all right," says Samuel. "Just like he meant it when we went into the Territories that very first time to try to forestall a border war. He finally relented, that time, and let me hide a dagger in my boot." Carew shakes his head in disbelief.

"Well, this time, I'm not worried we'll be searched, so you can hide as many daggers in as many places as you want to, so long as they're not visible. But no swords. Put a flail in your pack if there's room and you can still carry enough food. Just don't expect me to share my food if you run out." My humor doesn't seem to do much to allay Carew's concern.

"One small hand axe to cut saplings or brush for a fire. We'll camp to avoid being recognized anywhere. I'll leave it to you to decide if we take a bow and a sack of arrows, but no more than one. It can't look like anything other than what we might need to hunt our supper."

"I told you he hadn't completely given up hare-brained schemes," says Samuel with a grin. "But this one seems pretty tame. It certainly worked for us back then."

"The place we're going is pretty wild, Carew," I add. "It's highly unlikely we'll encounter anyone at all, much less anyone intent on doing harm."

"If you say so, sir." Carew seems to have relaxed a bit. "I haven't seen it myself, so I suppose this is one of those times I'll just have to trust you."

"One other thing, Carew. See if you can find a map of that part of the kingdom and bring it with you."

"Whatever we have won't include the landmarks we'll be looking for," says Samuel.

"That doesn't matter. I just want to compare what it *does* include to what we see."

Thus it is that two nights later, three quite ordinary-looking travelers sit around their campfire beside a small stream about half a day's journey into Peveril's domain. The days are getting quite long, with the solstice merely three weeks away, so it's only just dark when we can finally spot Libra almost overhead – our cue to check the horses a final time before bedding down for the night.

The following morning, I ask Carew to retrieve his map. "Why so soon, sir?" he asks.

"Let's spread it out on the ground and I'll show you what I have in mind." I run my finger along the main road to a spot beyond Peveril Castle. "Our battleground, right?"

"Correct," says Samuel.

Then I trace farther along the road and stop at what appears to be a stream. "And this was roughly the back of Charles's supply lines?"

"That's right." Carew this time.

"With the long days, I think we can get there before dark and camp by that stream. It'll be a long day in the saddle, but worth it for what I have in mind." Neither of my companions comments. "The following day, I want to turn south the first decent chance we find. If there's not a suitable track, then we'll just have to go through the fields. I don't want us seen anywhere near the border on the main road.

"It was half a day's ride on the trail through the wooded hills and then another hour on level ground to the southernmost site. So we'll make our way that far south before we turn east. I'm sure we'll have to turn and wind a bit to follow whatever track we find. We'll just have to judge as best we can when it's time to change direction. If we get anywhere near these fens," I point to the map, "we're too far south."

"Why all the caution, Alfred?" asks Samuel. "You said yourself it was unlikely we'd encounter anyone or any threat."

"I know it's not entirely logical, Samuel. Truth be told, I can't really explain it – it's just an unsettled feeling I have about these places that makes it seem unwise for us to let anyone suspect we're curious about them. So we'll camp after we turn east. And no campfire that night. Smoke where it shouldn't be would just attract attention."

What we find at the Roman wall merely augments my uneasiness. Footprints in the dirt alongside the wall north of us, pointed in both directions. We've dismounted and left the horses several yards away where there are some nice patches of grass. "Looks like the prints were made after the last rain," says Carew, "when this would still have been muddy. Whoever was here didn't bother to hide their presence though."

Samuel walks on toward the north end of the wall and beckons us to join him, all three of us instinctively keeping our voices low. "Whoever was here," he says, "was probably hungry." He points to several gooseberry bushes growing along the base of the wall, two of which have been stripped almost bare, the others still laden with fruit. We each help ourselves to a handful – to the noisy consternation of half a dozen magpies perched on top of the wall some twenty feet away. No sooner have we turned back to retrieve the horses than the magpies resume their pillaging of the bushes.

When we reach the north end of the wall, Carew dismounts for a quick look on the other side. "Anything interesting?" Samuel asks when Carew rejoins us.

"Just brush growing near the wall and open meadow beyond."

"I still haven't discovered if this was a fort or a villa," I remark.

"Hard to say," says Carew. "The meadowland is extensive enough it could have been either."

When we reach the hill fort, my companions are just as intrigued as Geoffrey was, both of them jumping off their horses to walk about and study the ancient earthworks. "Not a place I'd like to try assaulting," says Samuel.

"For those who survived the arrows and spears raining down from the top," Carew adds, "hand-to-hand fighting on those slopes and in those ditches would have been brutal." He hands his horse's reins to Samuel. "Wait here. I want to see what's on the other side."

"Take care, Carew. We don't want to be spotted on the wrong side of the border."

"Don't fret, sir. I'm not going any higher than that first ditch . . . just want to sneak a quick look over the top of the mound." He scrambles up the slope and drops down into the ditch, crouching low before circling to his right.

Samuel remounts, saying quietly, "Just in case we have to get out of here in a hurry."

Great. As if I didn't already have enough trepidations about this place.

When Carew's head reappears above the mound, he has his finger to his lips, signaling us to keep silent. Carefully avoiding anything that might make noise under his boots, he returns to his horse, mounts, and leads us at a walk some hundred yards north, just into the shadows of the woodlands, where he finally stops and turns his horse to face us. "It's a shame we don't have a whole troop of archers with us."

Samuel's posture tenses as he reaches for the dagger hidden at the back of his waist beneath his jacket, while my heart skips a beat . . . maybe two.

Finally, Carew breaks into a smile. "We could've fed the entire castle and the town for a year. Biggest herd of deer I've ever seen, grazing in the meadow without a care in the world. They never even looked up when I peered over the top of the mound. Good thing there wasn't much of a breeze. But truth be told, they weren't paying much attention to scents either. One doe on the far side of the herd raised her head and sniffed the air a couple of times, but went right back to grazing.

"The woodland is close enough for them to take shelter there at night and the meadows extend as far as I could see to the east with no hedgerows or anything to indicate human habitation – just clumps of bushes here and there that look like they're browsed frequently enough to prevent their getting overgrown.

"Sir, those deer were not afraid. That tells me they've never been hunted and have rarely – maybe never – come in contact with humans."

We point our horses' noses north as the woodland trail begins its ascent into the low hills. After a couple of hours, as we near the highest point, I start looking for tracks leading off the main trail. Most aren't suitable for anything bigger than a fox, but I finally spy one with deer spoor along the side. "Time to turn back west, I think," I tell them. "No point wasting all our stealth in getting here only to be spotted at the border crossing."

We wind along the ridge until the woods begin to thin and the land slopes sharply down toward the farmland below. There, the track runs out, leaving us to find our own way down. Carew takes the lead and eventually finds a spot where it looks like rainfall running off the hills has created something of a wash – dry now – with a narrow bank on one side, descending into the valley. It reminds me a bit of the path we followed when looking for a source of water to feed Harold's reservoir years ago. We give our horses their heads and let them pick their own way down.

Once we reach level ground, Samuel declares, "Enough for one day, I think. Carew, let's have a look at that map and see if we can figure out where the nearest stream is. That'll be our camp."

In less than an hour, we've found the stream, unsaddled our horses, and hobbled them for the night. Far in the distance, I spy something that appears to be buildings of some sort, so we'll forego the campfire once again. The next morning, it doesn't take long to reach the main road.

For two days, I steer the conversation away from what we'd seen at the border, telling them about our visit to the quarries, but mostly discussing the boys' training and how they responded to what they'd seen that morning in Jasper's office. I want Samuel and Carew to have time to absorb and think about what they saw at the border before we talk about it.

When we camp for the last night before the ferry crossing, it's time. "So what did you think, gentlemen? Do we have a huge vulnerability? Or is my anxiety unfounded?"

They glance at one another, deciding who'll begin. "It's still a very wild place," Carew offers. "One or two of our own people, living somewhere on a remote farm or at the edge of the fens, who know where to find good gooseberries . . . and that's about it."

"How do you know they're our people?" I ask.

"Because the footprints didn't continue on the other side of the wall. That's what I was looking for when I took that quick peek. The area's barely inhabited on our side of the border – we saw that for ourselves – and from everything I observed, it seems even less inhabited on their side. We'd have to actually get someone in there to find out where their habitation begins, of course, but there's no evidence of it along the border."

"What about in the woodlands?"

"If there *are* woodland folk, I think they must be farther east. Those deer were completely unafraid. Again, we'd have to have someone scout the animal tracks to the east of our own trail to know for certain if anyone lives there, but there were no obvious signs that I could discern."

"Samuel?"

My friend looks pensive in the dimming twilight. "Not much I can add to Carew's observations. It's very wild, but we have no clues whatsoever how far that wildness extends. And it's that unknown, I suspect, that creates your feeling of unease." He pauses. "I'm not discounting your feeling, Alfred. I actually understand it. In some ways, the area is peaceful and calming. Yet its very wildness is disconcerting. It brings up primal feelings our ancient ancestors must have had when the whole world was wild and a predator could appear seemingly out of nowhere."

I'm not sure if his words are comforting or disquieting.

"And don't forget," he continues, "that the last time you were in a wild place you were in dire straits. Desperate to find your family and with a raging fever. The imprint that left on your mind could be coloring your reaction to these places in ways you're not even aware of.

"But I know your fundamental question is whether we should put defenses there. Yes, we could extend that Roman wall to the hill fort, but that would attract a lot of attention. In truth, Alfred, the border north of the main road is just as vulnerable – perhaps more so. It just feels like less of a threat because we're more familiar with it.

"What I've been thinking a lot about over the past couple of days is that all those wild places offer a unique opportunity to infiltrate scouts to observe what might be happening farther east and north of those wooded hills. That could actually prove useful even when there's no overt threat from that quarter. Doing anything at all about defenses along that portion of the border would deprive us of that ability."

Everything they say makes perfect sense. So why can't I shake this feeling deep in my bones?

Our visit to the Far Nordic Kingdom is nothing short of spectacular. Brandr sent Captain Thorvald to fetch Laurence's family and mine. During our first night at sea, I wonder aloud to Gwen, "What do you think's behind Brandr's generosity? First, he puts Thorvald at our disposal for Richard's mission, and now, this."

"Why so suspicious, Alfred? I think it's a lovely gesture."

"Perhaps. But we could certainly have gotten ourselves to the wedding."

"Do you want to know what else I think?"

"Of course."

"I think you're letting the Teuton king get under your skin. Not all kindnesses are given with the expectation of payback. Especially not between friends as good as you and Brandr. Be careful, Alfred, that you don't harm that friendship."

Perhaps she's right. Words like that . . . "we both know you are twice in my debt" . . . words like that tend to stay in a man's thoughts. And when you wear the crown, it can be unwise just to brush them aside.

"Now . . ." she snuggles even closer in our small berth, "turn your mind to enjoying the celebrations. After all, this isn't just a wedding – it's the realization of that formal alliance you and Brandr have wanted for so long. It should be no wonder he's in a generous mood."

As soon as we enter the straits that lead to the main port, we're treated to scenery unlike anything we've seen before. The royal castle is but a short journey from the port, with an evergreen forest off to one side of the road and meadows filled with wildflowers on the other.

Brandr's welcome is expansive and Aunt Beatrix is overjoyed to see us, but Brandr's wife, Arnora, seems as uncomfortable as ever in her role as queen. She greets Gwen and me formally, largely ignoring Geoffrey and Edward, intent, it seems, on displaying her image of how she thinks a queen is supposed to act. Her greeting for Laurence and Estrilda – while proper – nevertheless lacks any of the warmth one might expect for the parents of the woman about to marry her son.

"Pay her no mind," Beatrix tells the Montforts as she shows us all to the rooms that have been prepared for us. "I've been *ever* so much happier since I learned to do that. It took Margery no time at all to work out how to stay out of Arnora's way, so I think she and my grandson are going to be quite content."

"That's a relief," says Estrilda. "It was my one reservation about the marriage."

When I meet the King of the Southern Nordics – whose name is Hasten – he's cordial but remains aloof over the two days of celebrations leading up to the wedding. On the morning following the ceremony, Brandr arranges for the three of us to go alone to his hunting lodge. Its setting – in the midst of a forest of majestic evergreens with glimpses of the snow-covered peaks in the distance – is breathtaking. Inside, enormous stone fireplaces hint at what winter temperatures must be like. "No one comes here in the depths of winter," says Brandr. "But even for the autumn hunts, the days are short and the nights quite cold."

"Brandr has told me, Alfred," says Hasten when we've settled into comfortable chairs in the main hall, "that I may have appeared rude over these past several days. That was certainly not my intent. It's merely that I'm a cautious man with a tendency to be wary of strangers and new acquaintances. One learns that of necessity when your next-door neighbors are the Teutons."

"Not an enviable position," I reply. "And why I'm grateful to you for receiving my envoy earlier this year and for helping to craft an agreement that suits both our needs."

"One must be prepared against catastrophe," says Hasten. "One must also be guarded lest those preparations become common knowledge. And that is why I cannot invite you to my court . . . why I prefer that our acquaintance not be widely known. I am content to meet you on any occasion that brings us both to Brandr's court, but beyond that, it is too great a risk to the balance of power I must maintain with the Teutons, lest they simply overrun my kingdom."

"You have my word of honor, Hasten, that I respect your needs. One never knows when a secret alliance might be what turns the tide in an open conflict."

"Brandr long ago gave me his assurances that you would share my view." A reference, I've no doubt, to the secret role Hasten played in our campaign to suppress the Teuton incursion Charles supported as a way to quash his rebellious nobles and effect my demise. "Our overt indifference to one another need not be an impediment to furthering our common interests, however. Brandr and I both have complete trust in Captain Thorvald, and we invite you to do the same."

"I've long suspected Thorvald's role was far more than a mere ship captain." Brandr and Hasten exchange knowing glances. "Truth be told," I continue, "I'd started to wonder if perhaps he was Brandr's spy in my kingdom." They both laugh out loud.

"No more than in mine," says Hasten. "Perhaps it is time I tell you a bit more about what I know of the Teutons' ambitions. Their relentless pursuit of territory to their west is driven by their desire for easier access to the sea. They have built a large port and have a rather substantial fleet, but access to the open seas requires that they sail through my straits. They have long had their eye on a port in warmer waters. I'm content to let them sail uninhibited through the straits as the price for protecting my own interests, and my fishing fleet keeps a keen eye on whatever they might be up to in the Northern Sea. It is an arrangement that they have, so far, respected."

"And the reason we believe," says Brandr, "that it would be unwise for your banners and emblems to be seen frequently in those waters. The Teutons would waste no time coming to the conclusion that the three of us are in league."

Now, at last, everything makes sense. Brandr's generosity is also his strategy for preserving a delicate balance between three kingdoms – four, if I count Denis. "Now I understand why you found my suspicion of Thorvald so amusing," I chuckle.

"It is also why," says Hasten, "I hope you will consider participating in a further bit of subterfuge."

"What might that be?"

"It finally occurred to me that the best way to protect our trade is to conduct it under the banner of my merchant guild. If you are agreeable to allowing your trading ship to sail under that banner, I think we can keep the Teutons from getting curious."

"I'm more than agreeable. I'll just have to work out with my Port Commissioner how to do it without raising suspicion among *our* people."

"We anticipated that," says Hasten. "And to that end, they need only fly that banner on the open sea and while in my port."

"I'm sure we can work something out. It's actually quite a brilliant idea. And my Port Commissioner is the new Crown Princess's father, so we can discuss it on the journey home – even get Thorvald's input."

"Excellent!" Hasten smiles broadly. "I will see that the banner is delivered to Thorvald before you depart."

Brandr crosses the room to a sideboard and returns with three small glasses of the brandy-like drink made from grain that was served with pickled fish last night to toast his son's marriage. He raises his own glass. "To the success of our little enterprise!"

I add "To good friends!" and we drink the toast, downing the peculiar liquid in a single gulp.

Gwen was right. I've been seeing shadows where there are none. After Samuel and Richard, I've no better friend in the world than Brandr.

The morning after our return, I find Ademar and Richard waiting for me at the stable. "Seemed like a nice morning for a ride," Richard remarks.

"Fancy a bit of a gallop, Ademar?" I ask when we arrive at the meadow.

"I'm an average horseman at best, Your Grace. And my horse has a bit of a lazy streak, so something a bit less frenetic is better, if you don't mind."

"Not at all. A bit hard to have any useful conversation at that pace, in any event. Which, I presume, was your intent, Richard?"

"Aye, Sire."

"Lord Devereux's told me . . ." says Ademar. My mind does its familiar hiccup at hearing Richard referred to this way. When will that finally begin to seem natural? Ademar continues, ". . . what you and he have in mind relative to the Assembly."

"Excellent!" I reply. "And what say you?"

"May I be candid, Sire?"

"I expect nothing less."

"I'm not sure I actually measure up to your expectations."

"In what way?"

"Sire, I'm truly no different from Devereux or Thorssen. What I do is manage a great estate. And I suspect that's exactly how the Assembly will view me."

"From where we sit, Ademar, that's absolutely right. But unlike Devereux or Thorssen, your greatest asset can't be rented out or replanted or sheared over and over, year after year. If Devereux's right, the merchants will see what you do through their own lens. You have a product to sell. And you have to produce that product, hire staff, find buyers, and set prices that turn the greatest possible profit. Not much different from the baker or the purveyor of fine fabrics except for the scale. I'm inclined to agree they'll see you as someone who actually understands what they do rather than as just an aristocrat who does little more than collect rents and feast at the king's table. So you see, Ademar, what it comes down to in the end is less about my expectations than those of the Assembly members."

"But surely you must have some expectations, Sire."

"Well, I'm pretty sure the Council would say they want you to convince the delegates to see that they need to contribute to the good of the kingdom rather than the other way around," I chuckle, and Richard laughs out loud. "We actually had a bit of success there in the early days, but I think that had a lot to do with the influence of two particular delegates. One thing I've come to realize is that most of the commercial interests measure their own worth and that of their peers by the size of their profits, and very few can see beyond that to the broader needs of society or that they should contribute in any way toward the betterment of lives other than their own. No doubt Devereux and Thorssen have told you about their frustrations."

"They have indeed." Ademar rolls his eyes. I'm sure Richard and Phillip didn't mince words about some of the more intractable men who've been Assembly delegates in the past.

"I have no expectation that you can change their thinking in some grand stroke," I continue. "What I hope is that you can allow them to see you as someone with similar concerns and that you can help them shape their contributions into something a bit less purely selfish."

"That's pretty much what Devereux said, but I'm grateful for the chance to hear your own views, Sire. I've been lucky to have had no greater responsibility so far than the running of our estate, so it's long overdue that I render some service to the Crown. I only hope there'll be occasions for me to go home from time to time to ensure things are still running smoothly."

"That goes without saying," says Richard. "We all do that. And it's my job to manage Council business to be sure everyone has those opportunities."

"Then I'll do the best I can with these unruly Assembly delegates."

"Welcome to the Council, Lord Ademar," says Richard.

As we turn our horses' heads back toward the stable, I switch topics. "There's one thing you should probably attend to straightaway, Ademar. The Council will be taking up the matter of new defenses in short order, so be sure to spend some time with Sir Jasper. His plans impact your estate directly."

"Already done, Sire. And I do have one concern. I'd like to keep anything associated with fighting well away from our quarry operations. I know that can't be guaranteed, but I'm proposing that the land we give up for the new garrison be on the south side of the main road and have written to my father for his confirmation. I think perhaps Sir Jasper wasn't quite as pleased with that as he might have been."

Jasper may not have been well pleased, but I am. "Leave Sir Jasper to me, Ademar." It least now I won't have to try to convince him to choose the site of his garrison based on my probably irrational anxiety.

If one summer can be considered more beautiful than others, this one is certainly a contender for the prize. Every plant in the garden seems intent on outshining its neighbors with brilliant color and enormous blossoms, and the meadows are a veritable celebration of wildflowers. Even the rain confines itself to short showers – often with the sun still shining above the small clouds – and leaves behind the smell of land and air cleansed and fresh and ready to renew its bounty. The absence of any new crisis to contend with this year may be coloring my view, but I'm grateful for the respite and the chance to really enjoy the glories of nature.

Time spent with Regulus reminds me just how much peace and contentment I get from helping a young horse learn what he needs to know to be a good mount. His most serious training will come next summer, when he's old enough to bear a man's weight, but for now, he's learning how to respond to the reins, how to remain calm when tied or hobbled for grazing, and how to be his rider's best friend. By the end of the summer, I'll introduce him to the feel of the saddle on his back so that's already familiar when we start preparing for that first ride. That I get to do this alongside my sons makes the pleasure even greater.

Geoffrey's grey has a bit of an independent streak and likes to make his own decision about when a day's training is finished. But with Elvin's help, Geoffrey's learning how to teach the colt there are times when someone else is in charge. Edward is proving to be as natural a trainer as he is a horseman. After spending hours in the library searching for just the right name for his colt, he settled on Fortis. "I'm sure it took a lot of courage to start his life in the midst of that storm," Edward told me. "And he's still very brave. He'll try anything I ask him to, even when it's something he's never seen or done before."

Peveril didn't answer Ademar's letter, but came home instead to be sure there was no doubt about his position. Something of a surprise, since he typically leaves the management of the estate entirely in Ademar's hands.

"Not that it isn't always a pleasure to see you," I remark when I invite him to join me for a brandy after the court dinner on the night of his arrival, "but I surmise from the fact that Emmeline didn't come with you that you don't plan to stay long. So what really brings you here?"

He chuckles. "Can't a man look after the needs of his estate without being suspected of ulterior motives?"

I laugh and clap him on the shoulder as we head for the staircase to go up to my private reception room. I pour two brandies from the special decanter I keep hidden away at the back of the cabinet under the sideboard. "Almost the last of that cask of St. Didier that Lucia sent last year. I've ordered more since then, of course, and it's excellent, but it doesn't compare to this. So it's your lucky day."

He takes a sip. "My lucky day indeed."

We chat for a bit about his general observations of the state of affairs in the Kingdom Across the Southern Sea. "In short, it's looking more and more like what I remember from Goscelin's time," he sums things up.

"Then what's your ulterior motive for coming home?"

He smiles. "You're right, Alfred. I could simply have answered Ademar's letter and that would have been sufficient for Sir Jasper. But the estate business gave me a perfect excuse to come home and update

Laurence – and you too – on some new developments. Petronilla's begun rebuilding Denis's spy networks. Slowly and quietly, but Laurence needs to know some details so his agents don't accidentally run afoul of what's afoot there."

"Sounds like good news if things are stable enough to get that underway."

"Good news on several fronts, actually. With Lord Greville's agreement, she's quietly put the Duke of Aleffe in charge of the operation. Agents can come and go from Aleffe Manor and avoid raising eyebrows at court."

"But isn't the Duke at court most of the time?"

"Much of the time, yes. But the Duchess travels back and forth quite a lot. Nominally, she's looking after the management of the estate. But it provides her the perfect cover for being the conduit between the agents and the regent. And we already know Tiece has a talent for stealth, given what happened during Charles's reign."

When the nobles opposed to Charles rallied around the Aleffe name, the Duke remained staunchly loyal to his sovereign. Tiece, however, disappeared from sight, and it was widely believed she was in league with the insurrection – perhaps even in overall command. One thing that's certain – though still a closely guarded secret – is that she successfully smuggled Denis out of the kingdom to keep him out of the hands of both factions and protect his life until the time when he could accede to the Crown.

"Do we have any idea how much Denis has been told about these developments?"

"Not really. But from everything Petronilla's told me in private, I'm inclined to think they're not keeping him in the dark. After all, he comes of age next June, so there's less than a year for him to be fully prepared."

And less than a year for us to prepare for what might happen when he takes the throne in his own right. God grant that the world simply moves on, accepting that there's no change to the status quo. But where the Teutons are concerned . . . "We both know you are twice in my debt."

"Alfred?" Peveril's voice jars me out of my musings.

"Sorry. So I presume you're headed to the port tomorrow and then back across the sea."

"That's what I plan. How long I stay with Laurence will depend on what he wants to put in motion and how long it takes him to do that." He finishes his brandy but declines when I offer to refill his glass. "Planning an early start in the morning, so I think I'll find my bed."

•   •   •   •   •   •

Jasper is now resigned to having the new garrison on the south side of the main road. It required adjustment to the geometry of the fort and the plans for cannon positions, but that's all been accomplished, the Council has approved the money, and building is getting underway. He was – and still is – puzzled by my insistence on four firing positions on the southeast-facing wall rather than the two he'd planned. But once I assured him there'd be no argument over the additional cost, he was happy to humor his king.

"I've no intent to put a damper on your enthusiasm for the new garrison," I also told him, "but I hope you haven't forgotten what might be facing us next summer, when King Denis comes of age."

"Not at all, Sire. In truth, much of our planning for the previous campaign is still relevant, but since we no longer have to concern ourselves with internal strife within that kingdom, there are some changes I want to make. And an idea I want to explore with Lord Goron."

"As long as we're ready when and if our support's required."

"We will be, Sire."

•   •   •   •   •   •

Toward the end of July, Laurence brings news of Gunhild's first outing as our agent. "It looks like Gunnvor took the bait. He's sent her back to try to discover the formula for black powder. Apparently, he's quite ambitious and wants to impress his cronies and seal their loyalty."

"Any idea where his ambitions lie?"

"We asked Gunhild that very question. Seems he currently has his eye on the lands to the east of his own domain. The lord there is old and infirm, and his elder son is thought to be feeble-minded. His other son – by his second wife, who's some thirty years his junior – is just fourteen. But the lad's mother has been scheming to get her son named as the heir, and one of her schemes involves collusion with Gunnvor to make that happen by force if her husband is too long dying or too stubborn to abandon his firstborn."

"How does Gunhild know this?"

"She claims her brother makes her serve the ale when he and his cronies are reveling in the great hall of an evening. Makes her sit in the corner of the room so anyone can snap their fingers for an instant refill when their mug runs dry. If she's to be believed, Gunnvor cares less about what she overhears than that the ale flows freely and with no delay. Treats her like a servant but seems convinced she won't gossip like one."

"And what's your opinion about her reliability?"

"Too early to say. And that's the difficulty with infiltrating new places in general – and especially if you have to do it with an unproven agent. The person I've chosen as her minder is particularly skilled at probing for inconsistencies – not just when Gunhild makes her report, but in ordinary conversation where the questions are shrouded in the mundane.

"It also turns out that Brother Nicholas is pretty astute at getting her to speak unguardedly about her home and what life with Gunnvor is like. That's probably because he's the only one she can communicate with easily, but it works to our advantage.

"So we're watchful and wary and testing everything as best we can. But it'll take more forays and more reports before we can get any sort of useful sense of whether our gambit is working or if we're just being played from the other side."

"Only thing you *can* do, I suppose. So what's next? Or should I not ask?"

"Well, we'll assume Gunnvor has taken the bait, so I need to slowly pull him in. It's completely implausible that Gunhild could learn everything about how to make black powder easily, so I want your permission to feed her bits and pieces to take back to her brother, saving the most important ingredient for last."

"You really want to arm them?"

"Alfred, he'll get the information somewhere if he's determined enough. And he'll get weapons eventually. It's all out in the world now. So if we can keep him believing Gunhild is getting what he wants, then maybe we can control the pace at which it happens. It's likely he doesn't have anything resembling a cannon yet. Gunhild says she talked to the blacksmiths and forgers, and none of them had been asked to try to cast anything new. No idea how true that is, but the fact that what he wants now is the formula for black powder might indicate that he's not far along yet in thinking about how he's going to use it."

"What does Rupert think?"

"That it's a dangerous game but one we have to play."

"Play it slowly, Laurence. I don't want to create an enemy where we've had none before."

"And yet we're putting our most modern defenses in the east, so apparently our military minds think that's where our greatest vulnerability lies."

"The situation in that part of the world is unsettling, at best, which is why I'm satisfied to let you try to get some insight into what's going on over there. Just play the game wisely – that's all I can ask."

As he rises to leave, I can't resist the question that pokes its head into my consciousness now and again. "By the way, Laurence, did we ever learn anything more about that extra body that was found in the barn when my mother died?"

"Not to my knowledge. The sheriff's done his best to try to figure out who the man might have been, but without any success."

"It just seems to me that amulet might have been a clue to where he came from – to where someone might be able to identify him."

"I know the sheriff's shown it all around, but no one seems to have ever seen anything like it before. He even brought it down to the port one day and showed it around the taverns, but no one seemed to recognize it. I know you'd like an answer, Alfred, but this may be one of those cases where the man took the answer to the grave with him."

Two weeks later, when I wander out to the stable to spend some time with Regulus, the boys are just finishing with their colts. "I had a letter from Denis today," Geoffrey announces. "He's invited me to visit him."

"Did he suggest a date?" I ask as I hand Regulus one of the carrots I'd liberated from the kitchen.

"The middle of September. Can I go, Papa?"

Regulus nudges my arm, requesting another carrot. "I don't see why not. In truth, it's been too long since we paid Petronilla a family visit. Would you object if your mother and I came along?" His shoulders slump. Clearly, he'd been hoping for an adventure on his own. "I promise we'll stay out of your way. You and Denis can get up to whatever you wish, completely without parental interference."

"You promise, Papa?"

"I promise. This is your visit. So why don't you arrange things with your mother and then reply to Denis? Let him know you'll have hangers-on, just so Petronilla can be prepared."

Thus it is that on Saint Deiniol's Day, Gwen, Geoffrey, and I depart the castle for a visit I'm looking forward to almost as much as my son is. Even aboard the ship, Gwen and I try to remain in the background, while Geoffrey spends all his time with the captain and first mate, peppering them with questions about sailing, navigation, commanding a crew, and dealing with the weather. This isn't the first time he's shown an interest in such things, leaving me to wonder if he might choose to be a mariner were he not heir to the throne.

Denis and Richenda greet us in the courtyard when we arrive at midafternoon, carefully welcoming Geoffrey first since the invitation was extended to him. Petronilla is waiting just inside the front door, an obvious sign of the transition in progress from her regency to Denis's personal rule nine months hence.

The change in the young king is remarkable. The budding confidence I saw a year ago, when he took the decision to accompany me to the rendezvous with the Teuton king despite the vigorous debate among his advisors over its wisdom, has matured into an air of dignity – of an innate sense of his role. He's taller than last year, naturally, but that's accentuated by an inescapable awareness of the respect he must command. The frightened lad desperate for someone to help save his life may still be in there somewhere, but he's long gone from the young man's external demeanor. That said, he still has the unruly blond hair and boyish smile that I'm certain charm friend and foe alike. By comparison, Geoffrey seems much younger, despite his growing understanding of what the future holds for him. Denis has had to embrace his role sooner and learn faster.

While Geoffrey walks on with Denis and Richenda, Petronilla embraces Gwen and extends her hand for my kiss. "So what do you think of our boy, Alfred?" she asks.

"I don't think we can call him that any longer," I chuckle.

She laughs and takes Gwen's arm in her right, mine in her left. "Let's go find your quarters so you can shed your traveling clothes and refresh from the journey. We'll have a private supper this evening in Richenda's sitting room, and I want to hear all the news from your side of the sea."

That evening's conversation proves to be lively indeed. Juliana's interest in the arts pales by comparison to Richenda's enthusiasm. "I simply *must* show you the workshop we've created for our artists, Aunt Gwen. It's just like the ones we saw in Lucia's homeland." She pauses for a bite of food then resumes. "Then there's the music school. We're only just getting underway with that, but I have big plans for it to be even grander than what we had in Papa Goscelin's time. I just wish we were going to have a big banquet while you're here so you could hear some of our new music."

"Well, *I'm* glad you wanted a simple family visit," says Petronilla. "Court functions happen all the time, so this is a rare treat."

Denis and Geoffrey have had their heads together, no doubt laying their own plans for the next few days. Taking advantage of a lull in the artsy conversation, Denis says, "Tomorrow morning, I'm showing Geoffrey what we've been doing with our horse breeding program. Would you like to come along, Alfred?"

"I think not. That was your and Geoffrey's project. He can tell me about it later." Anyone who knew to look for it would be able to see the relief wash over Geoffrey's face and posture as he realizes I intend to keep my promise. He knows that, of the things that might tempt me to break it, horses would be at the top of the list.

It's the third day of our visit before I have the opportunity to talk privately with Denis. Alone – just the two of us – the deference he's always shown me is still present, but it's no longer that of boy to man – more an earned respect similar to what I've always felt for the late Lord Devereux and old Lord Ernle. "I'm really glad you read between the lines of my invitation to Geoffrey, sir. I know you've encouraged me to avail myself of Lord Peveril for private messages, but that's hardly the same as a conversation, which is what I feel sorely in need of at the moment. I only hope Geoffrey won't take offense at my ruse, especially since I've thoroughly enjoyed his company these past two days."

"As long as I stick to my promise not to interfere in his visit, I doubt you have any cause for concern."

He chuckles. "Well, you certainly seem to be keeping your word."

"What's on your mind, Denis?"

"My birthday, mostly, and everything it implies. I think Lord Peveril's told you we're once again able to spy on the Teutons. Not deep within their kingdom, but well beyond the border villages. So far as we can tell, life there is boringly ordinary. No sign of soldiers in the towns or villages. No sign that men are being conscripted. No interruptions to farming or commerce. No weapons appearing where there were none before. Nothing. For the life of me, I don't know what to make of it – whether to be grateful there's no obvious, immediate threat or to be alarmed by what might lie beneath the apparent calm. And it doesn't help that Greville has no better idea than I do."

"To my way of thinking, your wariness is wise. I'm still convinced you gained the Teuton king's respect last summer. But we both know everything he does is purposeful, and it's impossible to tell, from what you know, what he may be signaling.

"There's one thing I *can* tell you. I've learned recently that he's obsessed with finding easier access to the sea than he now has through the northern straits. That could mean either our port or yours. But since he has a land border with you . . ." I let the thought hang in the air.

"The safe wager is that my port is the target," says Denis. "And the need for easy land access means Aleffe province is part of his grand design. But truly, Alfred, that does nothing but validate what we already surmised."

"Yes, but removing uncertainty from the target makes things far easier for your commanders to plan their strategy to counter the threat."

"I suppose it does." Denis rises and takes a turn around the room before returning to his seat – something I've seen his mother do when she grapples with a difficult decision. "Can I tell you something, Alfred?" he finally asks, then goes on without waiting for a reply. "I almost wish the attack would come straightaway so we could deal with it and I could get on with the business of ruling my kingdom.

"I should be out on progress, letting the people see their new king, cementing the loyalty of the nobility. Instead, I'm living here in seclusion like a monk once again, only this time my cloister is a castle rather than a monastery. The unrest here seems well and truly behind us. Even Suidbert is managing to fit into the court and the others have come to accept his presence. So it's time to look to the future. And yet Lord Greville continues to advise against any ventures into the countryside for the present."

After what he's weathered to get to this point, Denis's frustration is understandable and so is his youthful enthusiasm. But equally so is Greville's caution. "Do you want my advice?" I ask him.

"Please. More than anything."

"Your instincts are right, Denis. Don't be swayed from them. But temper them for now. Your throne isn't really secure until you have an heir. And you can be certain our mutual acquaintance is just as much aware of that as your advisors are. That doesn't mean you have to live in fear or postpone looking to the future. Set aside the idea of a grand progress throughout the kingdom for the moment, and just test the waters with small steps. One- or two-day journeys to places nearby. No doubt Greville will insist on an excess of guards to accompany you, but that's entirely reasonable and something I'm sure you can tolerate with ease."

His countenance brightens. "Indeed I can. Especially with the new captain of my personal guard. You were right, Alfred, that I'd find congenial and trustworthy men to rely on. Crespin is one of them. So is my new deputy commander. He's young – only six or seven years older than me – but he's risen through the ranks quite quickly because he's a superb strategist. It's said he actually plays chess blindfolded and rarely loses."

"Blindfolded?"

"From what I hear, the players call out their moves and Étienne can construct an image in his mind of where the pieces are on the board and all the moves to arrive at checkmate."

"Have you ever played him?"

Denis laughs. "Maybe one day I'll get the nerve. I think I'm pretty good at the game, but to be beaten by a blind man might be rather humiliating. And if I happened to win, then I'd probably think it was only because he let me."

It's my turn to laugh. "You'd better get used to that."

"To what?"

"To people letting the king win at any contest – even when you tell them not to. Probably goes back to a time when people thought their lives were at risk if they did otherwise, but now it seems to be a matter of protocol or a show of respect. In truth, though, it just means you don't know if you succeeded on your own merits."

"And to think I'd thought that was only in practice swordplay where no one wants to injure the king," Denis chuckles.

"That's where those congenial, trustworthy men around you are so important. Encourage them to be candid with you – in the right circumstances, of course – and they'll be invaluable."

He sits quietly for a moment before saying, "Thank you, sir. For coming. For sharing your wisdom." He pauses. "For guiding me as Grandpa Goscelin would have if he were still here."

"I'm pleased to do what I can. I think it's time I should tell you directly what I told Petronilla when she agreed to be your regent. You can count on my full support. And though I really can't speak for your other allies, I'm inclined to believe you can count on them as well."

"And my most fervent prayer is that we never actually need it. Now," he rises from his chair, "let's make our way to the stable. I told Geoffrey the three of us would go riding when we finished here, and I rather suspect he'll be there waiting for us. Besides, I want you to meet Crespin. I think you'll like him."

It's five days before Christmas, and I'd much rather be back at the castle watching Alicia's irrepressible delight in guessing what her Christmas gift might be. One day she hopes it's a pony of her own; the next she wants two new frocks; the day after, it's a basketful of ribbons for her hair.

But instead of enjoying my daughter's antics, I'm sitting with Rupert and Laurence in front of the fire in the drawing room at the country manor. "We've pressed our luck as far as we can, I'm afraid," says Laurence.

"In what way?" asks Rupert as he pours each of us a glass of wine.

"It seems Gunnvor's given his sister an ultimatum – either she brings him the full and correct formula for black powder or he throws her out."

"Well, that was bound to happen. You've been toying with him for half a year now." Rupert hands out the glasses then takes his own to his favorite chair. "So what do you want to do?"

"We have three options. We can abandon the field and put her away somewhere where she can't do us any harm. We can give her the proper formula and continue to run her as our spy. Or we can throw her out and see what she does. If she runs straight back to Gunnvor, that's probably a sign that he's been playing us rather than the other way around. If she hangs around here – maybe goes back to the brothels – that's a fair indication that she's telling the truth and still trying to get what her brother wants before she dares go back home."

"Play out all those options for me," I say. "What do you foresee happening in each scenario?"

"The first one carries the least short-term risk for us. We've revealed our new port defenses, but those are out in the open anyway. We've gotten some things from Gunhild in the way of insight into her brother's activities. We choose not to be responsible for arming him. And Gunhild's put away where she can never cause us any more trouble." He pauses for a sip of wine.

"But?"

"But . . ." another sip of wine before he sets down his glass. "There's no doubt Gunnvor will look elsewhere to get his hands on black powder, and it's a safe wager he'll have it by next summer."

My turn for the thoughtful sip of wine. "If that's the safe wager, then we'd best assume he'd have it by Easter."

"And while Gunnvor's busy courting a new ally," Laurence continues, "we're once again blind to whatever's afoot there. And that's the longer-term risk."

"And if we continue to run her as our spy?"

"The game becomes trickier. We're past the opening moves – the relatively safe plays – and into a phase where I'd rest ever so much easier if I could get independent confirmation of even a couple of the details she's given us. Absent that, all we can do is constant probing to try to discover any cracks in what she brings us. What it does give us, though, is control over what she reveals to Gunnvor. I'll want your wisdom more than ever, Rupert."

"I'll do what I can, naturally."

"So what about the last option? Why do I get the impression it's your preference?" I ask.

"Truth be told, Alfred, I'm not sure. It's high risk. But the rewards, if she doesn't run home straightaway, could be enormous." He pauses to give me time to ponder. "We'd have to handle it carefully, but we already have an example of her being more cooperative if she thinks she's being abandonned to her own devices."

"Oh?"

"She was making almost no progress on learning more than a few words of our language – to the point that Gunnvor would soon have become suspicious of what she was claiming to have learned on her own. Nicholas said she wasn't stupid – just lazy and easily bored."

"Reminds me of Gundrea," I chuckle, "before Father laid down the law."

"So, with my approval, Nicholas told her she was wasting his time, and he was needed back at the monastery. Of course, he didn't go there – just came to stay with Estrilda and me. It took Gunhild five days before she finally managed to put together the words 'Ask Brother Nicholas come back,' and her minder sent us word. Apparently, she got increasingly agitated as the days passed and there was no one she could talk to. We let her fret for one more day before Nicholas returned. She's been a much more diligent student since. Hardly perfect – she still throws a bit of a tantrum now and then when she gets tired of it all. But she can finally carry on a rudimentary conversation as long as the topic isn't too complex and no one speaks too quickly.

"The handy-dandy for me, though, is that her minder has a good ear for language and is rapidly gaining competence in the Eastern tongue. I've got to remember to thank Warin for that next time I see him."

"So how would you cut her loose?" asks Rupert.

"Thank her for all she's done, give her a purse with enough plain coins to live on for a few days if she doesn't run and a couple of silver ones – enough to look like we're still on her side, but not enough she could survive very long either here or in her homeland – drop her off in town, and see what happens. Her minder then becomes her shadow. If she does run, we need to know if she goes straight to Gunnvor or if she tries to disappear on her own and escape him and us too."

"And if she does try to escape?" asks Rupert.

"Her minder will grab her and bring her back, and she'll disappear on our terms. She knows too much to be let off leash in the wild."

Through this whole exchange, my mind's been wrestling with something neither Laurence not Rupert seems to be considering – or, at the very least, not verbalizing. "That's all well and good, but what if she's the one who's actually masterminding the game? Playing us against Gunnvor for her own amusement. After all, she's bound to resent how she's been used by other people in the past. Is she savvy enough to do that?" Rupert catches my eye and nods almost imperceptibly. "If so, she won't run – but that won't prove any loyalty to us."

Laurence finishes his wine and reaches for the pitcher to refill his glass. "Quite astute, Alfred. Remind me again why your grandfather didn't give *you* this job?" He tops up my glass and then Rupert's. "Oh, now I remember. You were too famous."

"And I seem to recall *you* jumped at the chance to take it." We all laugh at the memories.

"In truth, Alfred, that's part of the risk. But my instinct tells me that's not the case. I can't explain it rationally. It's just that, when she's being questioned – or even when she appears to be talking openly about Gunnvor – it's impossible to miss the fear in her eyes and her manner.

"Two trips ago, she came back with the news that Gunnvor was bedding the wife of the old lord whose lands he wanted. But it was the next trip that was so telling. Gunnvor's wife had disappeared and so had the feeble-minded son of the old lord. When Gunhild asked about them, he told her to shut her mouth or she'd be next. 'And if you don't want to see the old lord die and me marry his widow,' he added, 'then get out of my sight.' That's Gunhild's version of it, in any event, and she was clearly terrified as she told the story."

He pauses before adding, "Of course, another part of the risk is trusting one's instincts too much. I hope I'm mindful of that . . . and both her minder and Brother Nicholas think the fear is real. But to answer your original question, Alfred, I'm relying on a feeling in my gut."

Another pause before Rupert asks, "And what else does your gut tell you?"

"Gunhild says that, even though the deed is done and her brother now holds both his lands and those he married to get, he still wants the formula for black powder. And why else would he need it except to threaten others? So his ambition isn't yet satisfied. And my gut says he intends to challenge their king. Threaten enough of his fellow lords to get them to capitulate or join with him and then go after the ultimate prize."

The three of us sit in silence, staring into the fire, contemplating the decision facing us. My thoughts go back to the first time I learned about Abbot Francis's chronicle of my grandfather's reign and the first lesson I learned from it. When his fellow sovereign was threatened from within his own kingdom, Grandfather interfered to protect another man's throne – even though they weren't yet strong allies. He saw it as a chance to build an alliance and acted on the opportunity. Is this our opportunity to finally open the door with our neighbors to the east? Or is it a trap we're being invited to walk into with our eyes wide open and Gunnvor is the bait? Impossible to know with any certainty at this juncture.

Of one thing I *am* certain. If Gunnvor does oust his king and take the throne, he'll want more to feed his ambition. Flush with success, he wouldn't be able to resist the idea of expanding his holdings further. And the idea of payback for denying Gunhild's son – and thus his family – our throne would make us his prime target.

Another thing I'm certain of is that it's up to me to break the silence in the room. "The idea of Gunnvor, drunk with power, on our eastern border doesn't bear contemplation. We don't even know who the present king is, but at least he's not hostile."

"I'm sorry, Alfred," says Laurence. "It's my fault we're in this conundrum."

"Quite the contrary. It's thanks to you we even know we *have* a conundrum."

"He's right," says Rupert.

"Very well," I resume, "we arm Gunnvor as the necessary risk to continue learning what he's up to and to forestall his making an alliance we know nothing about." Laurence opens his mouth to speak, but I hold up my hand to stop him. "I may not be comfortable with the price, Laurence, but I've had enough time since we began this little adventure to live with the idea and weigh things in the balance. If your instincts are right about the overall situation – and I'd trust yours over anyone else's – then we have to see this through if we're to avoid a complete catastrophe. Or, perhaps almost as bad, have to turn Jasper's garrison into a border fortress and maintain a large standing army there.

"But we have to take responsibility for our actions. That means the nature of your mission changes, Laurence. In addition to keeping track of what Gunnvor's up to, we now have to find a connection to the Eastern king – we have to let him know we want to cooperate in putting a stop to Gunnvor's ambition. Unless their king's a complete daff, he likely has a spy in Gunnvor's household already, so Gunhild needs to work out who that is so you can send messages." I pause for a sip of wine before continuing. "I presume part of your plan is grooming Gunhild's minder to be another agent there."

"Damn shame you were so famous back then," Laurence chuckles. "You'd have been good at this."

Rupert smiles broadly. "Exactly what I told his grandfather."

"You're right, though, Alfred," says Laurence. "Which means the other information I need from Gunhild is which of the nobles are *not* cozying up to Gunnvor so we have another path to try to thwart his plans."

"So we're agreed on what we're going to do?" I look from one to the other of my companions.

"Aye," says Rupert.

Laurence takes a deep breath, then exhales audibly. "I just hope I'm up to it."

"You are, Laurence. You and the master of spymasters." I raise my glass to Rupert. Over the past couple of summers, my uncle seemed to age visibly. But I can already see his energy blossoming anew with his involvement in this extraordinarily complex game of spycraft.

"So how do you want to go about it?" asks Laurence.

"Isn't that your purview?" I grin. "Seems to me you've admonished me more than once that I shouldn't meddle in how you learn what you learn."

Laurence laughs out loud. "Nice to know you were paying attention."

"I suppose," says Rupert, grinning, "we can talk about it in front of him just this once. Probably less risky than telling the king to leave the room."

With the intensity of our conversation, we'd been ignoring the fire. A sudden chill makes me realize it's in danger of going out, so I cross to the hearth and add another log then turn my back to the flames to soak up their warmth. Rupert and Lawrence, seemingly oblivious to the temperature in the room, are already plotting Gunhild's future.

"I'd really like to test her a bit this time," says Laurence, "but I want to be sure she's back with Gunnvor in time to eavesdrop during the revels leading to Twelfth Night. There's sure to be enough ale flowing then to loosen tongues – likely enough that no one will remember in the morning anything said the night before."

"You can do that and still test her . . . and at the same time, play off her fear and bind her closer to you. Don't cut her loose. Just arrange for her to get separated from her minder on an outing in the town. If it looks like she might run, the minder can conveniently find her again. But if your gut is right, she'll panic at being alone with no idea how to get what Gunnvor wants so she'll start looking for you or the minder or start trying to find her way back to the place you've been keeping her. Rescue her a second time, when she's afraid, and you're one step closer to being certain she's *your* creature."

• • • • •

Alicia doesn't get all her wishes for Christmas. But that's soon forgotten in the excitement of a new frock and her own pony. The unenviable task of teaching her to ride will fall to Mervyn Lightfoot, Elvin's eldest son – the latest in that family's long line of Mervyns and Elvins – who's just been named as head groom. When I asked Elvin about the epithet, he said, "'Twere his mum what first be calling him that. When he were a boy, ye could barely make out his footsteps when he come into a room. Many be the time his mum be working at the cook fire, and when she turn around, there he be, just watching her. Give her a right fright that first time, he did. She well-nigh drop a pot of hot soup. So he be Mervyn Lightfoot ever since."

The day after Christmas, I get the best present of my life – perhaps the best I'll ever receive. Returning from the meadow through the woods, I catch a glimpse of Edward, riding alone, taking the left fork onto the trail beside the stream that leads to the hidden paddock. It's too early for new life there yet. But not too early to be sure the place is ready to shelter that life when it comes into the world. I'm tempted to follow and catch up to him but restrain my impulse. Leave him to it, Alfred. It's what you hoped for when you shared its secret with him. I'm overwhelmed with pride in my second son. Geoffrey may be my heir – the son of my mind – but Edward is the son of my heart.

Most of the lords choose to spend Twelfth Night on their estates this year, so it's mid-January before everyone is back at court. Everyone except Lord Bauldry, that is. He hasn't returned since the death of his wife. "And I suspect he never will," Guyat told me when I asked after his father. "I'd thought his grief would be spent by now, but, if anything, he's sinking further into the depths. Spends his days in his study writing. Says it's a chronicle of his life. But I took a look through some of the pages when we were home. Mostly, it's love letters to my mother. My sisters bring their children to visit, hoping to snap him back to reality, but it doesn't seem to make much difference. He fawns over them for a bit, then sends them to the kitchen for a sweet cake and goes back to his writing. I fear he's completely lost his will to live."

What a sad turn for a man who once was able to rise above my Aunt Isabella's scheme to ruin his marriage. Or perhaps that was what bound him so closely to his wife and why he's so bereft without her.

The surprise when Juliana and Rainard return is that Goron and Kensa are with them. "We visit Ernle Manor for what you call Twelve Night," Kensa tells us when we gather in Gwen's sitting room shortly after their arrival. She speaks our language more easily now but not as comfortably as Goron or Egon. "And Juliana invite us visit here. Not snow, so we say yes."

The following day, I retire to the library when I finish Coliar's stack of documents, still searching for some clues to the Roman wall and the hill fort on our southeastern border. While I'm paging through an old Latin text, Goron and Kensa walk through the door, and Kensa stops in her tracks, her eyes as big as saucers. "May we join you, Alfred?" Goron asks.

"Of course."

He takes a seat opposite me. Since Kensa's visits have always been to the country manor, it's her first time seeing this room. Clearly awed, she lapses into her own tongue. "Goron told me about this place, but I never imagined it was so grand – that you have so many books." She makes her way slowly to sit beside her husband but can't take her eyes off the shelves filled with books and scrolls. "This," she waves a hand all around the room, "this is why I want our sons to learn your language. I want them to be able read all these books. Goron teaches them when he can, but he does not always have so much time."

"Even then, they couldn't read *all* of these," I reply. "Many are in Latin."

"Then I want our sons to learn Latin. I want them be able to read everything about the world. That is how they will be better lords. Is it true, Alfred, if they know Latin, they can talk to other kings?"

"And to other educated men as well."

She pauses, seemingly unsure about what to say next. Goron comes to her rescue. "My Kensa has a request, Alfred."

"Is it possible," she asks, "for Brother Eustace to teach our sons?"

"That's not for me to say. But there's no reason you shouldn't talk to Abbot Warin about it."

"Who is this Abbot Warin?"

"He's Eustace's superior."

"Like his lord?"

"Something like that."

She turns to Goron and touches his arm. "If Alfred will introduce us, will you speak with this Abbot Warin?"

"I'll discuss it with Alfred. Now, shall we continue out to the gardens for some fresh air?"

After supper, Goron, Rainard, and I drain the very last drop of Lucia's special brandy from my hidden decanter. It's only just enough to make three small draughts, but Goron's visit seems a fitting occasion. He lingers when Rainard eventually excuses himself for the night.

"I hope, Alfred, that my Kensa did not offend with her enthusiasm for your library and her ambitions for our sons."

"Quite the contrary, my friend. Her pleasure reminded me a bit of the first time you saw our collection."

"I remember that day well – and what we spoke of in that moment."

"And what of your wife's ambitions for your sons? Do you share them?"

"They must be prepared for what the future will hold for them, so the more they know about the broader world, the better they will be able to chart a course for our land. On that point, Kensa and I agree." He pauses to drain the last possible drop of brandy from his glass. "May I be completely truthful with you, Alfred?"

"Of course."

"I do not want to enter into an arrangement where my sons are required to practice your religion. Please forgive my bluntness, but I know no other way to say it. We all know Brother Eustace and are very fond of him. But if he must answer to this Abbot Warin, then will he be required to teach my sons his religion if he teaches them other things?"

"Let me tell you a bit about Warin." I refill our glasses and settle in to relate the history Warin and I have together, from the day he found me, exhausted and starving, inside the gates of the western monastery through all we've shared since.

"That is quite a story," says Goron when I've finished. "Perhaps he is not so rigid a man as this cardinal you told my father about last summer."

I can't suppress a chuckle. "I think you'll find Warin to be quite the opposite of that popinjay."

"Popinjay?"

"A bird with fancy feathers who has a very high opinion of himself."

"This is a word I want to remember." Goron grins. "Popinjay. I quite like it!"

"By all means, let Warin know your concerns. And don't forget that, in all the time Brother Eustace has spent in your lands, he's never once tried to impose his beliefs on anyone."

When we visit, Warin offers precisely the sort of solution I expected. "Our calling in life is to serve others, Lord Goron, and sometimes this takes the form of teaching. So it would be perfectly acceptable for Brother Eustace to teach your children. As for the matter of religion, our calling also exhorts us to carry the message of God's word." Though Goron had relaxed in Warin's calm and genial presence, he bristles at this remark.

"But I have always been of the opinion," Warin continues, "that the message is better conveyed by deeds than by words. Words provide the explanation of what we believe, but it's our actions that reveal how we embrace those beliefs. You've already seen how Brother Eustace lives his life. What I ask is that you permit him to answer questions if people are curious about our faith. And in return, I give you my assurances that he will not compel anyone to adopt our beliefs."

Goron visibly relaxes once again. "*That* is something I can agree to."

And *that*, Cardinal Patrasso – not your prodigious proselytizing and coerced conversions – is how one introduces Christianity to a people who have no experience of it.

At the first Council meeting of the year we learn just how inspired was Richard's suggestion to name Ademar as liaison to the Assembly. "They're a stubborn lot," he reminds us, to chuckles all around the table, "but not completely intractable. Appeals for them to consider the common good land entirely on deaf ears, as Thorssen and Devereux can tell you. Where I seem to have found a chink in their armor, however, is by casting everything in terms of what's in it for them.

"It's taken a couple of meetings to get there, but at least they're now talking about the possibility of a second woolen mill. Once I showed them how the path they were on would eventually put them in direct competition with the great weaving houses but with an inferior product, they finally grasped that responding to the demand with more supply would serve them better in the long run than treating their product as a scarce commodity and constantly raising the price. Of course, they're now debating among themselves how much that will impact the wool trade and whether the herdsmen can be prevailed on to increase the size of their flocks, but at least they're actually trying to work things out rather than just hurling accusations at each other – which, as you might imagine, is where they started."

"Well done, Lord Ademar," says Richard, to hear-hear's all around the table. "Keep us apprised of their progress. Your next big hurdle, however, is the withdrawal of the subsidy for trade through the Southern Nordics port. Any idea if they're prepared for that or if we should gird our loins for more howls of protest?"

"We've discussed last summer's trading season. I wouldn't say they've absolutely found the goods they can't live without, though it seems there's quite an appetite here for that pickled fish the Nordics are all too happy to sell us. Can't stand the stuff myself," he wrinkles his nose as if he'd just smelled something putrid, "but apparently enough people like it that the merchants are eager to get more. So to answer your question, Devereux, they'll likely howl a bit just to show they haven't forgotten how, but I think I can keep that to a whine of protest rather than a full-on baying at the moon."

There's little other business requiring our attention. Sir Jasper reports progress on the new garrison. Building's on hiatus for the winter since it's too cold for the masons to work the mortar. But enough of the barracks and stable were completed over the summer for one troop to already be housed there and the expectation is that the full complement of three troops will be in residence before by the end of July. Hmmm . . . I wonder who he'll choose as commandant in the east? A quick vote to approve commissioning of the second new ship, and we're adjourned.

•　　•　　•　　•　　•

It's the end of January before Laurence has any further news. Truth be told, I've been skeptical we'd get much more from Gunhild once we gave up the formula for black powder. "Oh ye of little faith!" Laurence gloats. We're once again in the drawing room at the country manor with Rupert, having decided this is the safest place – for now, at least – to have these discussions.

"She came back with a treasure trove this time. It seems Gunnvor was so completely enthralled with his new capability that he paid her absolutely no attention. His big Twelfth Night celebration was to blow up an empty granary on the grounds of the manor of his newly acquired lands. No one who was there could have doubted his message that they'd best join with him if they didn't want to be blown out of house and home. What followed was three days and nights of drunken revelry with Gunnvor boasting to his cronies about everything he planned to do next and promising them vast quantities of silver and land and women in abundance if they'd do their part."

"I trust Gunhild found a way to eavesdrop?" Rupert asks.

"Apparently, Gunnvor didn't give a rat's arse for who might have heard anything that was said. Servants, the whores who came and went day and night, anyone who happened into the hall."

"So what else is in this treasure trove of yours?" I ask.

"Gunnvor's next target, for a start. He's after the lands to the east of the ones he's just acquired. That will give him control of everything north of the east-west main road from our border to the sea – and that includes their main port. His cronies control everything along the border with us and the Lakes, all the way up to Northern Kingdom, so if he can keep them loyal or afraid, they have the king and the last two lords boxed in on the south and west with the sea on the east."

"Any idea if their king has an alliance with the Northern Kingdom?"

"We asked Gunhild and she didn't seem to know."

"And the lord of this domain Gunnvor wants next?" asks Rupert. "Friend or foe to Gunnvor?"

"Gunhild's not sure, but she thinks what's being planned is raids into those lands, so she thinks maybe that lord won't just capitulate."

I shake my head slowly then prop my chin on my hands. "What have we unleashed?"

"From what we've heard, Alfred," says Rupert, "the question is really 'What have we accelerated?' Don't forget we were already convinced Gunnvor would likely be at this point by Easter no matter what we did or didn't do."

"I know, but I can't help but remember the innocent people who're in the path of Gunnvor's ambition."

"Then remember also that their fate is out of our hands. Short of a full-scale invasion, there's nothing we can do to protect them. And an invasion would put even more innocent people in danger . . . even if we had cause to invade . . . which we don't."

"I know that too, Uncle, but that doesn't mean I have to like it." I sit up straighter and shake off the momentary pangs of conscience. "So what else is in the trove, Laurence?"

"It seems there are two new faces in Gunnvor's household. The first is a priest. Gunhild says that, unlike her father, her brother has no use for priests and threw the last one out when Lord Erik died. But apparently, his new wife doesn't share that opinion and insisted on a confessor and someone to say mass and administer the sacraments. So this new priest is allowed to come for one day every week or two. Where he goes the rest of the time, Gunhild doesn't know.

"The other new face is a new master armorer. According to Gunhild, this isn't a surprise, as the previous one was getting old and had lost the use of one hand recently in an accident. Either one could be a spy, but my money's on the priest, since he can come and go easily and can move about within the household."

"Hmmm . . ." Rupert looks thoughtful. "Or maybe it's the new wife that's the spy and the priest is just the messenger."

"That thought occurred to me as well," says Laurence. "I've no idea what to make of the new wife, since we don't know where she came from or who might have a hold over her if it's not Gunnvor. Even if the priest is just the messenger, though, we might be able to use him as our own channel. But I don't want to use Gunhild for that contact. I still don't fully trust that she's working only for us."

"Is the minder ready?" asks Rupert.

"Near enough that I'm willing to risk it if I'm certain they can get in and out while Gunhild's away. Don't want her getting wind of what we're doing."

"Something you said earlier, Laurence." I've been turning it over in my mind while they talked. "About their king being boxed in from the south. Does that mean Gunnvor already controls the lands south of the main east-west road?"

"I wondered about that too and had Gunhild questioned about it. She says it's all wild . . . wooded hills that slope off quickly to marshlands down to the sea. According to her, the only things that live there are varmints, the hawks and eagles that prey on them, and waterfowl in the marsh . . . and nobody ever goes there."

"So what's next?" asks Rupert.

"We'll send her back with some details about the new garrison. The sort of things she would be able to pick up if she stopped to chat with the builders on her way back home. And her mission will be to learn more about Gunnvor's wife and about where this new priest goes and comes from."

Those may be Laurence's next steps, but I have something decidedly different in mind.

•   •   •   •   •

Back at the castle, I waste no time. "Could you have picked a colder day, Alfred?" Samuel shivers inside his cloak as we step into the rundown hut in the woods.

"Mother Nature didn't seem to be offering choices. Her exact words, if I recall, were 'Here's today – take it or leave it.'"

"So what's so important that you couldn't leave it for a warmer day?"

"Something I'm not sure can wait until April."

Samuel shivers again and rubs his upper arms for warmth. "In that case, why are you waiting now?"

"Remember when we went to the eastern border and you mentioned the wild areas looked like a good place to infiltrate a scout?"

"Yes."

"How much danger would there be for the scout?"

"Scouting's never without some danger. You know that as well as I do, Alfred. What's on your mind?"

"Laurence has recently come across some information that the entirety of the Eastern Kingdom south of the east-west road that leads from our border to their port may be uninhabited. I want to know if that's true."

"You know anyone we send in there will be one more person who's in on the secrets. Are you sure now's the time to do it?"

"I have a feeling it might be. But the scout has to be someone I absolutely trust."

"You're not asking *me* to go, are you, Alfred? My scouting days are long past. In fact, I'm not sure I was *ever* much of a scout."

"No. Last thing I need is to have to ransom you when you get captured." Samuel laughs out loud. "No, Sir Cedric's who I have in mind."

"Is he any good at scouting?"

"I have no idea. What I do know is that he's very, *very* good at keeping my secrets."

"Then talk to him about it." He pauses, his brow furrowed in thought. "But I don't think you dragged me out here in the cold just to hear me say that."

"What I need is something besides instinct to base a decision on – and I don't want to reveal what the three of us saw there to anyone else."

"Then consider this. If the area really is completely wild, then sending someone in will leave telltale signs. Footprints, broken branches – even markings on trees if the scout is worried about needing signs to find his way out. This time of year, there could be snow. No way for a man's movements in a snowy landscape to mimic an animal's. And whether there's snow or not, a man's going to need a fire from time to time just to stay warm. Not to mention there'll be no leaf canopy in the woodlands – any movement there would be much easier to spot. Once it's warmer and the trees have leafed out, the mission's far less risky." He pauses to pull his cloak tighter around him. "Is there really any urgency? Seems unlikely to me that any threat would come at us from there – or from anywhere, for that matter – in the dead of winter."

"Only that it's tied in with some other information Laurence is trying to verify."

"He has eyes inside the Eastern Kingdom now?" Samuel puts his gloved hand up straightaway. "Never mind – I know you're not ready to answer that yet or you'd have been more forthcoming from the outset.

"Consider this too, Alfred. What I said about telltale signs will hold true whenever we send a scout in. We won't have many chances to use that route before someone – either here or there – gets wise to what we're doing. So my advice is to save them for when it matters most."

So when *does* it matter most? If we discover Gunhild's telling the truth about this, it doesn't prove the truth of everything she says – only that part of what she says is true . . . and we're still on our own to untangle which parts. Remember Harold, Alfred, I remind myself. Don't let the fact that you *can* act overshadow your judgment of *when* to act.

"Does that help?" Samuel's words – and the fact that he's pacing around the hut and stomping his feet for warmth – draw me back to the present.

"I think so."

"Then can we get back to where I can find a warm fire?"

"Come on. Let's go." I lead the way out of the hut. "And Samuel . . . thank you."

Geoffrey's birthday has been looming in my consciousness since we celebrated the New Year. He'll turn seventeen, which means *I* must turn my thoughts to serious consideration of his bride. It seems I'm not the only one aware of the upcoming event – a letter from the King of Peaks tops the stack of papers on my writing table this morning.

My dear King Alfred,

It is my practice, during the quiet of winter after the revelry of Twelfth Night, to contemplate where I should direct my attentions in the year at hand. And as I have engaged in this year's contemplation, one thing continues to present itself as having great importance and some small sense of urgency.

I remain as keen as ever to cement the alliance between our realms through an advantageous marriage between our families. Though we mentioned the topic during my brief sojourn with you last year, I have decided that it might now be timely to pursue it with a sense of purpose.

To this end, I venture to offer the hand of my daughter, Eirwen, as a suitable match for your heir, Lord Geoffrey. My observations last year were that they seemed comfortable in each other's company. And your own daughter declared, when she visited here prior to her betrothal, that Eirwen would be perfect for your son. My daughter will celebrate her seventeenth birthday this year – on Midsummer's Day – which might be an auspicious time for the announcement of a betrothal, leading to a marriage when they both come of age.

With this in mind, may I venture a further suggestion that she might spend some time at your court in the coming weeks so that we can better assess their compatibility. While I know that fondness between the two parties is not necessarily required in a dynastic marriage, it is my opinion that this contributes greatly to the security and success of the alliance. Judging from the manner in which you handled your elder daughter's betrothal, I am inclined to assume that you share my view.

As for Eirwen herself, she has expressed that she found your son's company quite pleasant and would not be reluctant to explore whether this might be a suitable match.

It is my hope that you are of like mind, both with regard to a continuing interest in a marriage alliance and to the prospect of my daughter visiting your court. I shall look forward to your reply.

Yes, I'm of like mind . . . provided Geoffrey is . . . provided Gwen agrees . . . provided the senior lords concur . . . provided the young lady's head isn't turned by one of Geoffrey's mates . . . provided . . . Great God in Heaven! Whatever made me think settling on a match for Juliana was difficult?

I fold the missive and slip it into my pocket then make my way back to my dressing room in search of Osbert . . . who's nowhere to be found. As I return to the bedchamber, Letty pokes her head in from Gwen's side. "Ye be looking fer Osbert, m'lord?"

"Aye, Letty. Think you might be able to find him and send him to me?" She drops a little curtsey along with an "Aye, m'lord" and disappears.

Back to the stack on my writing table, the entirety of which turns out to be affirmations of sentences for miscreants. As I finish signing the last one, Osbert appears from the door to the bedchamber. "Ye be needing something, m'lord?"

"Indeed I do, Osbert. Drinks in the tavern this afternoon with Samuel, Richard, and Phillip. Not that I think they're likely to raise any objections, but for old times' sake, tell them I'm buying. And our wives to join us for supper – just like we've done so many times."

"Methinks it be right cold when the sun be going down. Mayhap the ladies not be so keen on going outside."

"I suspect if you arrange a carriage for them with lots of lap rugs, they'll be delighted to come."

• • • • • • • •

Once we've settled in with the first round at our favorite table in the back of the tavern, I hand the Peaks king's letter to Richard to read and pass around. "If I recall," says Samuel when he finishes and returns the paper to me, "the last time that young lady was here, she had no shortage of eager suitors."

"Which is precisely my problem," I say.

"Sounds as if it's going to be much like when Gwendolyn first came here," says Richard.

"As I remember it, you lot were perfect gentlemen, even if you did have some fun at my expense on that first day when we rode out to meet her."

"As *I* remember it," says Phillip, "every one of us was tripping over his tongue at any glimpse of the angel with golden hair."

"*You*," Richard nods toward me, "were just too busy trying to impress the angel to notice."

"Or," Samuel chimes in, "to notice how often Phillip and Laurence contrived to find a way to kiss her hand."

"You weren't the only one completely besotted," says Richard, "but we all knew she was here for you. So make it known that Eirwen's visit is about a match for Geoffrey, and the boys will behave accordingly."

"Well," says Phillip, "at least Ancel will. He knows if he misbehaves at court, Addiena will send him home to be dealt with by his grandmother." He pauses to down what's left in his mug.

"Although I rather suspect his grandmother does more to encourage him than to chastise him." Which elicits a laugh from all of us.

"How is the indomitable Lady Cecily these days?" I ask.

"Feeling her age in many respects. It's getting harder for her to get around, and her joints pain her when the weather's damp for long stretches. But she's as feisty as ever." He raises his mug to signal the innkeeper for another round.

"Well, if I can rely on you three to keep an eye on your sons, I guess my next question is for the first lord. I honestly have no idea what the proper protocol is for the betrothal of an heir to the throne. When Harold married, he was already king, and producing an heir took precedence over any question of alliances. And even though we all hoped John would never be king, he gave Father little choice when it came to choosing a match. So is seeking the lords' agreement something formal or is it more about private conversations?"

"In truth, Alfred," says Richard, "it's the king's choice. It was set up that way back at the very beginning of the kingdom, with the idea that every lord – including the king – was entitled to choose his own heir's bride. I suppose the reason it's never been changed is because there's never been a particularly disastrous outcome. It relies on the lords' responsibility to curb egregious behavior by a king. We always like to be consulted, of course, and Father told me your grandfather had private discussions with the lords about his choice of Berengaria for Harold. But that's entirely up to you."

"In which case, I'll leave it up to each of you to let me know if you have any concerns. It's clear I won't be able to consult Bauldry, but I do plan to have a chat with Papa Ernle." Lately, I've adopted Juliana's style of referring to Samuel and Rainard's father. It feels so natural and comfortable for the man who's been like a second father to me ever since he looked after me in that first week following my return from captivity.

"I think it's a first-rate idea, Alfred," says Richard. "Your marriage binds the Lakes to us. Richenda's marriage to Denis secures the alliance with the Kingdom Across the Southern Sea. Margery and

Thorbrand link us to the Far Nordics. If Geoffrey and Eirwen are a good match, that would cement our ties with the Peaks."

"So don't I count for at least as much as Margery?" Phillip gives his best impression of whining disappointment. His wife, Addiena, is, after all, the Peaks king's cousin.

"Oh, come on," Samuel teases him. "You're not nearly as pretty as Margery."

Phillip grins and raises his mug. "To pretty women!" We laugh and drink the toast.

"Now I just have to hope Geoffrey has no objections," I say.

"Or that Gwendolyn hasn't been planning something entirely different," chuckles Richard.

Thankfully, Gwen's reaction when I show her the letter during our bedtime conversation removes any doubt on that score. "I'm sure you expected this, didn't you? I certainly did. And it does seem like the right next step to bind all our alliances closer to our own interests. After all, it's too early for such a thing with the Territories. Until they're more unified, a marriage there might do more harm than good."

One of these days, I suppose I'm going to have to explicitly tell her about Egon's grand plan. She's pretty much figured it all out anyway. Do I need to seek Egon's permission, as I did when we brought Samuel into the picture? Or does Egon already assume I've confided in my wife? Something to ponder at another time.

"In any event," Gwen continues, bringing my thoughts back to the present, "I'm grateful the Peaks king is the one who suggested the visit. I'd have insisted on that."

"You want to give them the same choice our fathers gave us?" When our fathers signed the marriage contract, they each stipulated that if either of us found a serious objection to the union, the contract would be terminated. In Godwin's case, he knew that his educated, intelligent daughter who was determined to do something important in her life needed a husband who would appreciate and honor those qualities. In my father's case, I think he just wanted me to be happy, as he and Mother had been. Neither of us was ever expected to become king – me least of all – so dynastic concerns were not a particular priority.

"I think we should be sure they're compatible before we even contemplate a betrothal," she replies. "But beyond that, I need some time to assess whether she'd be a good queen for this realm. I found her nice enough in the brief time I spent with her last year, but that's a far cry from being confident she's a good choice for a future queen. I'll want Tamasine and Avelina, in particular, to weigh in as well."

"Maybe you should see what Lady Cecily thinks," I chuckle.

She giggles. "You may think that's a jest, Alfred, but it might be a rather good idea. The dowager certainly wouldn't mince words about her opinion."

•   •   •   •   •

My surprise comes when I show the letter to Geoffrey. I'd dressed quickly and made my way straight to the room my sons share in hopes of waylaying him before he got his day underway. "We were just headed out to the stable," says Edward. "Sir Tobin gave us a free day, so we were going to spend some extra time with the horses."

"Did you want us to go riding with you, Papa?" asks Geoffrey.

"Not this morning. But there is something I'd like to talk over with you, Son. Edward, is there something else you can do for a bit?"

Edward doesn't hesitate. "Of course, Papa. I'll be in the library, Geoffrey, when you're ready."

As Edward closes the door behind him, I perch on the side of his bed and hand the letter to Geoffrey, who takes a seat on his own bed to read. When he finishes, he slowly folds the missive, returns it to me, and rises to go stand in front of the fireplace. He's almost as tall as I am now – something that still takes me aback when we come upon each other unexpectedly. In my mind, I suppose, he's still a lad; but the young man now standing before the hearth with his back to me has, in the past year, put that phase well and truly behind him. He has the dark hair and blue eyes that dominate in my family, and his trim build reminds me increasingly of my father. But the twinkle in his eye when he smiles and his almost constant good humor come straight from his mother.

When, at long last, he turns his back to the fire to face me, neither the twinkle nor the good humor are anywhere to be found in his aspect. "I suppose I'd hoped to delay for a while longer." His tone carries a tinge of sadness.

"Delay what, Son?"

"Delay taking up the burden all this will surely bring. I know my marriage will be scrutinized by everyone from the turnspit to the Holy Father in Rome, and every last one of them will have an opinion to proclaim. I just don't know if I'm ready for that."

"And why do you think that burden will fall on you? You're right – there'll be scrutiny – and lots of it. But it'll all be directed at me. Most people will assume you had little or no choice in the matter, so it's *my* motives they'll be searching out – *my* reasons that will be questioned in foreign courts and local taverns – *my* decision that will garner approval or displeasure. It really won't reflect on you at all, so there's no reason for you to feel burdened."

He wanders back and sits heavily on his bed opposite me. "Be that as it may . . ." he begins, then hastens to add, "and I'm sure you're right, Papa. But be that as it may, I doubt I can completely escape being aware of the talk."

"Maybe not. But that's all the more reason we should choose well . . . so that any displeasure is drowned out in a roar of approbation."

Finally, a hint of a smile. "You said 'we.' Do I get a say in this?"

I extend the folded letter back to him. "Maybe you overlooked the fourth paragraph."

He waves the paper away. "Oh, I read it. The bit about assessing our compatibility. What makes you think he really means that and isn't just writing words he thinks you want to hear?"

"That's not out of the question, but I have no reason to doubt his sincerity. The only thing you need to be concerned about, though, is that your mother and I care about such things. Yes, sometimes an heir to a throne is forced to accept a bride for political reasons, even if the match is destined to be unsatisfactory to the individuals involved. But that's not the case here. We're just solidifying an existing alliance – not trying to end a war or forestall a future conflict. So yes, if you find something seriously objectionable about the girl, we'll listen to you. If I recall, though, you were rather taken with Eirwen last year."

"So I presume you also recall that William and Barat and Ancel were as well."

"I don't think that escaped *anyone's* notice." He finally manages a laugh. "But you'll have an advantage – everyone will know she's been invited here as a prospective bride for you. That should dampen your mates' ardor a bit. Doesn't mean they won't look for every opportunity to be in her company – or that they won't be clamoring for a chance with her if she's not right for you.

"Remember too, Geoffrey, that your mother and I also have to consider her as a future queen. If either of us – particularly your mother – discovers she's not well suited for that role, then it may turn out not to be a good match."

"So I shouldn't get my heart set on it?"

"Want my advice?"

"Yes."

"Talk to your mother before Eirwen arrives. Find out what your mother thinks will make a good queen. And then talk to her again from time to time throughout the visit. You and she will see different things – and both of you will benefit from the other's insights."

"What about you?"

"You know you can talk to me anytime, Son. About this or anything else that's on your mind."

"I know, Papa. It's just that this is the first big decision of my life, so I may need a lot of your advice."

"So . . . does this mean I should extend the invitation?"

He hesitates for a long moment, the import of his answer visibly on his mind. "I think I'm ready." Another pause, then, "And thank you, Papa."

I stand and take the three steps across to his bed, saying "It's what fathers do" as I tousle his hair. I don't get many opportunities anymore to do this. Will this be the last?

However momentous the milestones in my son's life may be, there's another birthday looming heavily on my mind. King Denis will come of age in June, assuming the throne in his own right. As yet, we've detected no signs of a threat emerging anywhere on his long border with the Teuton Kingdom. But somehow that does little to allay the anxiety that hovers at the back of my mind and occasionally pricks my consciousness. Neither does the letter I receive this morning from Denis.

My dear Alfred,

I am dreadfully remiss in not having written sooner to send you our warmest wishes for this new year. Richenda joins me in expressing our hope that the coming days bring only joy and contentment for you and all of your family.

For the two of us, the year holds many changes, and while I naturally have some small trepidations when I contemplate the enormity of what's soon to fall on my shoulders, I still find myself eager to take up my destiny and try to be the king that my people deserve. I suspect no thinking man is ever fully prepared for the mantle of rule, but I've received the very best possible tutelage, and for that I feel deeply grateful to you. Had you not possessed the insight to recognize the importance of having Petronilla as my regent – and the determination to make that happen – I fear the time of my minority would have been continuing chaos rather than what has been an extraordinary period of reconciliation and preparation for me to step fully onto the stage.

Petronilla is gradually ceding bits of authority to me, a smoother transition than a sharp change on my birthday. We are of like mind – Petronilla, Greville, and I – that it's best to avoid taking notice of the event lest it become a touchstone for any who might not have our best interests at heart. And to that end, I will forego any celebration of my birthday beyond my immediate family.

This year is nevertheless momentous for us in other ways. My darling Richenda turns fifteen next month so we can at last take up our lives together as man and wife.

Gwen once pointed out to me that children understand the milestones of life in terms of birthdays. Of late, I'm beginning to believe that experience is not limited to children.

It's something we've both longed for. I think Lord Greville has as well, given the number of times he's mentioned how precarious my rule is until I have an heir. I've actually come to find that rather amusing, given how eager I am to get on with producing one.

We plan to host the King of Lakes for a state visit in midsummer. To that end, I'm dispatching Suidbert to that court near the end of March to convey my invitation. He suggested sailing from our port in Lamoreaux to theirs on the Western Sea as a means to evaluate what that journey might be like. My first reaction was that he was merely seeking to avoid the obligation of paying respects to you – and I still think that's at least part of his motive. But the more we discussed it, the more Greville and I have become convinced there might be some merit in his proposal. Knowing that our main port on the Southern Sea is a prime target for the Teutons, it seems wise to have a reliable back door, as it were, should surreptitious action ever be necessary. And having an experienced mariner who's sailed those waters before would ensure we wouldn't be stepping off into the unknown in such an event. I'm therefore assigning my most trusted captain to the voyage.

If the peace continues undisturbed through this state visit and the weeks following, then I plan to go on progress to celebrate the harvest season as a way to reassure my people of my concern for their interests. I'm aware of the risks but am convinced that remaining aloof any longer poses just as great a risk to peace within the kingdom. I've not yet completely won Greville over to this line of thinking, but I believe his reticence arises from wanting to see what the summer brings along the border before committing himself to a highly-visible journey. I value his caution just as much as I know we must look to the future.

Nothing has been discovered, so far, to hint at impending danger. Nevertheless, we remain on guard and diligent in our efforts.

The last authority that will come to me is control of the military. I'm keenly aware that military men dislike ambiguity and would be reluctant to take orders directly from me while a regency is still in place, so delaying this step in no way distresses me. The fighting forces that we've rebuilt over the past two years are impressive. Anyone skulking around to assess their readiness will be in no doubt of their skill or determination.

It's almost certainly a breach of royal dignity, Alfred, to tell you of the enormous feeling of delight I take in writing this missive without others reading over my shoulder. Given our history, however, I trust you'll permit me this small bit of self-indulgence. And I hope this will be only the first of a lifetime of exchanges between us.

The man who brings this letter is my personal courier, so you may rely on him to convey any reply directly into my hands.

Finally – and just this once – I shall speak for Petronilla (rather than the other way around) in sending her love and best wishes to you and to Gwendolyn.

Denis

I'm truly impressed with Denis's acquiescence in foregoing any fanfare associated with his accession to power in his own right. Not many young men would be able to resist the temptation to blow their own horns. Perhaps his time among the monks taught him virtues that other young men require more years to grasp – if they grasp them at all.

What draws my eye, though, is the short paragraph about the continuing absence of any sign of activity along the Teuton border. Brief as it is and buried as it is within an otherwise voluble letter, there can be no doubt it's his purpose in writing to me at this time.

I step into the outer chamber to find my secretary busy at his writing table. "Is the man who brought King Denis's letter still here, Coliar?"

"Yes, Sire. He went down to the servants' hall to find some food and said he'd come back later to see if there was a reply."

"There will be, but not before tomorrow. So see that he has lodgings for the night and anything else appropriate. I'll let you know when my letter is ready."

"Of course, Sire."

"Any idea where Lord de Courcy might be?"

"Not at the moment, but I believe he spends quite a bit of time with Sir Jasper of late. Shall I send for him?"

"No, I think I'll go look for him myself. The fresh air will clear my head. But would you make sure there's a fire in the old library?"

"Of course, Sire."

I wander back into my dressing room for a cloak, grab Denis's letter from my writing table, and set out in search of Samuel, finally finding him perched atop the fence of the riding arena watching the trainees at swordplay. I remember those exercises – trying to keep your attention focused on your opponent's moves while the loose soil and sand underfoot scream for that same attention lest you fall on your arse and leave yourself vulnerable to the kill. Thank God and all the saints those days are well and truly behind me.

Samuel's attention is focused on the fight his son is waging with another trainee. Without turning his head, he acknowledges my arrival. "Barat asked me for some pointers so I came out to watch this morning." Then, as if willing his son to hear his thoughts, he says quietly, "He's off balance, so attack. Left foot's out of position, so go for the right side – force him backward – when he steps back with the right, he won't find firm footing to recover." Barat prepares to attack but hesitates just long enough for his opponent to recognize what's coming. The effort to rebalance and fend off the attack is clumsy though, and the man goes down in the dirt.

Samuel then turns in my direction. "He had the right idea – just didn't move quickly enough. You know, for a kid who was so awkward when they first handed him a weapon, Barat's become a pretty decent swordsman." He swings his legs over the railing and hops down to join me outside the fence. "So what brings you here, Alfred? Somehow I don't think it was to improve your fighting skills."

"Not with a sword – you're right about that." I clap him on the shoulder. "But I do need your strategic mind. Let's go somewhere we can talk."

The fire in the old library really hasn't had time to break the chill, so we pull the chairs close to the hearth. I hand Samuel Denis's letter and warm my hands while he reads. Finished, he folds the paper and returns it to me. "Seems like things are quiet there now, and they're doing everything possible to keep it that way."

"And yet that's what bothers me. Laurence says his agents haven't discovered any sign of Teuton activity either. It's *too* quiet. The Teuton king knows precisely when Denis will rule in his own right – he's too crafty not to. And I don't believe for one moment that anything has altered his ambition to get his hands on Aleffe province – and more importantly, the port. His self-imposed restraint comes to an end in just a few short months," I continue, "so why hasn't he begun putting the pieces in place to pursue his goals?"

"Why are you so convinced he'll move the moment Denis comes of age?"

"Because the longer he waits, the more time Denis will have to bolster his defenses and build loyalty within his fighting forces. Strike immediately, while Denis is still young and inexperienced, and he can create doubt and discord within the kingdom, making a campaign to grab the port and maybe even overrun the entire country that much easier."

"That's one approach. The other is to lull your target into complacency. Play the longer game. Bide your time until they least expect you to act – and then act with such speed and ferocity that they can't assemble their defenses in time to be effective."

We sit in silence, watching the fire, for a long moment before Samuel adds, "From what you've told me about the Teuton king, I suspect he's spent the past two years with his commanders, preparing both options. And he's got his spies strategically placed, watching for just the right signal to tell him which one to execute." He pauses. "You're right to be concerned, Alfred."

"I just wish I knew what to be concerned about. And what to tell Denis. He's certainly hoping for some advice in my reply."

"Remember how you kept Charles off balance when he asked for our help with his Teuton problem?"

"Aye."

"That's exactly what Denis should do now. He should be seen spending time with his commanders. Give the spies something to scratch their heads about, wondering what's afoot – some uncertainty to report back to their master. Plan for both scenarios and for how to surprise the Teutons regardless of which path they choose. Give the Teutons cause to be off-balance. You know how to do this, Alfred. You did it brilliantly in the last campaign. I'm not sure why you're so uncertain now."

"Back then I was the puppet-master – even though Charles thought he was, I knew it was the other way round. Now's different. I know the Teuton king's up to something – I can feel it in my bones – but it's shrouded in a fog so dense I can't even begin to make it out. And that's what worries me."

"Then tell Denis that. Not to frighten him but to enlist his help in figuring it out. His commanders are accustomed to thinking in terms of how to defend that long border. And don't let him overlook the possibility of an attack on the port from the sea. I know the defenders have a huge advantage in that scenario, but the Teutons could have the advantage of surprise if everyone's attention is focused on a land assault."

The room is warm now so we move our chairs back to their usual positions. "Will you be at court for the next few weeks?" I ask him.

"Well, I need to check in with my estate manager sometime, but it's not urgent."

"I'm going to the country manor the day after tomorrow to meet with Laurence. Something tells me I'm going to want some more of your wisdom after I hear what he has to say."

"I'll be here, Alfred. For whatever you need."

• • • • • •

Back at my writing table, I dip my quill in the ink pot then pause a moment before beginning my letter to Denis. I'd originally thought my reply should be as circumspect as his prompt. After talking with Samuel, I've changed my mind. Denis wants real insight, and I owe him nothing less.

My dear Denis,

This is indeed a momentous year for you. My pleasure that it has finally arrived is dampened somewhat by the fact that you can't enjoy the grand celebration you deserve. But the decisions you're making, given the uncertainties surrounding this time, tell me you've grown enormously in your understanding of what it means not just to rule but to do so thoughtfully.

As I'm sure Lord Peveril will have told you, our information sheds no more light on what to expect than does your own. But the very fact that there are no signs whatsoever of future aggression is enough to give me pause. I cannot credit that our mutual acquaintance would so easily relinquish his ambitions.

We both know that everything he does – or doesn't do – is purposeful, so our task is to look beyond his immediate moves, to avoid an instinctive reaction that plays into his plans, and to find ways to keep him off balance. I'm not suggesting this will necessarily be easy, and it will almost certainly involve making some difficult decisions. But you've already taken the first step by foregoing a public celebration of your coming of age, thereby eliminating an "occasion" he can seize upon as a cause for action.

He'll be weighing the merits of acting early – while your personal rule is still in its infancy and might be fragile – against biding his time – allowing your commanders to grow weary of constant vigilance, perhaps even lulling them into belief in a lasting peace – and then striking when their guard is down. But you can take steps to unsettle that simple assessment.

Be seen spending ample time with your commanders. His spies will recognize this as the action of a mature reign. Your idea for a progress is a good one for building loyalty among your people so they're ready to fight if called on – another sign that your kingdom will not be easy prey. But consider doing it in smaller segments, with frequent returns home to consult with your commanders. Don't offer up a long absence in the countryside as an opportunity for an attack. And don't overlook the possibility of a direct assault on the port from the sea. You have an enormous advantage if your defenders there are at peak readiness. Such an attempt might be a diversion, intended to draw your attention away from the major onslaught overland, or it might be a tactic of surprise if the opponent thinks you've become complacent in the belief that the port is unassailable from the sea. And with each of these things, there are opportunities for you to mislead the spies and to draw any aggression into a trap of your own making.

I'm confident your commanders have both the strategic and tactical skills to support these endeavors. But might I venture to suggest delving into Goscelin's papers to see what they might contain about how he established a largely peaceful coexistence with his neighbors to the east.

Much of the burden for how to deflect any threat falls on you, but you are in a far better position to do so now than at any time since your grandfather's reign. The alliances you've created and the friends you've made have common cause with you in subduing any aggression. Together, we'll find a way to force our acquaintance to look elsewhere to satisfy his ambitions.

Alfred

I read the missive twice over before pouring wax and applying my seal. I'll ask Coliar to send for the courier in the morning. I want him to be able to tell Denis that he accepted the letter directly from my hand.

A visit to the country manor usually means a time to step away momentarily from the responsibilities of the throne. But of late, my trips there have been anything but relaxing. This time, though, there's a second purpose in my going, which will actually give me great pleasure.

Sending the invitation for Eirwen's visit made me realize there was another task I needed to attend to in preparation for Geoffrey's coming of age. "It occurs to me, Osbert," I said during my bath the following morning, "that it's probably time we got on with finding a squire for Geoffrey. You'll need time to train him before he takes up the role officially."

"That be fer certes, m'lord. I not be letting just anyone take care of that boy."

"Any thoughts on where we should look?"

"Well, talk in the servants' hall is that 'twon't be long afore Lord Bauldry's squire be needing a new master to serve. And even if that not be fer several months yet, 'twouldn't be like he be needing much training from me. He already be knowing how to serve a lord, so he only be needing to learn Geoffrey's habits and his likes."

"An interesting idea, Osbert. But isn't Lord Bauldry's squire closer to our age – maybe even a little older?"

"Aye, he be."

"What I want for Geoffrey is someone about his own age so they can be together for a long time and so Geoffrey will have someone he already trusts when he becomes king – rather like you and me."

"That make sense, m'lord."

"I'm sure if we both put our minds to it we can find the right person."

Three days later, it was Osbert who brought up the topic once again as he was finishing my shave. "I be thinking on the business of a squire fer Lord Geoffrey, and I be talking to Timm too. See, 'twon't be too much longer afore he needs be thinking on the same thing fer Lord Barat." The adventures Samuel and I have shared have led to our squires becoming fast friends, so it's no surprise Osbert would consult Timm on such a matter.

"Anyways, Timm, he be remembering something what Lord Rupert's squire have to say last time he were here." Rupert's spending most of his time at the country manor these days. His excuse is that it's easier to help Laurence from there – which, no doubt, it is – but I rather suspect as he gets older, he prefers the peace and quiet of the country to the constant activity of the court.

"Seems there be a butcher in Great Woolston," Osbert continued, "what have five sons, and that be too many to take over the butcher shop. The oldest one not be wanting to stay in Great Woolston on account of the girl he want to marry getting betrothed to the mayor's son. So he give up his inheritance and join the knighthood. That mean the second son be taking over when his father canna' do the butchering any longer."

I chuckled to myself, but took care to keep my expression neutral. Leave it to Osbert to know the whole family history. I wondered, though, how many sons we'd go through before we got to the one of interest.

"So the third son, he be all at loose ends. He dinna' want to be a knight and he dinna' want to be a monk, so he dinna' know how he be making his way in the world. He apprentice to a stone mason fer a bit, but he never be getting the hang of working the mortar. Seems that be something a man have a talent fer or he dinna'. So the mason tell him he best be looking fer another trade.

"Anyways, he like horses, so he think mayhap he try to become a stable master, so he get work at the stable in the town. 'Cept the only thing what they have fer him to do be mucking out, and there be no promise of when he be getting better work. So Lord Rupert's squire say he be all down in the dumps over not having any better idea what to do."

By this time in the narrative, I'd almost finished dressing, needing only to pull on my boots. "So, anyways, I be thinking," Osbert wrapped up the story, "mayhap he be a good fit fer Geoffrey."

"Any idea how old the lad is?" I asked.

"Me and Timm be thinking he likely be somewheres about the same age as Barat, but we dinna' know fer sure."

"Well, I suppose we have to start somewhere. Why don't you and Timm take a couple of days to go to Great Woolston and see what you think of the lad? You can spend the night at the manor, naturally. Then if you think he might be a possibility, I'll talk with him next time I visit Rupert." I wiggled my left foot to settle it in the boot then rose from the stool, ready to start my day. "And, Osbert?"

"Aye, m'lord?"

"This is really important. If you don't think the lad would be a good fit – if you don't think he could learn to do the job just as well as you do – then tell me that. There's no reason we have to settle for the first person we find unless we're sure he's the *right* person."

"That be fer certes, m'lord."

When the squires returned, Osbert couldn't conceal his excitement over the butcher's third son. So I've arrived at the manor a day before Laurence and am chatting with Rupert in the drawing room while Osbert goes to fetch the young man.

"The father has a good reputation in the town," Rupert tells me. "Of course, that says nothing about the character of the son, but I don't remember ever hearing of those boys being in trouble as they were growing up."

"I suppose that's a good start."

"Just trust your instincts, Alfred. Better still, trust Osbert's. And don't forget you can always make a change if things don't work out."

"I know. I just hope I can get it right the first time, like Father did for me."

A soft knock on the door precedes Osbert stepping just inside the room to say quietly, "He be waiting fer ye in the study, m'lord."

"Well, Uncle," I say, rising from my chair, "guess I'd best be getting on with this."

Rupert grins. "Maybe having daughters wasn't such a bad thing after all. At least I didn't have to find them both a marriage partner *and* a squire."

I open the study door to find a young man looking out the window, his back to the door. I leave the door open, knowing Osbert will be discreetly out of sight in the corridor – I want him to hear this. At the sound my entrance, the young man spins around and drops to both knees, his head bowed. "Rise, my good fellow. Take a seat." I choose my own chair and sit quickly so he doesn't have to stand around awkwardly, waiting for his king to be seated. When he remains standing, his cap in his hands in front of him, I gesture to the chair nearest me and invite him once again, "Please."

Still he hesitates. "I . . . I not be sure if that be right and proper in front of the king, Yer Grace. I never be taught court manners. And this be too important to do ought that not be proper."

I smile, attempting to put him a little more at ease, but he's right – this may be the most important thing he's ever done in his life. "Then why don't we make this your first lesson? If the king invites you to do something, then it's perfectly permissible. So, please . . ." I pause briefly. "Well, this is awkward. I'm afraid I don't know your name."

"Robin, Yer Grace. Me christened name be Robert but on account of that also be me da's name, I always be called Robin."

"Well, then, Robin, please do take a seat."

Very tentatively, he perches on the edge of the chair I indicated, a hand on each knee, his cap still held firmly in the left one. He's clearly taken a lot of trouble with his appearance today, though it's impossible to know if this was on his own initiative or at Osbert's behest. Either way, it speaks well for his wanting to impress. His light brown hair is neatly combed, and I suspect the clothes he wears are his very best, saved for wearing to church on high holy days and perhaps his saint's day. His boots look as if they've been cleaned and polished, though they're a bit down-at-the-heels from constant wear.

"So tell me, Robin. Why do you think you might want to be a squire?"

"I dinna' think on it meself, Yer Grace. But when Master Osbert tell me mayhap it be possible I could serve a great lord, it seem like God really were listening to me prayers. See, I have to make me own way in the world, and I were not much good at the things I be trying. So mayhap it be that God dinna' let me be good at those things on account of He were saving me to be a squire." He scrunches his cap and looks down at his feet before adding. "But Master Osbert never tell me the man I might serve be royal."

"What *did* Master Osbert tell you?"

"He say a good squire be knowing what his lord need even afore the lord know it hisself. And he say he can teach me how to do that, but I have to be willing to do whatever the lord be needing and never complain and never act like I be better than any of the other servants."

"And do you think you could do that, Robin?"

"I dinna' know fer certes, Yer Grace, but I think mayhap I could."

"What would you think if you had to go with your lord to some place that was quite dangerous? Maybe even to war. Would you be afraid?"

"Master Osbert say that be part of the job – that a squire go everywhere his lord be going and the squire have no say in the matter. But, begging Yer Grace's pardon, methinks any man be a little afraid when he go to war, even if he be a great lord."

I like this young man. His answers are honest, but he's not cocky. "How old are you, Robin?"

"I be seventeen me next birthday."

"And when might that birthday be?"

"That be Saint Aldhelm's Day, Yer Grace."

"Not so far off then. Close enough for your second lesson in court manners. Whenever we meet, once you've addressed me as Your Grace the first time, it's quite acceptable for you to simply say Sire thereafter."

"That be a good thing to know, Sire."

"You're still rather young, Robin. If you take this position, you'd be committing to serve your lord for the rest of your life. That could be a very long time. Are you ready to sign up for that kind of service? Have you thought about whether you'd be willing to give up the idea of having a wife and raising your own children?"

"Master Osbert, he ask me that selfsame question, Sire, so I be thinking on it ever since. Mayhap a wife and family be nice. But I be a third son, so there be nought fer me to inherit. And if I not be good at a trade, mayhap I not be able to feed meself, much less provide for a wife and children. So if God be sending me this chance to be a squire, then mayhap He already make the decision this be how I should spend me life."

As I start to rise from my chair, the young man is on his feet in an instant. "Thank you for coming to talk with me, Robin. Osbert will let you know my decision."

"It be an honor, Yer Grace. Sire." He bows repeatedly as I make my way across the room.

At the door, I turn back, one more thought coming to mind. "I'm told, Robin, that you like horses. Is that true?"

"Aye, Sire. Ever since I be just a boy, if something be troubling me, I talk to me da's horse about it. He never say much – maybe he nicker or something – but he always make me feel better."

I smile. "So does mine." I turn and walk through the door, gesturing to Osbert to show the lad out and send him on his way.

Osbert makes no mention of the interview while he helps me bathe and dress the following morning, keeping his usual banter to the topic of Laurence's expected arrival and how long we'll be here before returning to the castle. As I step out of the tub, I ask him, "So what did you think of my conversation with Robin yesterday? Do you still think he might be suitable for Geoffrey?"

"He be respectful, but he dinna' act like he be afraid of ye. That were what I couldna' be guessing aforehand. Whoever be Lord Geoffrey's squire going to be always around nobles and knights and state visits and all such at court. So he have to be just going about his business and doing his job and not be all anxious about whoever be around." He pauses while he fetches my boots. "And methinks ye be liking what he have to say about his da's horse."

"That I did, Osbert. Sounds like you and I are both coming down on the same side as God in this case," I chuckle. Osbert gives me a puzzled look then breaks into a big grin when it dawns on him I was referring to Robin's remarks the previous day. "I'll leave it to you then to convey my decision and to decide how long he needs to be in training – when he needs to come to court and such."

"Aye, m'lord. Methinks he and Lord Geoffrey get along just fine – mayhap even as good as ye and me."

"I certainly hope so. And, Osbert?"

"M'lord?"

"If you don't think he needs to come to court straightaway, see to it that he has some money to live on until the time comes. He should understand from the outset that he'll be taken care of in return for his service."

•　•　•　•　•

Laurence arrives at midday, just in time for our meal, his demeanor leaving no doubt as to his state of mind. The instant Rupert dismisses the servants, he gets straight to business, foregoing the usual pleasantries. "Gunhild's latest news is . . . I suppose the right word is 'unsettling.' And truth be told, I'm not sure what to make of it. Coupled with the fact that we haven't really made any progress on finding a conduit to their king, I'm growing increasingly concerned about what's at play in the Eastern Kingdom.

"Gunhild's been back about a week, so we've had time to try to punch holes in her story and so far it holds up. There were three men in Gunnvor's court this time that she'd never seen before – two of them appeared to be retainers of some sort for the third. She described the third man as being very tall and with an air about him as if he knew his own importance and was accustomed to being in charge. She swears he wasn't the Eastern king – who she claims to know on sight. When questioned about whether it might be a lord from some other part of the kingdom, she was convinced she'd recognize any of them and that this man was a complete stranger.

"Which led us to the question of whether Gunnvor might be in league with the Northern Kingdom. She couldn't shed any light there. Seems she's never traveled to the Northern Kingdom or spent enough time at her own king's court to have encountered any visitors from that part of the world. So that's still a big unknown. All we can be sure about is that Gunnvor has another compatriot in his midst."

I've never seen Laurence like this – not even two years ago when he was so exasperated by encountering blank walls at every turn in our search for who was behind the papal inquisition and Peveril's kidnapping. Then, he was frustrated, questioning his own abilities. What I see today is more visceral – as if he's desperate to tell someone else what he knows and to share the burden of what it might mean. He barely pauses to put food in his mouth, and when he does, he keeps on talking while he chews.

"Another disturbing thing Gunhild described is the nature of Gunnvor's relationship with this stranger. Most of the time, they act like great friends. But she says there's an undercurrent of something else that rises to the surface now and again. She's unsure if it's distrust or fear, but she's in no doubt that her brother is, in some way, not entirely on a firm footing with this stranger.

"It seems the stranger is more circumspect than the rest of Gunnvor's cronies about talking in the presence of the servants and even of Gunhild herself. He's more inclined to watch and listen while the others go on and on about their ambitions and their plans. And those plans still seem to be to remove their king and put Gunnvor on the throne.

"That new master armorer she told us about after the previous trip seems to have wasted no time in preparing for their little adventure. Gunhild says the forges are going night and day making weapons, and there's talk among the servants that they're also casting what they call iron tubes but sound suspiciously like cannons to me. So I'm increasingly certain the new armorer was found specifically for the purpose of helping Gunnvor make use of his ability to produce black powder."

By now, I'm feeling the same burden Laurence must have been carrying for all the days since Gunhild's return, and Rupert's furrowed brow speaks of his own depth of concern. Laurence finally pauses to down what's left in his wine glass and pour himself a refill before pressing on with his news.

"What we still don't know," he continues, "is how much the Eastern king is aware of the plot. I sent Gunhild's minder in behind her on this last trip. The minder followed discreetly to be sure Gunhild actually went to her brother's stronghold – we've had no way, prior to this, to be entirely certain she wasn't just going to ground somewhere once she crossed the border and making up fanciful stories to keep us on a string. She went straight home, without any deviation, and the servants' chatter seemed to verify her story about Gunnvor making her serve the ale for his cronies."

Laurence's pace is no longer as frantic as when he first started. Even his posture is more relaxed.

"We did have a stroke of luck that the priest Gunnvor's wife insists on was there when the minder arrived so we got our first chance to discover where else he goes. For the first three days, he went from one small village to the next, saying mass and administering the sacraments. Then he spent an entire day traveling, finally going into a bishop's compound and not emerging for two full days, at least. By then the minder had to call off the hunt in order to be back home before Gunhild returned." I still find it fascinating that Laurence so carefully avoids revealing whether this minder is a man or a woman.

"I seem to recall, Alfred, that there was a bishop somehow involved in that business with John marrying Gundrea. What do you remember about that?"

"I remember a letter from a bishop, certifying the marriage, but I'll be damned if I can remember the bishop's name."

"Asgaard of Styrvangen," says Rupert quietly.

Three simple words. But three words that might prove pivotal to our ability to get word to the Eastern king that we're aware of the plot and ready to come to his assistance. Over the years, I've come to realize that Rupert's ability to take note of even apparently inconsequential details and recall them as needed to fill in the picture of what's happening around him is the genius that makes him the master of all spymasters. And even his advancing years haven't diminished his skill. I thank every god ever imagined by man that Rupert's talents belong to us and not to someone who might wish us harm.

"Styrvangen," says Laurence thoughtfully. "That's the name of the town where this priest went to ground."

"We can be reasonably certain this bishop was friendly to Lord Erik," says Rupert, "since he was complicit in ensuring there was no question about John and Gundrea being properly married. But what does he think of the son?"

"Perhaps Gunhild knows," Laurence muses.

"Tread carefully, Laurence," says Rupert. "We can't risk her telling Gunnvor we have an interest in the bishop until we know more about where he stands – or even if he's the same bishop. It certainly sounds like events are coming to a head there sooner than later, so time is short. But my inclination would be to see what more this other agent can turn up before showing our cards to Gunhild."

While I've listened to Laurence's news and Rupert's guidance, I've had little to say. My mind's been occupied searching for other possible explanations. "What if," I now offer, "we've got this all wrong?

Remember our speculation back when we were looking for who was behind the papal inquisition?"

"Aye," says Laurence. "That the Eastern kingdom was feeling threatened by our expanding alliances and feeling squeezed between us and the sea."

"Well, what if that's still true? What if it's actually the Eastern king behind all this? With Lord Erik dead and Gunnvor freed from any restraints on his actions, he's the perfect choice to be the point of the spear in a move against us. What if, instead of being that elusive king's spy we've been searching for, Gunhild's stranger is actually an entirely different kind of agent of the king – possibly even in charge of the entire operation? Have we been wearing winkers? Too willing to accept Gunhild's tales at face value because we're too focused on Gunnvor to see what might be an even more menacing picture?"

"As if I didn't have enough to worry about." Laurence sighs heavily.

"It's all part of the game," says Rupert. "Watching the opponent's moves and trying to anticipate his strategy. Alfred, your scenario is plausible and one we should be prepared for. Especially since we've no way to know yet if knowledge of this stranger is serendipitous for us or if it's a carefully staged tableau to mislead us."

"Or if this whole venture with trying to use Gunhild was a terrible mistake." Laurence sighs again.

"Getting more information is never a mistake, Laurence." Rupert is quick to try to bolster Laurence's spirits. "It's simply that it sometimes takes longer than we'd like for the pieces of the puzzle to come together in a useful way. Without what you're learning, we wouldn't even know there *was* something to worry about."

"What worries me is that time is closing in," I tell them. "I've kept this to myself until now, but I don't think I can any longer. I think I have no choice but to bring Jasper into the picture so he's ready however this plays out. Same with the Council. It's time for them to weigh in."

"I agree that's prudent," says Rupert. "But I hope you share my view that no one needs to know precisely *how* we've come by the information."

"Without question, Uncle. Now, Laurence, what else do you need?"

"The one thing I don't have. Time." He pauses to finish his wine. "But we've no choice but to act with dispatch. Is there a patron saint of spies?"

"No idea," I reply.

"Well, maybe you should get busy finding one and pray for him to intercede so we don't make any terrible mistakes."

As we ride home the following morning, I ask Osbert about his conversation with Robin. "He be right happy, m'lord. As near beside hisself as I ever see."

"But you're not bringing him back to the castle with us?"

"Nay, m'lord. See I be thinking if'n he be smart and eager, I not be needing a whole year to teach him. So I be telling him to come to the castle at Whitsuntide."

"But you did give him some money?'

"Aye, that I do. But I not give him all of it. Enough to get by on if he be careful and count his coins, but not enough so's he can show off. I be going back down there after Easter and see how he be faring. If he already spent all his money, then I know he not be right for Lord Geoffrey and I tell him so. But if he do well, then I give him the rest and tell him what kind of clothes he be needing and what else he best do afore he leave home."

"That's quite wise, Osbert. I can always count on you."

"Ye can at that, m'lord," is all he says aloud, but the broad smile on his face says how much he relishes the praise.

•　•　•　•　•

"Anything there that can't wait, Coliar?" I gesture to the papers on my writing table as I make my way through the private reception room on the way to shed my traveling clothes.

"I think not, Sire."

"Good. Because I need to talk with Devereux, de Courcy, and Sir Jasper straightaway. Think you could find them for me?"

"Of course, Sire. One at a time or all together?"

"Together, please. And this room will be fine."

It takes the rest of the afternoon to bring them fully into the picture of what we think we know about what's happening in the east, the gaps in our information, and the two scenarios we've imagined relative to how things might play out. "I know it's a lot to take in in a single gulp," I finish.

I let them sit silently, each man with his own thoughts, for several moments before asking, "Jasper, how many troops are assigned to the new garrison right now?"

"Just one, Sire. But if the weather holds and we get some early spring warming, I'm told the barracks could be finished by May Day."

"If we get that early spring warming, could the full complement of troops be assigned there by Easter, even if some of them have to camp inside the perimeter of the garrison? Maybe they could even help with the ongoing building?"

"Aye, that's possible. But don't forget that building isn't just about manpower. Getting the mortar properly set is the limitation on how fast we can build."

"What about the exterior walls?" asks Samuel. "Are they complete?"

"Mostly. The cannon placements facing southeast still have work to be done, but I made the decision that getting started on the barracks was more important."

"So we have the ability to signal, by Easter at the latest, that we have forces in the east?" I ask.

"Barring a late March freeze, Sire, yes."

"Truth be told, Jasper, I hope that's all we need do, but you should make your plans for all possible scenarios."

"Yes, Your Grace," Jasper formally acknowledges what he takes as an order, before adding, "And shall I assume this in no way changes the fact that we need to be ready to support King Denis, should that be necessary?"

Samuel laughs out loud. "Wishful thinking, Jasper? It wouldn't be Alfred if he wasn't making his commander's life complicated."

"I've noticed that," Jasper grins, and everyone gets a chuckle at my expense.

"You know I won't interfere, Jasper," says Samuel, "but if you need me to do anything, you only need to ask."

"Thank you, sir."

Richard's been quiet, his brow furrowed, something obviously on his mind. "I can't help but wonder, Alfred, why you haven't brought this to the Council sooner. A threat lurking on our border? That's not like you."

"In truth, Richard, until yesterday, I was convinced the matter was no more than an internal revolt within the Eastern Kingdom, and you know how determined I've always been that we not involve ourselves in squabbles between other kings and their lords."

"Be that as it may, you made sure we were all aware of the situation between Charles and his rebellious nobles."

And with this admonition, I truly understand – perhaps for the first time – the wisdom of Father's and Grandfather's practice not to involve themselves in the details of our intelligence gathering. I don't fault Laurence for bringing me into it – he had little choice since Gunhild was involved. But I realize now that I've allowed myself to get too close to the actual operations and, in doing so, have lost some of the perspective that comes with distance.

"You're right, Richard. And you're right, as first lord, to question my actions. I'd convinced myself all we had to worry about was finding a way to get word to their king of what we'd learned and that we had no intention of taking advantage of the situation – a job for our agents. But with this latest information, the situation has gotten both clearer and murkier at the same time. We have to be prepared . . . all the while hoping our preparations are a complete waste of time."

"I'll convene the Council the day after tomorrow, in the afternoon. That should be sufficient time to get word to Rupert and for him to get back here. Thankfully, everyone else is already at court. Do you want Geoffrey in the meeting?"

"Not this time. He's not yet privy to our spy networks, and I don't want the lords having to guard their tongues when we're discussing something so important. I'll tell him what his maturity and his intellect can absorb when the time's right."

"Besides," Samuel grins, "I think he's about to be otherwise occupied entertaining a Peaks princess."

"There's one thing that still puzzles me," says Richard. "How will we be able to discern if this is just civil war within the Eastern Kingdom or a threat to us? Especially if specific details are hard to come by."

"We watch Gunnvor's forces," says Samuel. "Where he assembles them and what stance they take. So long as their backs are to us, we can be reasonably certain that the target – at least the first one – is internal."

• • • • •

The Council doesn't disguise their consternation at learning of this matter late in the game. Richard allows them all a chance to express their exasperation, and my penance is to sit quietly through it all. Rupert occupies his usual place at the opposite end of the table, his expression a mask of neutrality except for the brief moment when he catches my eye and offers the faintest of supportive smiles, for which I'm grateful.

When the remarks around the table start rehashing the same complaints, Richard intervenes. "Perhaps it's time for us to hear the king's perspective. Sire?"

"I can't argue with anything I've heard here this afternoon. You all have legitimate concerns – you, in particular, Lord Ademar, since whatever this turmoil turns out to be, it's at your doorstep." As the newest member of the Council, Ademar had been restrained in his comments, but the expression on his face said he was deeply concerned.

"Let me offer you some additional insight," I continue. "The agent involved is new and unproven, leading me to a high level of skepticism around the early reports. Only in the last week or so has Lord Laurence been able to establish some bits of corroboration – and as fate would have it, that coincided with the most recent report that opened up a whole new scenario about what might be afoot in the east. In hindsight, gentlemen, one might argue that I was too skeptical."

Heads nod around the table at that last comment, but everyone's posture is somewhat more relaxed. "I can affirm the king's assertion that this agent was unproven," Rupert comes to my defense. "A new agent in a place that's previously been impenetrable . . . I had doubts as well. But Lord Laurence has consulted me frequently, and I now share the king's view that what we've been told is sufficiently concerning to begin preparations for what might come next. Laurence is working hard to further corroborate the agent's reliability, but meanwhile, we need to decide what to do about what we think we know."

With Rupert's reassurance, they've all finally sat back in their chairs, ready to take up the business at hand. We leave the meeting in agreement that the next steps are to inform the Peaks, the Lakes, and the Territories without alarming them, for Jasper to accelerate his preparations, and for Laurence to stay the course with as much dispatch as possible.

As I walk slowly back to the king's apartment, deep in my own thoughts, Lord Montfort catches me up. "A word, Alfred?"

"Of course."

"I just wanted you to know . . . I've been thinking about how that meeting unfolded. Your mistake, if one can call it that, was in revealing there were suspicions long before any confirmation. That caused everyone to look at things from the vantage point of hindsight. Had you brought us your suspicions sooner, I can imagine there'd have been a very different conversation – and probably even doubt about putting much credence in uncorroborated stories."

"Perhaps, but doesn't the relationship between the Crown and the lords —"

He cuts me off. "There's nothing dishonorable, Alfred, in withholding details that are at best, unproven – perhaps even untrue. There's actually merit in not being alarmist. Your father and grandfather were masters at that, and for the most part, so are you. I think you can be forgiven the rare lapse." He smiles.

Another reminder – as if I needed it – of the risks of getting too involved in the operations of gathering intelligence.

"The way you conducted yourself today was beyond reproach. And nothing's lost except time for Jasper to prepare, but he's at the mercy of the mortar as far as the garrison's concerned nor can he deploy an army in any strength until there's greater certainty we're actually under threat."

"Thank you, Montfort. Coming from you, that helps bolster my confidence in my own judgment."

"My friend Ernle would tell you the same thing had he been in the room." He claps me on the shoulder. A familiarity few would assume but that doesn't feel out of place from this man. The last of my father's generation sitting on the Council. A man whose wisdom and advice I've always trusted.

"I'll be off to the Lakes tomorrow," he says. "They need to know there's unrest brewing along their eastern border."

At the next corridor, he turns toward his rooms while I make my way up the staircase, my confidence renewed, but praying fervently to every god I've ever heard of that Gunnvor keeps his back to us.

Eirwen and her party arrive just before the feast of Saint Patrick. She's accompanied by her younger sister, Ceri, a personal maid, and an aunt, whose name is Morfyl. The plan is for them to stay several weeks, returning home on May Day. During the formal reception, Morfyl seems severe and over-protective, holding both girls' hands and only reluctantly releasing them to curtsey and to greet Gwen and me.

Geoffrey's emotions had gone from eager, school-boy-like anticipation, to anxiety, to romantic wistfulness, to utter dread all in the space of the week leading up to Eirwen's arrival. But when they saw each other in the reception room, it was impossible to miss the spark that flashed between them. While our visitors were being shown to their quarters to rest from the journey, he had only one question for me. "How am I ever going to have a chance to get to know Eirwen with that woman hovering like a vulture all the time?"

"Give your mother and Lady Thorssen a few days to help them settle in. You have plenty of time, Son."

The visitors dominate our conversation this evening as Gwen and I climb into bed. "Poor woman looked like she'd been sent into a lions' den to protect her nieces," I remark.

Gwen laughs. "How apt!"

"Oh?"

"Just think about it, Alfred. All your family symbols. The king's banner flying from all the towers. She truly did come into a den of lions."

My turn to chuckle. "Well, when you put it that way . . . When she finally caught sight of Addiena, though, it looked like she'd found a port in a storm." Phillip's wife, being the Peaks king's cousin, would at least be another family member, no matter how distant the relationship might be.

"Mixing metaphors, are we?" Gwen's in a particularly playful mood this evening.

"If the metaphors fit . . ."

"Don't worry." She pats my hand. "All will get better. I'm holding a gathering for all the ladies tomorrow afternoon and the following day for the express purpose of putting Eirwen and her aunt at ease. Especially the aunt."

"I hope it works. I wouldn't want to have to do battle with that woman for Geoffrey to be able to have some time together with his prospective bride."

"Been saving up your metaphors all day, dear?"

"Just for you, my love." I kiss her hand. "But you should know . . . Geoffrey's terrified of the battle-axe. Though he referred to her as a vulture. There you go – another metaphor for your collection."

She laughs and snuggles close, clearly interested in a different kind of play.

•　•　•　•　•

It takes more than just a few gatherings of the ladies of the court to win Geoffrey his first hour alone with Eirwen. Well, as alone as the sons and daughters of kings are allowed to be in such a situation.

After a week with Morfyl showing no sign of letting Eirwen out of her sight or anywhere near Geoffrey, Gwen decides some subterfuge is in order. The conspiracy begins with her invitation to Morfyl for a private conversation. Addiena does her part by hustling Eirwen, Ceri,

A Feeling in the Bones 196

and their maid down to the garden, where I'd made sure Geoffrey was waiting. I watch from the window of the library as the young people take several turns around the garden, talking, while the maid and Ceri trail behind, always within earshot. Memories come flooding back of the times Gwen and I spent there, getting to know each other, with Letty as our chaperone.

Anticipating Morfyl's reaction when she discovers what's happened behind her back, Addiena makes it her job to be on hand to curb the battle-axe's fury before Eirwen's return to her room. But she can't prevent Morfyl from waylaying us as we enter the dining hall for the court dinner. "You tricked me." She points a finger at Gwen, stopping just short of touching her person. "Don't think I won't tell my brother about this."

"Yes, Lady Morfyl, I did trick you." Gwen's tone is kind, but in no way apologetic. "But the young people need some time for conversation . . . an opportunity to learn about one another. Otherwise, how will your brother and my husband assess their suitability as marriage partners?"

"That's *not* how it was done in my day. The children of kings did not have a say. Their duty was to marry as they were told. This whole business of conversation and suitability. It's utter nonsense."

"I believe," says Gwen, "that this visit was your brother's suggestion. And, of course, we were completely of like mind."

"Which is precisely why I insisted on coming along. To protect my niece's honor. To ensure your son takes no improper liberties."

Addiena rushes up just at that moment. "Come, Morfyl. Let's go in to dinner. The court is waiting for the king and queen."

"You haven't heard the last of this." Morfyl refuses to give up easily.

Addiena takes her in hand and leads her away. "Come, dear. I told you this afternoon there was nothing improper. Ceri and the maid were there the whole time. They can tell you everything that was said. Just ask them if you're concerned."

Gwen can't help but roll her eyes, and I have to suppress a chuckle. I've no doubt tonight's bedtime chat will be about the next ploy to give the young people more time together. May Day is starting to feel like a long time away.

•   •   •   •   •

And so the cat-and-mouse games begin. I prefer to think of it as slaying the dragon. Gwen is quick to chide me for being too harsh, but her barely suppressed giggle tells me she really thinks it's funny. It's to Addiena that falls the unenviable task of keeping Morfyl occupied, but she accepts it with aplomb.

Juliana takes Eirwen – and by extension, Ceri – under her wing and plans a series of activities for the girls. First, she hires Master Giorgio – the visiting artist – to paint a portrait of Eirwen and Ceri together as a gift for their father.

To no one's surprise, Morfyl insists on being present for the first session. "She told me artists were not to be trusted – that they have no morals at all," Juliana tells us over supper on that first night, her imitation of Morfyl's severe expression and stern voice eliciting smiles from everyone and peals of laughter from Alicia.

"Alicia," Gwen chastises, "remember your manners. It's not polite to make fun of people."

"But I'm not making fun, Mama. I'm just laughing at Juliana. *She's* the one making fun." As usual, my youngest daughter gets straight to the heart of the matter.

"Just remember," Gwen does her best, "that whenever you're around Lady Morfyl, you must be a proper princess, alright?"

"I will, Mama. But Juliana's right – she's awful." And also as usual, Alicia has the last word on the matter.

"Anyway," Juliana resumes, "Morfyl sat stiffly on her chair, watching Master Giorgio at work. After the first hour, she complained that it was all taking too long. It's true the silverpoint drawing is a tedious process, but it's worth it. From then on, every quarter hour she'd rise from her chair and go look over Giorgio's shoulder, only to complain that he hadn't made much progress and she was bored with it all. The fifth time she left her chair, she started criticizing the drawing, proclaiming it a terrible likeness. Giorgio called a halt to the session. 'I cannot work with that woman here. I *will* not work with her here,' he practically shouted.

"Morfyl was already headed to the door by then, but she called over her shoulder, 'And *I* will not waste my time watching this charade. Lady Ernle, I hold you responsible for protecting the girls' virtue.' And then she swept out of the room." Juliana pauses for effect before adding with a huge smile on her face, "Which was exactly what I'd intended." Morfyl gets invited to sittings from time to time, but only so she gets fed up and storms out, leaving the coast clear for Geoffrey to drop by.

Market days are an excuse for an outing, with Juliana arranging to meet Geoffrey and his mates as they wander the stalls. Gwen holds her afternoon gatherings frequently enough that Morfyl soon tires of them, giving Gwen and the other ladies of the court an opportunity to converse with Eirwen without the interference of her aunt. We invite Eirwen and Ceri to private family suppers two or three times a week. On the other nights, Juliana invites them to join her and Rainard – and, of course, invites Geoffrey as well.

When Juliana suggests an outing to the monastery to visit the kennel, she's quite surprised that Eirwen asks her aunt to go along. "I was certain she was going to spoil everything, Papa," Juliana tells me later, "but it seems Eirwen's quite clever. Morfyl said 'At last! A sober activity befitting your status as a maiden princess. But I will not accompany you. I have no need of the company of monks or of dogs. I have to spend far too much time with those beasts at your father's court.'"

What no one chooses to mention to Morfyl is that Geoffrey and I are riding up early in the morning, ostensibly to spend some time with Warin and Frery, both of whom are delighted to be part of the grand subterfuge. When the carriage arrives, the ladies make their way straight to the kennel where Brother Adam has a litter of puppies just approaching six weeks of age. In due course, Gwen brings Eirwen to join us in Warin's dining room.

Geoffrey jumps to his feet as soon the ladies enter, taking Eirwen's hand and raising it to his lips in greeting. "The orchards here are only just beginning to bud," he says, "but it's still a pleasant walk. Would you care to join me?"

"That would be lovely," she replies. Gwen and I follow at a distance, only close enough that they're never completely out of sight.

As we watch them walking side by side – close, but careful to avoid touching one another – I take Gwen's hand. "I wonder what they're talking about."

"I can assure you it's not the same things we discussed."

"Oh?"

"She's not like me, Alfred. She can read and write, but she's not had much education beyond that. At first, I thought she was a bit flighty – utterly unconcerned with the serious business of what it means to be a queen. But I'm coming to see that she just has a different view of that than I do. She has no interest in making her own mark on the kingdom. Where her heart lies is in making life easy for her husband so that he can make *his* mark. What I first thought was frivolousness seems, in fact, to be a genuine interest in the social graces and the trappings of the court. More traditional than I am, certainly, but not necessarily an undesirable trait in the wife of a king. She seems to be naturally generous, and Morfyl's iron hand has taught her to be clever about getting her way."

"Seems like it's teaching *us* that too," I chuckle.

"What's striking though is how people are drawn to her. Not just the young men. She has a way of making people like her. It's in no way disingenuous – she's just a delight to be around."

"Sounds like maybe she's captured you as well," I chuckle once again.

"Perhaps she has at that." Gwen laughs softly. "But if so, I'm in good company. Tamasine and Avelina agree that the people would love her. So if Geoffrey loves her too, then I think she would make him a lovely wife and a lovely queen."

We all share the midday meal with Warin and Frery before returning home. Geoffrey and I take a detour through the meadow to the woods to guard against being spotted arriving at the same time and from the same direction as the carriage, in case Morfyl is keeping a lookout at the windows – which she almost certainly will be.

As Easter approaches, we all breathe a bit more freely, knowing we've gotten through the first half of the visit unscathed. I'm rather surprised to find a letter from the King of Peaks on my writing table on Good Friday morning.

My dear Alfred,

As Easter will soon be upon us, I take up my quill to send you good wishes both for the season and for the success of our little venture.

My dearest cousin, the lovely Addiena, has written to me of the challenges that my sister imposes on allowing the young people to make a comfortable acquaintance, but she also tells me there have been opportunities – schemes, shall I say? – to circumvent the problems. When Morfyl learned of Eirwen's visit to your court, I found myself unable to convince her not to make the journey. I could, perhaps, have confined her to my dungeon, but that seemed a bit extreme.

My sister, unfortunately, adheres strongly to the old ways and refuses to embrace any modern innovations, no matter how reasonable they may be. Here, at least, Eirwen is very adept at avoiding her aunt's scrutiny, but I can imagine that scrutiny there is multiplied manifold in the face of what we all know is at stake.

If Morfyl makes too great a nuisance of herself and you should choose to send her home, I would not be displeased. Nor, I suspect, would Eirwen.

I shall write separately to my dear Addiena thanking her for undertaking what I'm certain is a thankless task.

I send my best wishes to you and Gwendolyn and look forward to the discussions we shall have in May.

I immediately go in search of Gwen to show her the letter. At one point, while she's reading, she laughs softly. When she hands the page back to me, she says, "I'm sure Eirwen wouldn't be unhappy to see her aunt go home. But you know, Alfred, I've decided having Morfyl here is not entirely a bad idea. It's actually a bit like what we had to endure with the seemingly endless rainy days and with John's boorishness. If Geoffrey and Eirwen find their way to each other in spite of Morfyl, then I think we can be confident it will be a good match."

"I'm glad to hear that. I wasn't looking forward to doing battle with the dragon to get her into a carriage back home." Gwen laughs again. "And as much trouble as the dragon is – especially to Addiena – I completely agree with you."

• • • • •

After early morning mass, Gwen holds a splendid Easter court. The sun does its part, delivering an early-April day warm enough to permit games and nuncheons on the lawns throughout the afternoon before the usual end-of-Lent banquet in the evening.

At one point, I notice Eirwen make her way, alone, through the hedge into the garden. Seeing no one follow her, I decide the best way to stay in Morfyl's good graces would be to make sure nothing's afoot that anyone could deem inappropriate. A quick glance around the corner of the hedge reveals that she's alone, walking the paths and occasionally stooping to smell the early spring flowers. Sensing my presence despite my effort to be unobtrusive, she says, "It's odd, isn't it, Your Grace, that the daffodils and tulips don't have much of a scent."

I take that as an invitation and join her where she's just rising from an enormous clump of daffodils. "I've never really thought about it, but I suppose you're right. Those daffodils were planted by my great-grandmother when she first laid out this garden. I find it remarkable that they return year after year, always more lush than before."

"It must be her spirit revisiting a place that she loved."

A Feeling in the Bones 202

We continue down the path to a bench beside the rose bushes where I first cut a rose and placed it in Gwen's hair. How could that have been so long ago? The memory is as fresh as if it were yesterday. I invite Eirwen to sit. "I hope our side-stepping your aunt's strict rules hasn't made her too angry."

She smiles. "Aunt Morfyl is grumpier even than usual, I fear. I've decided it must be because I'm to be married and she never was. Most women of her station who never married would long since have retired to a convent. But my father puts up with her . . . for my mother's sake, I think."

"Oh?"

"Mother was very ill for a very long time before she passed into the next world, and Aunt Morfyl took care of her. I think Father shows his gratitude for that by letting Morfyl do what she wants." She fondles the leaves of the nearest rose bush, carefully avoiding the thorns. "Of course, he also allows me to ignore Aunt's admonitions most of the time, which is good because otherwise, she would have me locked away in some tower like a cloistered nun, doing nothing but saying my prayers and practicing my needlework." She laughs. "Your court is delightful, Sire."

"My wife has a lot to do with that."

"She told me your mother encouraged her."

The mention of my mother brings a pang of grief to the surface, something I'd managed so far to keep in check on this first anniversary of her death. Over the past year, the wound has begun to heal, the hurt no longer so raw. But her absence is still palpable and will forever color the Easter season for me, though I know the color will fade with time.

Eirwen seems to sense the change in my mood. "Is something wrong, Sire?" she asks gently.

I push the pain away, not wanting to dampen her joy. "Not at all. Just remembering how welcoming my parents were when Gwen first arrived here. I hope we're able to do the same for Geoffrey's bride."

"I really should thank you, Sire, for all you've done to make it possible for Geoffrey and me to become acquainted . . . despite Aunt Morfyl. In truth, the only concern I have about marrying is that I'll be leaving Ceri behind to cope with Aunt on her own."

"If I know anything about younger siblings, my dear – and I *was* one myself – they learn an enormous amount from watching their brothers and sisters. I learned what I *didn't* want to be. I suspect Ceri has been studying your tactics carefully so she'll know how to deal with Morfyl when the time comes."

I see what Gwen means. Whether it's highland magic or simply a genuinely likeable young woman, I'm completely captivated. I rise and offer her my arm. "Now . . . we should probably rejoin the others before your aunt organizes a search party to find you."

"This has been delightful, Sire," she says as we make our way toward the opening in the hedge. "I hope this won't be the only time I get to enjoy your company."

So do I. But I won't voice that just yet. Not until I've talked with Geoffrey.

•　•　•　•　•

Easter Monday is given over to preparation for a visit to the country manor. Gwen wants to see how Eirwen adapts to the more relaxed style of life we adopt there. Richard and Avelina are coming as well, both for Avelina to have some time to visit with her parents and also to serve as a foil for Morfyl, giving Addiena a respite from the task. My purpose is a meeting with Laurence at the end of the week.

To no one's surprise, Morfyl insists on having the biggest room with the biggest bed so that she, Eirwen, and Ceri can all sleep together. "And it must have a lock on the door," she demands. "I'll not risk my nieces' virtue by making it easy for some man with low morals to sneak in during the night." I wonder what she thinks she'd be doing while this imaginary man is having his way with one of the girls.

I'm inclined to tell her she can make do with whatever room is assigned to her, but Gwen prevails. "It won't hurt us to give up our room for a few nights. Hardly a battle worth fighting, my love. Just think how miserable the girls would be with all three of them crammed into a room usually meant for one or two." I acquiesce, but not without making sure Morfyl knows she's seriously inconveniencing a king and queen that her brother wants to impress.

To everyone's surprise, it's Catherine who takes Morfyl in hand, dragging her to the dressmaker in Great Woolston, putting her in charge of what's to be served at mealtimes, taking her along to the pastures to check on the new lambs. By the time we all gather in the drawing room in midafternoon, Morfyl is too exhausted – or too put out – to cause much trouble.

Laurence arrives on the feast day of Saint Alphege, just after the midday meal, and Rupert and I retire with him to the study for the latest news. "We instructed Gunhild to stay a bit longer this time, Easter being the perfect excuse for that. But my real purpose was to give her minder more time to investigate. Unfortunately, what we'd hoped to find was not to be. Asgaard went to meet his maker several years ago, depriving us of the pretext of inquiring about his memory of John's marriage as a way to start asking questions.

"Gunnvor's wife's priest appears to stay with the bishop when he's not on his way to or from Gunnvor's stronghold. But he does enjoy spending evenings in the tavern. My agent is suspicious that's where he may be transmitting messages, but we have no proof of it yet. We don't believe he's transmitting anything in the villages he visits."

"If the villages are small," says Rupert, "I'm inclined to agree. Everyone knows everyone else's business in those tiny communities. Anyone going away for a week – especially on any regular basis – would be noticed."

"Gunhild says the tall stranger was still with Gunnvor when she arrived, but left a few days later. Seems Gunnvor's given him the use of the wife's former manor house for whatever time he chooses to spend there. Gunhild seems to think there's some connection between the stranger and Gunnvor's wife, but she hasn't been able to work out what it might be.

"The cronies all went to their homes for Easter, every last man of them carrying a wagonload of arms. Gunhild's minder confirmed that."

"I thought the minder was watching the priest," I say.

"For the first few days, yes. But my real objective was for the minder to observe the comings and goings around Gunnvor's fortress. We need to better establish Gunhild's reliability so I can have them working together rather than wasting one of them spying on the spy."

Rupert chuckles. "So what did you learn?"

"At least three wagonloads of arms departed the fortress. Two headed north, one east. My agent wasn't in a good position to observe the eastbound one, but the other two were loaded with battle axes, halberds, and crates that we assume would have been filled with swords. There may have been others that left under cover of darkness – we can't be sure.

"According to Gunhild, her brother expected all his cronies to return immediately after Easter. Presumably, they're all under one roof again by now. So there's activity, but we're still not sure to what purpose." He pauses. "In truth, Alfred, I was hoping for more, but I have to remind myself this business doesn't always move at the pace I'd prefer."

"News?" Richard asks when we emerge midafternoon.

"Yes and no," I reply. "More confirmation that something's afoot. Arms being transported from Gunnvor's fortress to the strongholds of the lords who've joined with him. Conventional arms though, as far as can be observed – swords, battle-axes, and the like. So there's ongoing activity. What we still can't confirm is to what purpose."

"Do you want a Council meeting when we return?"

"Until we know something more definite, it's probably sufficient for you just to make sure everyone's informed of the latest observations. But of course, if anyone wants a meeting . . ."

"Agreed," says Richard.

As May Day approaches, decisions loom. Three days before the visitors from the Peaks are to depart, I find Geoffrey waiting in my private reception room when I return from my morning ride. "To what do I owe this great honor? I thought you'd be spending these last few days with the lovely Eirwen."

"I have a request, Papa. I want to escort her back home. Me and my mates."

"You know what message that would be sending."

"I do, Papa, and it's the message I want to send. Eirwen too."

"Your mates as well?"

"So I'll have someone to keep my spirits up on the journey home . . . while I wait for you and her father to reach a decision."

"And have you discussed this with your mother?" I already know the answer. Gwen and I both think they're a good match, the only missing part of a final decision being Geoffrey's own view. This conversation is rescuing me from having to ask him directly.

"She quite likes Eirwen – thinks she'll make a good queen one day. But she reminded me you have the final say." He pauses – that pause I know so well that means there's something else he wants to say but is weighing in the balance whether to say it or not. And as always, when I give him time, he finally says what's on his mind. "Please don't say no, Papa."

"Have you arranged everything with your mates?"

"Aye."

"And with Carew? You'll need guards, you know."

"That too."

My pause is just for the perverse joy of keeping him on tenterhooks for a few moments longer. Something a father's entitled to now and again, I tell myself, especially when that father's also a king. "Then I think it's a splendid idea. And I'm quite proud of you for thinking of it."

"Thank you, Papa." The joy on his face warms my heart.

"Think you four can cope with Lady Morfyl for that many days?"

"I've already worked that out too. Carew says we can post a guard outside the ladies' door every night and tell the dragon it's to keep all us lecherous lads away from her charges." He grins. "I guess I'd best be off to tell my mates the good news."

"And I guess I'd best put my mind to writing a letter for you to deliver to Eirwen's father."

On the day, when Geoffrey and his friends mount up and take their places – two in front and two behind the ladies' carriage – my pride in my son is almost overwhelming. Two guards lead the column out of the courtyard, one carrying the banner of the heir to the throne, and the rest fall into formation in the rear. Gwen takes my arm and I look down to see her eyes glistening, as I'm sure my own must be.

To preserve the king's dignity, we turn to go inside. "I only wish his grandparents could have been here to see him," I tell her.

"What makes you think they aren't watching?"

The second day after their departure brings another post-morning-ride surprise. "This just arrived," says Coliar, handing me a folded paper. "The messenger was rather breathless – said he'd ridden hard all the way and barely slept."

Turning the message over, I recognize Egon's seal and break it open quickly.

My dear Alfred,

I have no time to say more than that I need your help. If you value our friendship, come as quickly as you can. Samuel as well, if possible. The future may depend on it.

Egon

The expression on my face must look troubled. "Is something amiss, Sire?"

"It seems so, Coliar, though precisely what, I don't know. Send for Carew and Lord de Courcy, if you will. Tell them to hurry."

"Right away, Sire."

Samuel arrives first, and I hand him the message. "Sounds dire," he says, returning the page to me.

"Indeed. You'll come with me?"

"Well, I suppose my estate manager will just have to be patient a little longer," he chuckles.

"If you really need to attend to something—"

He cuts me off. "Of course I'll come, Alfred. Squires?"

"I think not."

The door opens quietly and Carew joins us. I hand him the message. "Samuel and I are leaving this afternoon."

"And I'm going with you. Cedric can look after things here. Just give me time to organize a troop of guards."

"No troop, Carew. Nothing to slow us down. No banners. Samuel and I aren't even taking our squires."

"Sir?"

"Egon wouldn't invite us into danger without a warning. Whatever it is, it's urgent but not a threat to us. But we can go armed, if that makes you feel any better," I chuckle.

"Sir, the queen will have my *hide* if—"

I raise my hand to interrupt him. "The queen will probably have *my* hide even before we leave, so let's keep it just the three of us. Can you both be ready right after the midday meal?"

"As you wish, sir," says Carew, resigned but not completely convinced. "Permission to go arrange things with Cedric?"

"Certainly. We'll meet at the stable. And let's each ride one of Elvin's stable horses – good ones so we can move quickly, but ones we can trade along the way to keep up the pace."

"Elvin's not going to like that," says Samuel.

"We'll trade them back on our way home."

When Gwen reads the message, her first words are, "When are you leaving?"

"This afternoon. Carew's going along. Cedric will be in charge here."

"Do be careful, Alfred. I know Egon wouldn't invite you into danger, but what if he wrote that message under duress?"

"He'd have written it in his own language so whoever forced him to send it could read it."

"Possibly. Juliana and Rainard were thinking of going to Ernle Manor for a couple of weeks. I think I'll suggest they wait until you return."

"You think that's necessary?"

"Just until we know what's up in the Territories."

"Whatever you think best." I take her in my arms for a farewell embrace and kiss. "We'll be back as soon as we can."

The longer spring days give us more daylight, and the moon waxing full allows us to ride well past sundown. We arrive at the border midmorning of the fifth day, having trimmed more than a day and a half off the usual time for the journey. Egon must have had a scout out because he and a group of his men meet us well before we arrive at his fortress.

"I am beyond grateful that you arrived so quickly, Alfred." He nods to Samuel and Carew. "I hope you are prepared to keep moving. There is no time to lose if we are to get to Korst in time to prevent a disaster."

"Then let's not spend a moment longer in greeting," I tell him. We fall in side by side, Samuel and Carew just behind and Egon's men bringing up the rear.

An hour later, when we slow to a walk to give the horses a brief respite, we finally learn what brought us here. "There has been a collapse in one of Korst's mines," says Egon. "His youngest son was inside the mine at the time. He is convinced it was deliberate – sabotage by the two men he had recently hired."

"What makes him think that?" I ask.

"The two of them almost made it out. Their bodies were found with very little digging at the edge of the collapse."

"Isn't it possible they just happened to be nearest to the entrance when things began to cave in?"

"It is not out of the question, of course, but you will never convince Korst of that. You see, these men came from the Kingdom of Peaks looking for work. Korst was reluctant to hire them but his son convinced him they needed the extra manpower. Finding them at the edge of the rubble served only to reinforce his original opinion – which he then expanded to a belief that they had been sent purposefully by the Peaks king to create discord among us.

"He sent word to Goron to gather an army and come to his fortress so they could cross the lowland border and exact revenge. Goron had little choice but to go. Had he refused, everything would have been in jeopardy. In his current mood, Korst would as likely turn his fury on Goron as on the Peaks. My son planned to proceed as slowly as possible, gathering men along the way, but there is a limit to how much he can delay without further enraging Korst. I expect they have arrived by now and can only hope they have been able to avoid a precipitous march to the border. That is why we have no time to waste."

"What makes Korst think the Peaks have any interest in disrupting life here?" asks Samuel.

"That I do not know, my friend. My fervent hope is that he is simply crazed by the loss of his son – the youngest was his favorite. He does not often lash out without a sound reason, but perhaps his reason is clouded by grief, and in his current state, the presence of the two men from the Peaks appear to him as evidence of betrayal.

"We must hear him out – he deserves that respect. But you have been friends with the Peaks far longer than we have, Alfred, so your voice will be important in the judgment we must make. And I believe you know Korst well enough to know he must hear the words directly from you if he is to give them any credence."

"My first thought," says Samuel, "is that a mere two men seems like a completely inadequate complement if someone were intent on sowing discord. Have there been other reports of strangers where one wouldn't expect them to be?"

"None that I am aware of," Egon replies.

"What if these two were a test?" Carew speculates. "Sent to determine how easy creating disruption might be."

"If such is the case," Egon again, "then it is all the more reason we must dissuade Korst from overreacting."

"Until we know more," I say, "it seems at least as likely they were just a couple of renegades as they were saboteurs acting at someone's behest."

"I am inclined to agree," says Egon. "I am also inclined to believe our horses have rested sufficiently to resume our former pace. My sense of urgency grows stronger with every hour that passes."

We urge the horses to a canter. Conversation for the remainder of our journey is subdued – even around the fire when we camp late at night for a few brief hours of sleep. Pleasantries seem out of place. Yet there's no merit in speculating further on the situation in the west until we can assess it for ourselves.

Our arrival at Korst's stronghold is barely noticed amid the frenzy of activity. The mine in question, it seems, is quite near the fortress, and there are men going back and forth constantly. Goron's army, while relatively small, is encamped on both sides of the approach to the fortress, with men there polishing arms or exercising horses and the camp followers tending the fires and preparing food.

Hedrek spies us first and takes us straight to the tent he and Goron are sharing. Goron can't disguise the relief that floods his face and his manner. "Father! Alfred!" He offers me his arm in the warrior's greeting and briefly embraces Egon. "And Samuel!" Again, the warrior's greeting.

Carew hangs back, and Goron hesitates. "The captain of my guard, Sir Edmund Carew," I supply. "He's rather disinclined to let me wander off alone."

Goron extends his arm and Carew steps forward to accept the greeting. "Welcome, Sir Edmund. My name is Goron, and I am in charge of this . . . well, whatever this is. We have not yet fully worked that out. This is Hedrek, without whose advice and assistance I would be at even more of a loss."

"If it please you, my lord, I rather prefer simply 'Carew.'" I'm surprised when Carew needs no translation and replies straightaway in Goron's tongue. Then I remember Samuel made this a requirement for every commandant of the western garrison, and Carew almost certainly held that post at some point.

"It's a long story," I add, "from a time when the number of Edmunds in our senior ranks was more than a little confusing."

"Then Carew it is," says Goron. "Please, join us. May I offer you some ale?"

"That would be most welcome, Son," says Egon. "It has been quite a hurried journey."

The six of us gather around a small camp table where mugs of ale quickly appear, brought by Goron's squire, who leaves just as quickly and closes the flap of the tent.

"I have gone to extremes, you will discover," says Goron, "to limit the amount of ale available. Small ale only for the men. This place is a tinderbox at the moment, and I cannot risk igniting a flame.

"Korst has been drunk ever since it happened, and he shows no sign of changing his habits. Owen, Narth, and Rusk are here, and they spend most of their time trying to reason with him – to no avail so far. He set all his men the task of digging through the collapse, which is an incredibly tedious process. There is no doubt Korst wants to retrieve his son's remains, but the eldest son told me it is equally important to find a way to regain access to the rich vein of tin they have been working in that mine. So I have allowed my men to help, in part to give them something to do, but I will not permit them to work at the edge of the rubble, where the risk is greatest. At least this single-minded attention on digging out has kept Korst from pressing me to march."

As Egon drains the last drop from his mug, the sounds from outside the tent start to escalate and the tent flap is flung aside as Goron's squire rushes in. Before the man can say a word, Goron's on his feet, headed outside. "This happens a couple of times a day," he says. "Come with me. You might as well see it firsthand."

We follow him toward the growing commotion along the path from the fortress toward what must be the mine. Trailed by several servants, Korst is weaving his way toward the mine, shouting at anyone in his path, with men scrambling to get out of his way. "Work faster, you bastards!" he rails, waving the mug he's carrying, the ale sloshing out right and left. "Can't you bastards do *anything* right? *Dig*! Dig with your hands if you have to." He downs a gulp of ale, apparently emptying the mug, which he tosses aside then turns on the servants behind him. "More ale!" he orders, then gets right in the face of the nearest man and shouts, "You saddle-goose, where's my ale?" The poor man takes off at a run back to the fortress.

By now we've arrived on the spot, and Goron takes Korst in hand. "Alright, Lord Korst, you've made your point. The men know you want them to work as fast as they can, so let's let them get on with it." He manages to get Korst pointed back toward the fortress. "Come on, sir, the ale is waiting for us back in the dining hall. Let's go."

Korst allows himself to be shepherded like a child as men scramble off the path and we follow behind. "You promise, Goron?"

"I promise, sir."

"They're digging to find my son, you know. They're going to find him, aren't they?"

"I'm sure they are, sir. They're working very hard."

The belligerence suddenly returns. "They damn well better be! I'll have every one of them thrown off the cliff if they don't find my son." And then just as suddenly, the broken child is back. "He's a good boy, my boy is. You know that, don't you, Goron? A good boy."

When we finally reach the dining hall, Owen, Narth, and Rusk are waiting. "I'm sorry, Goron," says Owen. "We couldn't stop him."

"Think nothing of it, Lord Owen."

Korst lurches for the mug of ale that the servants have left for him on the table and downs half of it in one gulp before turning around and realizing there are new people present. "Egon! You come at last. Where have you been?" He sways on his feet then, thankfully, sits down on the nearest bench before he topples over.

"We waited for Alfred, my friend."

"Alfred?" He stares, bleary-eyed, in my direction and then recognition penetrates the fog of inebriation. "Alfred!" He jumps to his feet, embraces me awkwardly, then plops back down on the bench. "You, I know." He points to Samuel. "But you?" The pointing finger moves to Carew.

"My name is Carew, Lord Korst. Captain of King Alfred's Guards."

"What happened to Tobin?" Korst may be drunk, but not entirely forgetful.

"He now trains our knights," Carew replies.

"Then you will have good knights." Korst pours what remains in his mug down his throat then bangs the mug on the table. A servant scurries up with a pitcher to refill it. "Ale for everyone!" he orders as he takes another swallow of his own.

The servants, clearly terrified of their master's mood, rush to do his bidding. No sooner do they return, handing each of us a mug, than Korst orders "Drink!" and glares at us to be sure we comply. The toast – if it can be called that – finished, he goes on. "Now that everyone is here, we can finally do something about that villainous Peaks king. How *dare* he send his minions to mess with me?"

"Are you certain he did?" I venture.

Another swig of ale and then, "And how dare you question me, Alfred? I know what I know, and don't you forget that. It was *you* who convinced us to trust that bastard. Maybe *you're* the one responsible for my son's fate." He empties the mug, turns to put it down, and slumps over the table, passed out. The servants rush to collect him and carry him from the room.

"Pay him no mind, Alfred," says Egon. "None of us blame you."

"This is what happens every day," says Narth. "He will sleep for a couple hours then be back down here for the evening meal."

"And afterward, he drinks brandy until he passes out once again," adds Rusk.

"Brandy?" Samuel asks.

"Aye," says Owen. "My boats bring it from across the sea during the summer trading season."

"It is rather dreadful stuff – not at all like what you serve, Alfred," says Egon, "but fit for purpose if a man is not too picky."

"We have tried our best to get him sober," Narth resumes. "Even poured out a whole barrel of ale, only to discover that he had another cellar half full of more barrels."

"We considered shutting down the brewery for a time," says Rusk, "but somehow Korst got wind of it and threatened to lock us all in his dungeon if we interfered with the brewers."

"When we discovered how much brandy he was drinking," says Narth, "we ordered the servants to hide the casks. That worked for exactly one day before Korst figured it out and demanded that every cask be moved into his room."

"And it's useless to try to sneak anything out of there while he's abed," says Owen. "No matter how deeply he sleeps – how loudly he snores – he comes awake at the least sound, in an utter rage, shouting and throwing things until the intruder leaves. I tried it one time, hoping to remove at least one of the casks, and was lucky to escape without him realizing who I was. I have no wish to attempt that again."

"But you're right, my friends," I say. "We have to get him sober before we can get to the bottom of this."

"I may be able to help with that," says Carew. "Let me fetch my pack from Lord Goron's tent."

While we wait, I ask those who have been here through most of the chaos, "Have you been able to discover any clues as to what really happened?"

Narth seems to be the spokesman. "Very little beyond what I am certain Egon has already told you. The bodies of the two newly hired men were found near the outer edge of the rubble. In fact, you can see them for yourselves if you can stand the stench. Korst refuses to let them be buried until his son is found – says they can rot like the devils they were."

"I think we should have a look," says Samuel. "Perhaps there's a clue in their clothing or their weapons, if they had any."

"Very well," says Narth, "we will go when Carew returns. But I hope you will not be offended if my friends and I choose to stand well back. We have already had our noses assaulted sufficiently." Owen and Rusk both grimace.

"There is one thing that continues to puzzle me, Alfred," Narth continues. "I was here when those two were hired. They spoke our language quite badly, but enough to say what they wanted. When they spoke between themselves, they did speak the Peaks language if others were around. But when they thought no one was listening, they used a tongue I have never heard before."

"Is there any possibility it was a dialect from the far north highlands?" I ask.

"I cannot say with any certainty. I know only that I could not understand them. And that has made me suspicious of their origin."

By now Carew is back carrying a small vial of clear liquid. "What is this you have?" asks Egon.

"A tincture to ease a man's pain, given to me by our healers. Whenever my king goes off on one of his adventures without a proper entourage, I carry a vial of this in case he should be injured or in pain and I need to ease his suffering in order to get him back home. It has another property that I think may be useful here. A few drops in a small draught of brandy will cause a man to sleep uninterrupted for many hours. And we need Lord Korst to sleep until the toxins of excess drink have left his body. That's the only way to get him sober."

He hands the vial to Narth, who asks, "And how do we administer this? Will Korst notice a vile taste in his brandy?"

"Our healers tell me the brandy disguises the taste. Put three drops in his brandy tonight and he should sleep until morning. And then I recommend another dose of the medicine when he wakes – and another if necessary – so he sleeps all through the following day and night. He'll be a growling bear with a ferocious headache when he finally wakes up, but he'll be sober. And then perhaps we can discuss things with him more rationally."

"Will not the brandy in which we put the medicine keep him drunk?" asks Rusk.

"It requires very little brandy, my lord. And the medicine acts rather quickly, I'm told. When we finally get him sober, he'll need broth and bread to counteract the headache and the sour stomach he may feel after so many days of inebriation."

"Thank you for this, Carew," says Narth. "Perhaps we should also beseech our various deities that it may succeed. Now, shall we go view the bodies?"

"Let's get it over with," says Samuel.

We could have simply followed our noses and not imposed the grizzly ordeal on anyone else. The three western lords stop well shy of the site. Five more steps and the rest of us instinctively pull some part of our clothing over our noses and mouths, though it does very little good. Absent any attention from an embalmer, the bodies are decaying in the sun. "It's astonishing that predators haven't already made short shrift of them," I remark.

"Probably because there's round-the-clock activity at the mine with fires burning all night," says Goron. "But it looks like the maggots are moving in." He kicks the leg of one of the dead men, exposing a white, wormy mess.

Flies hovering around the corpses encourage us to make our observations quickly. The facial features offer no specific hint as to their heritage. The clothes are quite ordinary – nothing to identify where the men might have come from. A small emblem decorates each tunic, but offers no clues. It might be a clan sign from the highlands, but it could equally be no more than a talisman to ward off evil. It's certainly not the dragon and castle of the King of Peaks.

We turn back to rejoin those who are waiting for us.

"Someone should bury them no matter what Korst says," Egon remarks.

"I had some men try once, Father," says Goron, "and they almost wound up in the dungeon for their troubles."

"Perhaps we should take advantage of the time while he sleeps to do the deed," Egon suggests. "If it should rain, this rot will wash into the stream and foul the water for days or even weeks. If Korst objects, then we appeal to him on the basis of keeping his water supply safe for brewing."

"I wish I had thought of that," says Goron. "My men will take care of it as soon as Korst is carried to his bed tonight."

"Considerations for the water aside, Goron," I say, "it may be just as well they weren't buried before we arrived. At least this way, all of us have seen them and Korst can't argue that we don't know what we're talking about."

The others join us as we return to the fortress. "What did you think?" asks Narth.

"That I'm very glad Goron is going to have them buried while Korst sleeps off his drunkenness," I reply.

"That can't happen soon enough," says Owen, wrinkling his nose.

We spend the following day exercising our horses and catching up on events in our lives. Egon asks about Geoffrey. "Does he not come of age soon?"

"A bit less than a year. Osbert helped me find a young man to be his squire and will begin training him in June."

"And surely the time is near when he must have a wife," says Rusk.

"That's a project that has begun to weigh heavily on my mind of late."

They all laugh. "Finding a woman that pleases both the father and the son is not an easy task," says Owen.

Not wanting to draw further attention to Geoffrey's prospective bride at this point, I steer the conversation toward the horses we acquired from Denis – the ones from across the Roman Sea. They're all quite keen to see the breed. And, quite logically, the question of Denis's impending birthday arises. "I should quite like to meet this young king," says Goron. "Especially since we played a part in preserving his kingdom."

"I believe he is of like mind, though a bit uncertain how to arrange it."

"Perhaps you could host a visit, Alfred," says Narth.

"That's certainly a possibility. Or perhaps Goron could organize a gathering of the lords here so that all of you could converse with Denis without having to consider my sensibilities." I hope I haven't overplayed my hand. The barest hint of a smile when Egon catches my eye dispels that concern.

It's midmorning of the following day before Korst finally reappears, wandering into the dining hall where we've been debating how to pass the time. The ominous clouds quickly vetoed a ride, none of us wanting to get soaked should the skies open while we were out in the meadows. Korst is utterly disheveled – hair uncombed, clothes wrinkled and awry from having been slept in – and he holds one hand to his head. "How long did I sleep?" he asks, settling onto a bench beside the main table.

"A night, an entire day, and the whole night following," says Owen.

"And with a herd of cattle stomping on my head?"

"My friend," says Narth, "you exceeded even your own prodigious capacity for drink. What you feel is what lesser men suffer after too many rounds of ale of an evening. It will pass."

A servant brings a bowl of broth and half a loaf of bread, sets it in front of Korst, and hurries out, apparently eager to avoid his master's wrath. Korst looks at the steaming broth and turns to us, "What is that?"

"The fastest way to ease the pounding in your head," says Owen.

Korst eyes the bowl again then picks up the bread and tears off a corner, plopping it into his mouth. He chews with some difficulty then pronounces, "It's dry."

"The bread is fresh," says Owen. "It's your mouth that is dry."

"Try dipping the bread in the broth," I offer. "That's how I was taught to do it when I was near starvation or recovering from illness."

"But I haven't been ill," says Korst.

"Perhaps not," says Owen, "but the sooner you eat that bread and drink that broth, the sooner you'll feel like yourself once again."

While we encourage Korst to eat, we're all hoping the servants are engaged on another matter. Narth gave instructions this morning that, as soon as Korst was with us, they were to remove the brandy casks from his room and return them to the cellar.

Once Korst finally gets all the bread and broth consumed, he predictably asks for ale. "Best stick to broth for now," says Owen, "unless you want to turn your stomach inside out and spew everything you just ate all over us." Korst's glare would intimidate a servant, but Owen remains steadfast. "Trust me, my friend. It is how those lesser men recover their senses. Something even *I* have had to do more than once."

"Then get me some more broth. I'm so dry I won't be able to piss for a week."

Owen heads for the kitchens and returns with the broth – a smaller bowl this time. Korst won't thank us if he makes himself sick by overdoing the cure.

With that bowl emptied, Korst seems ready to take charge. "Now, my friends, it's time to do something about the Peaks. Goron's men are ready. It's time to march." Our worst fears are realized – that once he was sober, he'd turn his attention to revenge.

"Perhaps we should discuss that," says Goron. "Right now, my men are helping yours dig out. If we leave, the work will go ever so much more slowly."

"Then let it. If we delay, we'll look weak."

"I'm still curious, my friend. I know you're certain the Peaks king is responsible, but could you explain that to me?" I do my best to appeal to Korst's good sense. "Could those men not have been renegades just bent on causing mischief somewhere for their own amusement?"

"Mischief? Is that what you call it?"

"Destruction then."

"Who goes to another man's domain to wreak havoc unless they've been ordered to?"

"Maybe you've forgotten that I was taken captive because some renegades did just that."

"That's irrelevant. The saboteurs came from the Peaks. The Peaks must pay. Goron, when can you be ready to march?"

Before Goron can answer, Narth intervenes. "I know you think time is of the essence, my friend, but it seems to me we should try to discover the truth before we act. If we invade the Peaks and later discover they were not responsible, we'll have caused irreparable harm to a neighbor who's done us no wrong."

"Let me help you get to the bottom of things," I offer. "Something about this doesn't seem right. Something here stinks, and it isn't the bodies of the saboteurs, if that's even what they were."

"Something stinks, alright," says Korst. "And I want to get rid of the stench. Goron, when can you be ready to march?"

Goron has little choice but to answer. "In two days, my lord."

"Then two days it will be." Korst is single-minded.

There's nothing for it – I have to put a stop to the madness. "Lord Korst, I beg you. Don't invade the Peaks. My son is there at this moment, with his prospective bride."

"*And my son is at the bottom of that mine!*" Korst lunges at me in fury, stopping with his face only inches from mine.

Carew is on his feet in an instant, but I quickly wave him away. Samuel hasn't moved. He knows. If I'm to retain Korst's respect, I can't show even the slightest bit of fear.

And then it all comes out. Korst falls to his knees, his head in his hands, tears flowing down his cheeks. "It's all my fault, Alfred. *Mine.* I hired those men. My gut said they couldn't be trusted, but they said they'd worked the copper mines. So I hired them anyway because we needed more workers. And now my son lies buried at the bottom of a pile of rubble." He slumps to the floor, hands covering his face. "The boy I loved. He's gone, and I've only myself to blame." The twin pains of grief and guilt that he'd suppressed with drink come pouring out in a flood of tears. It's more than any man should have to endure.

Goron steps in and crouches beside him. "Come with me, Lord Korst. Let's go upstairs so your manservant can get you cleaned up and into some fresh clothes. Then you'll feel more like helping us all figure out what's best to do."

When they've gone, no one says a word until Goron's return. "Thank you for helping him preserve his dignity, Son," says Egon.

"Goron has a way with Korst," says Narth. "More even than any of us. I've been grateful for his presence over these terrible days."

The man who returns an hour later is the Korst I remember. We join him in a midday meal of broth and bread, and as he wipes his bowl clean with a morsel of bread, it seems even his sense of humor has returned. "Don't tell anyone, Alfred," he says conspiratorially, "but I've seen Owen even drunker than me."

"Really?" I play along.

"But I'd wager you a barrel of ale he's never had as much broth as I've drunk this morning." He roars with laughter and pops the morsel of bread into his mouth.

Sober – and having finally faced his demons – Korst's good spirits return. He's even able to shrug off the fact that we buried the rotting corpses against his orders. "You did it for the sake of the ale, my friends. That, I can forgive." We owe Mother Nature a debt of gratitude for the day's stormy skies that give credence to our explanation.

Over the course of that afternoon and the following day, we manage to get him to agree to let me try to get to the truth about the two renegades. "And how long will this take?" he finally asks.

"I can't be certain," I reply. "How long will it take to finish excavating the collapsed mine?"

"If Goron will leave some men here to help, maybe a month."

"Very well. Once you've given your son a proper burial, we'll meet again and talk about what I've discovered and what, if anything, is to be done."

"That, I can agree to, my friend."

"Good. And when we meet, I'll bring you some proper brandy and we can drink a toast to your son."

"I'd like that, Alfred. I'd like that very much."

As Samuel, Carew, and I ride away the next morning, Samuel asks, "Do you think he'll stay sober?"

"I think he just might – at least as much as he ever does." We both chuckle. "The pain won't go away any time soon, but he's finally faced it. And the sooner we can find something that helps him know he's not to blame, the sooner he can start to heal."

The relief I feel at seeing Geoffrey's horse in the stable when we arrive back at the castle can't be expressed in words. We turn our own horses over to Mervyn Lightfoot, the other grooms being busy with feeding. "The same ones what ye be leaving with." Mervyn grins. "Me da'll be pleased."

"They deserve a bit of extra ration tonight, Mervyn. We've been riding since just after sunrise."

"Yer own mounts be glad ye be back, m'lords. I be giving 'em some exercise now and again, but it not be the same as the routine when ye be here. And I work Regulus a bit too, when I not be teaching Miss Alicia, on account of I know ye be planning to ride him soon."

"How's Alicia doing with her pony, Mervyn?"

"She learn fast, m'lord. And now she be wanting me to teach her how to jump. I try to take her mind off'n it, but she be onto me in a flash."

"Mervyn, *please* tell me you're not letting her jump that pony."

"Dinna' ye fret, m'lord. Only thing I be letting her jump be a fallen branch here and there, and nought bigger than a man's forearm. The pony could step right over it, but he seem to be knowing she like him to leap across."

"I'll make sure she knows that's all she's allowed until I say otherwise."

"I be thinking mayhap that be a good idea, m'lord. That girl have a mind of her own, fer certes."

It being Thursday and quite late in the afternoon, I only have time for a hot bath and a change of clothes before it's time to go down to the court dinner. Geoffrey is less than forthcoming when I ask him about his journey. "It was good, Papa. We can talk about it tomorrow." There's no way to tell from his manner if this is because he's had some sort of disappointment or if he just doesn't want to fuel court gossip. So it's the first question out of my mouth when Gwen and I climb into bed.

"Oh, he's just missing Eirwen. Probably a little tired of people asking him questions when he doesn't know what the final outcome will be. But mostly, he's just missing Eirwen."

"Oh, dear. Are we going to have a love-sick goose on our hands for the next year?"

She laughs softly. "Well, you wouldn't know anything about that since we married only a month after I arrived here." She kisses my cheek. "Don't worry. As soon as he knows what the future holds, he'll be back to his old self. And probably writing letters to her every chance he gets."

"Sounds like you know something I don't."

She opens the drawer of her bedside table and retrieves a folded page. The seal has been broken. "I took the liberty of reading it, not knowing when you'd be back. And I have to admit, I was quite proud of Geoffrey that he didn't succumb to the temptation to open it himself."

My turn to chuckle as I take the page and begin to read.

My dear Alfred,

I write this letter as much to please Eirwen as to affirm my own satisfaction with the results of our little experiment. It is difficult for me to say which gives me the greatest delight: that our kingdoms will soon be allied by marriage, that your son chose to honor my daughter by escorting her home, or that you so successfully thwarted my sister's efforts to impose her outdated ideas on the young people.

Observing Eirwen and Geoffrey together during his brief stay here confirmed for me your assessment that they are quite well suited for each other. So there remains only for us to agree the terms of the contract and announce the betrothal to our respective courts.

Morfyl will no doubt think it necessary to place even greater strictures on Eirwen's behavior once the betrothal is known, but rest assured that it would please me to know they are corresponding or even contemplating the occasional visit during this time before their marriage.

I fold the page and set it aside. "We should tell him in the morning – not keep him fretting any longer."

"Why don't we tell him now?" Gwen asks.

"Why not indeed." I climb out of bed and step into my dressing room to ask Osbert to fetch Geoffrey.

He arrives in short order, a robe thrown over his nightshirt, running a hand over his hair as if trying to get fully awake. "You sent for me, Papa?"

Gwen and I have donned our own robes and moved to the seating area beside the hearth. I hand him the letter. "Take a seat. I think you should read this."

Still a bit sleepy-eyed, he unfolds the page. As he reads, his face lights up. He starts to fold the page, then smooths it out and reads it again before handing it back to me. "Tell me I'm not dreaming."

Gwen reaches over to touch his hand. "Feel that?"

"Aye, Mama."

"You're not dreaming."

"I'll be sending Lord Thorssen straightaway to negotiate the contract," I tell him. "Eirwen's father wants to announce the betrothal as part of her birthday celebration."

"Can I go back for that?"

"Sounds like a wonderful idea to me, Son, so I'll make sure Phillip asks that very question. Of course, you know that means you have to put up with Lady Morfyl again."

"To hell with Morfyl!" Gwen and I both laugh out loud. "Sorry, Papa." Geoffrey tries but doesn't quite succeed at being contrite. "It's only that . . . well, I'll get to see Eirwen again and that's what matters."

"Very well, off to bed with you." Gwen rises and kisses our son on top of the head. "I'm really glad you're happy. She's quite a lovely young lady."

Geoffrey kisses his mother, gives me a quick embrace, then practically dances out of the room. As we climb back into bed, Gwen says, "You goaded him into that outburst about Morfyl."

"Aye, but wasn't it fun to see him let his guard down?" We both laugh.

We talk long into the night as I tell her everything about the trip to the Territories. "The other part of my mission for Phillip is to find out if the Peaks king has any clues as to what might have happened at that mine."

"You don't think—"

"Not for a minute. I can't believe he'd negotiate with me so openly over this marriage while at the same time striking at those I also consider allies. I can't even imagine what kind of strategic reasoning would lead *anyone* to do something like that. There's something wrong that I can't yet figure out. That's why I want Addiena to go as well. Her cousin might say something to her that he wouldn't reveal directly to Phillip. Do you think she'll forgive me for sending her into Morfyl's lair?"

"This soon, you might be pressing it a bit. But it occurs to me that commiserating with her cousin over his sister's old-fashioned notions might be just the sort of conversation that would get him to open up to her about anything else. Just tell her what you need and why."

"Maybe you should tell her."

"Oh, no. I was the one who begged her to help out with Morfyl. Now it's *your* turn to ask for favors."

• • • • • •

I'm surprised to find Rupert at court, but soon learn why. He waylays me as I return from the stable after my morning ride. "Care for a turn around the garden?"

"Why not? Coliar's pile of documents can wait."

"News from Laurence," he says. "He thought you'd want to know straightaway rather than waiting for your next trip to the manor, and I agree."

"That sounds ominous."

"It may be. It's looking as if Gunnvor is almost ready to launch his campaign. The lords he's gathered around him have sent another two wagonloads of arms back to their strongholds – and each man went with the last wagon. Speculation is that they went back to lead their own men in whatever's about to happen. The minder had more information than Gunhild this time. It seems Gunnvor isn't speaking as freely around his sister as has been his custom."

"Any better clues as to Gunnvor's intentions?"

"Gunhild still thinks he plans to attack the king and try to put himself on the throne. According to her, he's still heard to boast, 'My time's almost here. Won't be long until I get what I deserve.'"

"Not the news I wanted to hear."

"Nor I. But hardly a surprise."

"I just wish we could get even a glimmer of what their deployments are."

"Laurence has sent both Gunhild and her minder back in with that as their mission."

"Very well. I'll tell Jasper to be prepared. He's ready to send three more troops to the garrison on a moment's notice, and I suspect he'll do just that. I don't know if Richard will call the Council together now or if he'll want to wait until Laurence's next update."

"I'll talk to Richard," says Rupert. "You see to Jasper."

Jasper chooses to act, ordering the three troops to leave the following morning. Richard chooses to demur. "I've spoken with all the lords privately," he tells me, "and to a man, they want whatever we can learn about the deployments before we meet to decide our course of action. I just hope that insight's not long in coming."

Two nights later, Gwen and I are enjoying a quiet supper in her sitting room with Juliana and Rainard – the boys dining with their mates and Alicia with Nurse – when there's a sharp, insistent knock on the door. Gwen rises to answer it, and Carew rushes in.

"Forgive me, Your Grace." He's somewhat breathless, as if he's run to get here. We're all instantly on edge, not knowing what the danger might be. "Sire, I thought this couldn't wait. I—" He stops short, as if suddenly aware we're not alone.

"Go on, Carew. If it's that urgent, you can speak freely."

"Sire, it's just come to me. Those emblems on the tunics of the saboteurs at Korst's mine. I've had this nagging feeling for days that I've seen those emblems somewhere before, and it's finally come to me. They're the same emblems we saw in the forest – worn by the Teuton king's guards."

"Are you certain, Carew?"

"As certain as I am the sun rises in the east, Sire. Those men were Teutons."

"Please, Carew," says Gwen, indicating a vacant chair. "Sit."

"But how, Carew?" I ask. "How ever did they get there? And why?"

"God only knows how they got there, Sire. But I've no doubt about who they were. It explains what Lord Narth told us about their speech – their accents and the fact that they spoke another tongue when they were alone. As for the why, Lord Korst has the right end of that stick. Disruption among our allies. I suspect that if they hadn't botched the mine collapse and gotten themselves killed, they had orders to move on and create more havoc elsewhere. Pitting the Territories against the Peaks would have been step one. Then they'd try to turn one or the other of those against us."

"There's logic in what you say, but why not do it all masquerading as Peaksmen or someone from the Territories or even us? Surely that would be a more effective way to create discord and distrust."

"I've thought about that, Sire. Perhaps they assumed no one would take notice of the emblems – or if they did, put them down to some kind of talisman or religious symbol. But I think it's more than that. I think we're being sent a message." He pauses for effect. "Think about it, Sire. If they hadn't gotten killed and had carried on with their orders, people would have started noticing – men wearing the same unfamiliar emblem. Word would get to us."

The room goes utterly quiet. My mind is overwrought with the import of Carew's words. At long last, I break the silence.

"Truth be told, Carew, those emblems have troubled me since I first saw them. But since I couldn't pin anything down, I've tried to explain them away. Your scenario makes far more sense than the notion that the King of Peaks would be behind this. We need to get word to Goron and Korst straightaway – before Korst loses faith in my promise to get to the bottom of things."

"I'll go," says Carew. "I can leave Cedric in charge here."

"I appreciate that, Carew, but it needs to be someone they have a history with. Something tells me there's some urgency and that there's not time to send for Lord Emaurri and have him carry the message. Samuel would be ideal, but I need him here." In truth, I'm thinking out loud in the moment.

"I'll go, sir," says Rainard. "I think Goron now counts me as a friend. And, of course, they all know my wife is your daughter."

"And I'll go with him," says Juliana.

"No, my dear," says Rainard. "A man on horseback can travel more quickly than the carriage."

"Are you sure, Rainard?" I ask.

"Quite sure, sir. Give me a letter in your own hand, and I'll see that it reaches those who need to know. I may not be able to get there as fast as you or my brother could, but get there I will."

"Then I'll write the letter tonight."

"And I'll leave at first light."

At first, I lie awake, my mind whirling with the implications of Carew's revelation. And then I fall into a deep sleep, my dreams peopled with Teutons, drunken cardinals, ginger-haired kidnappers, trading ships, and deer in flowery meadows. When Osbert touches my shoulder to wake me – "Ye said ye be wanting to go riding early, m'lord," he whispers – I'm instantly awake but momentarily disoriented.

Shaking my head to snap myself back to reality, I climb carefully out of bed, hoping not to disturb Gwen, and tiptoe into my dressing room. "Thank you, Osbert." He closes the door behind me. "Strange dreams last night. Let's hope a hot bath will clear the cobwebs."

At the stable, I'm surprised to find Samuel saddling his horse. "Just saw Rainard off and thought you might use some company this morning."

Mervyn Lightfoot leads Altair up, saddled and ready to go. As I check my gear, I ask, "How'd you know I'd be coming out early this morning, Mervyn?"

"Word from Osbert. He always try to be sure we be ready fer ye and not be surprised." Another glimpse into the complex world of squire to a king. Ah, young Robin, you've no idea yet how much you have to learn.

As soon as we're out of earshot of the stable, I ask Samuel, "Rainard told you?"

"Aye. Don't be miffed. He wanted my advice to be sure he got this mission right, and he knew I'd been with you at Korst's."

"Actually, I'm pleased. You've had time to think about it. All I've had is nightmares."

"Teutons, Alfred?"

"That's one thing I did manage to think clearly about. Carew's right. I don't know why I didn't make the connection sooner. Too intent on just proving that it had nothing to do with the Peaks, I suppose."

"How did they get there?"

"Any number of ways. They could even have just walked off a ship and wandered our own roads like ordinary travelers. No one would've paid them much mind."

"But why?"

"Distraction? Denis's birthday is coming up and maybe the Teuton king wants to divert our attention while he plots something across the sea. If he can keep us looking in the wrong direction and create in-fighting with our allies, it would be harder for us to support Denis in a conflict there. But the latest reports from Denis and from Peveril say everything is quiet."

"Just as well, though, that Jasper's ready."

"There's something else."

"What?"

"I know Richard told you about the latest reports from the East. I think it's time to send a scout in. We have to find out which way their backs are turned, and I don't think the people Laurence can get in there right now are equipped to assess a military deployment."

"I agree. Do you still want to send Cedric?"

"I do."

"If he doesn't know anything about scouting, I still think you'd be better served by an experienced scout."

"Only one way to find out. You find Cedric, I'll find Carew, and we'll meet at the hut."

We urge the horses to a canter and hurry back to the stable. In less than half an hour, all four of us are perched on stools inside the abandoned hut. It takes another quarter of an hour for me to bring my guards into the picture on what's afoot in the east – the carefully edited version, of course. "What we have to know without delay is what Gunnvor's deployments look like – if they're any threat to us. But Samuel and I can't agree on how to get that information. He says it has to be an experienced scout. I insist it has to be someone I already trust to keep my secrets."

A half smile appears on Cedric's face. "What if I could keep you both happy?"

"Oh?" I ask.

"I scouted quite a bit as a young knight. My great-uncle recommended it – said it was the best way to learn how to get inside the enemy's head." The Sir Cedric of legend. My grandfather's most trusted knight. The man who taught Samuel and me everything we know about fighting. "The question is just how to get in."

"That, we have an answer for," says Samuel, sharing a knowing look with Carew. "Have you ever patrolled our southeast border?"

"No. Patrols rarely go there."

"Well, the three of us have been there. It's completely wild and a perfect place to infiltrate without being seen by a soul. What few maps there are don't have any of the landmarks and very few of the trails, but Carew has one that we marked while we were there. He can show you the best ways in and out without going anywhere near the main border crossing."

"So when would you want me to go, Sire?" Cedric asks.

"How soon can you be ready?"

My anxiety through the week that follows knows no bounds. It's impossible to know how long it will take Cedric to complete his mission, yet each time there's a knock on a door or a rider comes into the courtyard, I can't help but experience a spark of hope that it's him. Sparks that are all extinguished as quickly as they flare. Carew dispatched a fast courier to Phillip with a message about the identity of the saboteurs. But until Phillip returns, I can't rest easy that the Peaks king knows the truth of what was being perpetrated in his name. And until Rainard returns, there's no assurance that Korst might not get bees in his head and do something rash and unfortunate. On top of all this, Denis's birthday looms like a beacon on a hill.

Coliar's stacks of documents fill barely an hour of each day. Working with the horses is usually soothing, but I dare not try riding Regulus for the first time in this frame of mind. He'd pick up on my nervousness in a flash and associate it with the idea of a rider on his back. Even a visit to the monastery is out of the question lest something crucial should happen while I'm gone.

I'm strung as tight as a bowstring, so when Coliar announces "Lord Peveril, Sire" I almost literally fly out of my chair, so unexpected is his arrival.

"Why so jumpy, Alfred?" he asks as we take our seats in front of the hearth.

I spend the next half hour relating all that's happened here in recent weeks and watching his expression grow increasingly cloudy. When I finish, he says, "I'm afraid my news is only going to add to your worry. Petronilla sent me home. Partially for my own safety, but mostly as a messenger to you. Things have changed drastically in the ten days before I left. All of the villages within a day of Denis's border are now occupied by Teuton soldiers. Most of the villagers fled when the soldiers arrived. And there's an armed camp, growing by the hour, just two days away from Aleffe province. They must have been assembling their army deep inside the Teuton kingdom – far deeper than any spies could reach – and are now moving things into position. There's little doubt, Alfred. Aleffe province and the port are the targets."

I drop my head into my hands in dismay. It couldn't be any worse. And yet, we couldn't have acted before the threat was manifest. Struggling to take it all in, I step to the door and ask Coliar to send for Richard, Samuel, Jasper, and Carew, then make my way back to my chair. "If there's more, let's save it for after they arrive so you don't have to repeat yourself."

Coliar must have threatened his messenger with the king's wrath, because all four of them arrive in a rush and stop short just inside the door when they catch sight of Peveril. "Find a chair, gentlemen," I say. "Peveril, tell them what you just told me."

Richard's face goes white. Jasper and Carew are stoic, but their expressions tell me they're already doing the mental calculations for what our next actions should be. "What's Denis's response?" asks Samuel.

"He's concentrated his forces in Aleffe province, but he has a thin line spread south along the border in case of an assault from any of the villages. That's where he's most vulnerable, but he can't risk leaving the back door wide open. His ship captains all have orders to put to sea at the first sign of a Teuton vessel. Their job will be to try to block access to the port from that direction.

"The moment we saw movement begin, Denis sent a fast courier to his ally in the Kingdom East of Rome, asking them to fortify their border with the Teutons and be ready to launch an attack to create a two-front war. The messenger returned just before I left. They'll be no help. They're under orders from the Pope to do nothing. The Holy Father's message, it seems, was that this is a simple dispute between two neighboring kingdoms, and it's God's will that they should sort it out between themselves. But just to be sure his message was heeded, he added a promise of excommunication of every living soul in the kingdom should God's will be ignored."

Everyone in the room sits in stunned silence, each communing with their own thoughts. After several moments, Peveril breaks the tension. "You know, gentlemen, I've been thinking about that business with the two Teutons in the Territories. This is only speculation, but if I'm right, it may add another dimension to what we're all pondering." He pauses.

"Go on," I tell him. "It can hardly get much worse than this."

"Just before Easter . . . when Denis sent Suidbert to the Lakes to arrange another state visit . . . I think Denis may have told you, Alfred, that they were sailing from Lamoreaux to the Lakes port on the Western Sea."

"Aye. His logic was sound – having mariners who knew those waters in case that route ever became of tactical importance."

"Well, they were delayed several days in returning, and it had nothing to do with the weather or the sea. Seems two of their seamen went missing. That happens from time to time so it wasn't really a surprise. Usually, the miscreants are found in a brothel or tavern somewhere, passed out from drink or otherwise neglecting duty. Occasionally, they'll turn up at the ship a day late, much the worse for wear. But these two couldn't be found anywhere. It was as if they had vanished into thin air. The captain had to hire two men from the Lakes to complete his crew, and all that took time to organize. As I said, I'm just speculating, but in light of what happened in the Territories, I can't help but wonder if Suidbert is somehow involved. It was, after all, his idea to use that route."

"You think he's in league with the Teuton king again?" asks Richard.

"More likely," I supply, "the Teuton is using Suidbert, still dangling him on a string with threats of the dungeon master. But that doesn't make Suidbert any less of a threat to Denis. We have to get word to Denis to watch out for sabotage from within his own court."

Silence descends again, interrupted by the door opening to admit a rather scruffy-looking individual. A week's growth of beard, well-worn clothes, a farmer's cap in his hands, but sturdy boots. What is Coliar thinking?

And then recognition dawns. "Cedric! Good God, man, what's happened to you?"

"Scout's disguise, Sire, but this can't wait. It's Teutons, Sire. Hundreds and hundreds of them. Maybe thousands. In those big meadows you described. Nary a deer or any other creature in sight. Not even a bird. Nothing but Teutons as far as the eye can see."

"Were you spotted?" asks Jasper.

Before Cedric can answer, the door opens once again to reveal Laurence shoving Gunhild inside. Her hands are tied behind her back and her clothes are disheveled and soiled.

"What the hell, Laurence?"

"I'm sorry, Alfred. She came back armed. Stabbed her minder but didn't do any serious harm. Either she's completely inept with a dagger or she just used that as a distraction to get away. By the time the minder got to me with word of where she was going, she had a good head start. We caught up with her not far from town, and she put up a hell of a fight. Bit two of my men and kicked the third one in the bollocks. But we finally got her subdued. Then she started screaming she had to see you or she'd be killed. She wouldn't shut up, so I just gave up and brought her here." He shoves her ahead of him a few more steps so she's facing me.

"Give me paper," she says. When Laurence doesn't comply straightaway, she shouts, "Give paper! Untie and give paper. Stranger with black eyes say I no put paper in king's hands myself, he kill me."

My mind is reeling. Holy Mother of God! How is it that no one thought to mention the stranger's eyes?

By now, Coliar has fetched the guards, so Laurence reluctantly unties her, retrieves a folded page from his pocket, and hands it to her. She steps toward me, the message in her outstretched hand. "Take." When I don't do so immediately, she shakes it in my face and shouts, "Take!" As I extend my hand, she spits on my boots and mutters, "Swine. All men swine."

Seven pairs of eyes are trained on the message in a hand that I struggle to keep from trembling. My heart pounding, I slowly break the nondescript seal and unfold the page.

Now you must choose. Your kingdom or the boy's. It is time for the debt to be paid.

Author's Notes

As cannons became more widely used, it soon became apparent that traditional hilltop fortresses – which relied on the terrain and skilled archers to repel an assault – were not well suited for the new style of warfare. Their walls could be breached fairly easily by cannon balls, and the circular towers (and the often curved shape of the curtain walls) resulted in blind spots that the defenders could not cover with crossfire. By the middle of the fifteenth century, bastion forts – sometimes called star forts because of their shape – had displaced hilltop fortresses. Bastion forts have lower, much thicker walls, and their rectilinear geometry provides better sight lines for the defenders. Such forts often have ditches in front of the walls as an impediment to keep the enemy at a distance where fire from within the fort is most effective.

In this volume, Alfred's commanders are just beginning to come to grips with the deficiencies of the hilltop fortress and trying to work out what new style of fortification might be better suited to cannon warfare.

Near the end of the fourteenth century, the new forms in art and music that would blossom throughout the Renaissance began to appear. These included the use of oil (rather than egg yolks) as a base for paints, highly realistic renderings of people and of textures, and the spread of polyphonic music once the Church lifted its ban.

Silverpoint is a technique for drawing that uses a fine silver wire held in a stylus (in some sources, the silver wire and not the holder is referred to as the stylus). The artist draws fine lines on a sheet of paper prepared with some sort of primer, such as gesso. To create shadows or features such as hair or even eyes, many such fine lines must be laid down close together. Over time, the silver tarnishes, rendering an almost pencil-like image. Silverpoint drawing requires considerable technique, since the lines cannot be erased. But in the hands of a talented artist, silverpoint can produce a very lifelike result.

Medieval and Renaissance artists routinely used silverpoint to produce studies before actually beginning a painting. Many of these studies have been preserved, and it is intriguing to see them side-by-side with the finished painting. Some later artists carried the technique well into the 17th century. But after the discovery of graphite, silverpoint fell into disuse.

Alfred's frequent visits to the monastery bring him into regular contact with the rhythm of the monastic day and the services associated with specific hours (the Divine Office). There are ample sources of information online about this topic and how the Divine Office evolved over the centuries. I've used the hours and services of the monastic day from the Middle Ages. The first hour of the day was considered to be 6:00 a.m., and the hours and services are as follows:

- Prime – the first hour, 6:00 a.m.
- Terce – the third hour, 9:00 a.m.
- Sext – the sixth hour, noon
- Nones – the ninth hour, 3:00 p.m.
- Vespers – around 6:00 p.m. – at the time for the lighting of the evening lamps

- Compline – often around 7:00 p.m. – a service held just before retiring for the night
- Matins – held during the early morning hours (what we would call the "wee hours of the morning"), typically around 2:00 or 3:00 a.m.
- Lauds – the dawn service, its precise time varying through the seasons

This novel is a work of fiction that tells the story of what might have been in a world that doesn't precisely correspond to the one we know. Readers will note similarities with northern Europe, but my decision to fictionalize the setting was a matter of practicality for my characters. European history from this period and its major actors are too well known for it to be plausible that a different set of kings and nobility might actually have existed.

I began this series as an allegory of modern times, and the allegory is still there for readers who care to look. Since then, however, so many readers have commented on how attached they've grown to Alfred and the people around him and how eager they are to discover what happens next. For a novelist, such remarks are truly heartwarming, and I'm deeply grateful that the characters I've come to love also touch the hearts and minds of my readers. I'm also grateful for all the readers who've chosen to come along with Alfred on his journey.

About the Author

Pamela Taylor brings her love of history to the art of storytelling in the *Second Son Chronicles*. An avid reader of historical fact and fiction, she finds the past offers rich sources for character, ambiance, and plot that allow readers to escape into a world totally unlike their daily lives. She shares her home with two Pembroke Welsh Corgis who remind her frequently that a dog walk is the best way to find inspiration for that next chapter.

Other Books by Pamela Taylor

Second Son
My Father, My King
Pestilence
Upon this Throne
Shadows
The Weight of the Crown
Destiny

Note from the Author

Word-of-mouth is crucial for any author to succeed. If you enjoyed *A Feeling in the Bones*, please leave a review online — anywhere you are able. Even if it's just a sentence or two. It would make all the difference and would be very much appreciated.

Thanks!
Pamela Taylor